EVA CHASE

ROYALS OF VILLAIN ACADEMY #8

Vicious Arts

Book 8 in the Royals of Villain Academy series

First Digital Edition, 2020

Copyright © 2020 Eva Chase

Cover design: Fay Lane Cover Design

Ebook ISBN: 978-1-989096-56-7

Paperback ISBN: 978-1-989096-57-4

❃ Created with Vellum

CHAPTER ONE

Rory

A moment before my phone chimed, the four guys waiting in the scion lounge with me had been casually shooting the breeze. Malcolm Nightwood and Connar Stormhurst were facing off over the pool table, Jude Killbrook and I had launched into another round of his favorite racing game, and Declan Ashgrave was nursing an espresso in the armchair next to me.

At the thin sound, every mouth snapped shut and every pair of eyes shot to me. I'd never seen a text alert met with such solemn anticipation. Jude paused the game. Malcolm lowered the pool cue he'd been about to aim with, the base rapping sharply against the floor.

I jerked forward to grab my phone off the coffee table. It wouldn't necessarily be the message we'd been waiting for... but it was. My mother's name stood out starkly at the top of the text. *I need you at the main residence this afternoon, 4pm. We have things to discuss with the other barons.*

I'd bet we did. I rested the phone on my knee, my mouth gone dry. I wasn't supposed to know what she was referring to—none of us in the room were. My mother didn't realize I was getting inside info from her assistant, Maggie, who didn't agree with the barons' recent plans any more than I did. Mostly because their recent plans had involved using the magic we all could wield—magic fueled by fear—to terrorize the nonmagical locals we'd previously kept ourselves secret from.

Apparently the barons planned to blow up that secrecy on a nation-wide scale. We'd secretly ruined their attempt to rule over the town just off the university campus, but rather than take that failure as a signal to back off or at least slow down, they were dreaming up ways to exert their influence on the highest levels possible.

Maggie had warned me that my mother would probably want to loop me in today. The five of us scions had been distracting ourselves, waiting for that call.

"She wants me to meet her at the Bloodstone residence for a discussion with the barons." I glanced at Declan, who was nearly a baron himself, even if the others had been shutting him out lately because of his family's known sympathies for the Naries. "Nothing on your end?"

He took out his own phone to check and shook his head. "Obviously they can't be bothered to include me in this discussion. If they're willing to make decisions this big without any Stormhurst baron at all, they can't feel that guilty about leaving me out too."

The former Stormhurst baron, Connar's mother, had died at my mother's hand just a couple days ago. Her loss should have shut down any further major changes, but it seemed the remaining barons had decided to throw the laws out the window.

"They're leaving *all* of the rest of us out," Malcolm said, his smoothly confident voice gone ominously dark. "We're scions just as much as Rory is, but no one's summoning me or Connar or Jude to join the discussion."

"That's hardly a surprise in my case or Mr. Musclehead's," Jude said wryly with a tip of his head toward Connar's brawny form. "Baron Killbrook wants me *dead*, and Conn was openly defying his mother before she kicked the bucket. I suppose your dad realized you're the one who got your sister out of there and figures that can't mean anything good."

His assessment of the situation sounded about right. Jude had been assaulted and nearly killed once already this month, by an attacker we had to assume had been sent by his supposed father to cover up the fact that Jude wasn't really his son. Connar had refused to spend any time in his mother's presence since his parents had temporarily magically manipulated him into hating me, and Malcolm had removed his younger sister from the Nightwood home just a couple days ago to keep her out of reach of his father's anger.

He hadn't done anything to piss off Baron Nightwood directly yet, but chances were high he'd do that soon. Also two days ago, the five of us had agreed that we wanted to be there for each other in every way for as long as we possibly could, both as colleagues and as lovers, and Malcolm refused to continue pretending he supported the man who'd tried to ruin my life more than once. After we'd gotten the news about the barons' new focus, we'd agreed that we were done trying to play their political game.

People had already died because of the new campaign to rule over the Naries. *Children* had died. The memory of the little boy lying limp and bleeding on one of the town's driveways made my stomach turn with a jab of guilt because I hadn't managed to intervene.

We couldn't stand by and wait for the perfect opportunity anymore. This might be the best chance we got, with only three barons to contend with and their allegiance no doubt shaken by the fact that the evidence Connar and I had planted suggested Baron Stormhurst had sabotaged their experiment in town. Standing up to them was a huge step, but with the five of us presenting a united front, I didn't think they could outright ignore us.

I stood up. "Well, you're coming anyway, whether they like it or not. We should leave in the next hour—she wants me there by four." I hesitated, the enormity of the step we were about to take looming over me. "That is, assuming you want to go ahead with our protest."

Malcolm tossed his pool cue onto the rack. "It's been a long time coming—I'm not leaving it any longer." He walked over to me, his hand rising as if to rest on my back, but at the last second he stopped, his fingers closing. His arm dipped down toward the arm of the sofa for a second before he offered the touch after all.

That kind of uncertainty wasn't like the Nightwood scion. He'd acted a little strange with me right after he'd gotten back from moving his sister to her new apartment, but we'd gotten caught up in dealing with the bigger news. Now wasn't the time to try to hash out a possible personal issue either. I set my hand on his shoulder, hoping the gesture would at least reassure him about whatever was on his mind.

Beside us, Declan's mouth twisted into a thin smile. "If they're going to shut me out anyway, it doesn't benefit me to keep playing by the rules."

Jude sprang up from the sofa, flicking his dark copper hair back from his eyes. "Watch you tell off those three jackasses, Fire Queen? I wouldn't miss it for anything."

A solemn expression tensed Connar's chiseled face as he set his own cue on the table. "Since we have time, should we ask some of the Guard to come along? There are only three full barons now, but they *are* still barons. Extra backup might be useful."

The barons did have plenty of power that went beyond their political status. The five families that ruled over fearmancer society were the strongest mages around, and our parents had far more practice at using their skills than we did.

I nodded. "And having people from the Guard along will give us witnesses—they'd be able to spread the word that the scions are on the Naries' side now. I don't think we should bring a huge crowd, but if we each have one person along for support, that should be a decent size. We're still trying to solve this by talking if we can. We don't want to look like we're marching into battle with them."

Baron Nightwood had accused me of trying to form an army when he'd first found out about the Scions' Guard—a group of fellow students the guys and I had recently started recruiting. Our official story was that we simply wanted to ensure our safety after Jude's attack and the chaotic magical aggression that had broken out on campus once the nonmagical students had become open targets. The baron hadn't been completely wrong, though. We'd picked people we believed were against the new policies victimizing the Naries in the hopes that they'd support us on those matters too.

It was time to find out exactly how loyal those allies would be when called to a real conflict like this. I just hoped we wouldn't end up leading them into literal battle.

"We'll meet at the garage in forty-five minutes?" Declan said.

I let out a shaky breath. "Sounds like a plan."

My heart thudded as I headed up the stairs to my dorm, figuring that was the best place to look for the current members of my part of the Guard. My first two recruits had come from among my dormmates.

One of those girls, Victory Blighthaven, was lounging on a sofa in the common room when I came in. A couple of our other dormmates were eating lunch at the long dining table. Victory looked up at my entrance, and I tapped the front of my shoulder, the same spot where she had her Guard badge pinned on her sweater.

I didn't want to say anything in front of the others. If

their families were particularly devoted to the barons, word might get back to my mother and the others before we could make our appearance.

Victory followed me into the hall and then the stairwell with a toss of her auburn waves. Even now that she was on the Guard, she seemed to feel she needed to make a point of not caring *that* much what I might have to say. For most of my time at Blood U we'd been at odds; I didn't think we would ever become actual friends. But that was part of the reason I trusted her. While she might not like me, she'd proven that she could set aside her ego enough to recognize my authority when our goals aligned. And I never had to worry that she'd lie to me to spare my feelings.

I cast a quick deflective spell around the stairs to temporarily ward off anyone who might have otherwise passed by. "The barons are getting ready to push their agenda against the Naries even more," I said. "All of us scions are going to confront them and make it clear we don't agree with the direction they're taking. We're hoping to bring a little backup just in case things go sour —or, I'd prefer, to make it less likely that they will. Are you in?"

Victory frowned. "I'll be openly going against the barons myself, then."

"You would," I said. "It's okay if you're not ready to do that. They'll probably mostly see it as us ordering the rest of you to help us rather than an idea you came up with on your own, if that makes you feel any better about it. And… I don't think they're going to back down until enough people stand up to them. If you want all the crap on campus to stop, we could use your help."

She shifted her weight from one foot to the other. "Is it true what they're saying—that your mother killed Baron Stormhurst?"

I'd known that incident couldn't stay under wraps for long. "She found evidence that Baron Stormhurst was the one who called in the joymancers to defend the Naries in town. That's how she responded."

Victory's gaze turned more considering. The scions hadn't told our Guard what we were planning, but she had to suspect, given what she knew about me, that I was a heck of a lot more likely to think of turning to the joymancers for help than any of the barons were. Most fearmancers saw the mages who worked with joy as the enemy—and the feeling was mutual. But I'd been raised by joymancers for most of my life, and I'd seen how generous and loving they could be too, even if they rarely extended those attitudes to fearmancers.

"All right," my former nemesis said. I wasn't sure what had convinced her, but maybe she'd simply decided that she was safer throwing her lot in with the scions than the three remaining barons. "Do I need to come now?"

"We're meeting at the garage in about half an hour. Grab your jacket and maybe something to eat if you haven't already—it's going to be a bit of a drive."

Back in the dorm, I ducked into my bedroom to grab my own jacket, bundling myself in the thin but down-filled layers of fabric. Far from the first time, a pang of longing ran through me to have my familiar here, to tell her what I was about to do and let out my hopes and my fears.

Deborah had been much more than a mouse. The joymancers who'd stolen me away from my real home had transferred the consciousness of a dying woman into her so she could keep an eye on me. But she'd become a friend as much as a guard over the time we'd spent together. Last month, she'd died protecting me. The physical pain of the severed connection had faded, but the emotional loss lingered on.

I took some time to sit on my bed and compose myself, imagining how I wanted this scene to play out. Then, girding myself, I headed out.

Declan was already waiting in the garage with his younger brother, who was part of the Guard. The Ashgrave scion had been hesitant to involve Noah in our political conflicts at all—he'd spent most of his life doing everything he could to keep his brother out of the line of fire. But the younger guy was pretty insistent, and he'd managed to convince Declan that they were both better off if they stuck together.

"I'm thinking we split up between three cars," Declan said as I joined them. "The more cohesively we can arrive together, the easier it'll be."

"Agreed. And we'll want to keep an eye on each other as we're driving to make sure we do arrive at the same time. I don't want anyone to end up literally shut out."

Malcolm, Connar, and Jude showed up a few minutes later with three more members of the guard in tow and Victory trailing behind them. I was pretty sure all of those three were among the many classmates Malcolm had gotten on board. I didn't always agree with the Nightwood scion's methods when it came to imposing his authority, but he had formed connections with our peers from all across the school. Which was a good thing, because Jude, at least, hadn't really chummed up to anyone outside the pentacle of scions, so he was relying on his friend's social circle for support.

I waved Jude over to join me at my Lexus. His father's attack had left his capacity for magic severely damaged—he could barely gather enough energy to cast fairly simple spells, and only one or two of those before he drained himself. I was the only one of the scions who was strong in all four areas of magic. If anyone could offset the power he'd lost, it'd be me.

And I'd be damned if anyone hurt him again.

"We'll ride together," I said, including the guy who'd followed him in my gesture. "And we really should get a move on."

Jude raised an eyebrow at me, so I suspected he guessed at my line of thinking, but he didn't argue. All he said as he slid into the back was, "Next time, I drive."

We reached the Bloodstone manor with the wind warbling around the car and Declan's and Malcolm's cars right behind mine. Several vehicles I didn't recognize cruised out through the gate toward us, forcing me to ease the Lexus closer to the right side of the lane. My stomach tightened as I watched them leave. It looked as though the barons had already started—and finished—a different meeting even I hadn't been invited to.

I spoke a casting word to keep the gate open and drove on in. The guys parked on either side of me. We all got out together, our Guard flanking us. Ignoring the stutter of my pulse, I raised my chin and strode up the front steps at the head of our pack.

The house manager, Eloise, came into the front hall to meet us and blinked at the size of our group. "Miss Bloodstone?" she said tentatively. "I'm not sure—"

"It'll be okay," I said with as much assurance as I could summon. "Where are they?"

"Well, I…" She dragged in a breath. "All right. They're in the main dining room. Come along."

I didn't really need her to guide the way, but I let her anyway. I hadn't spent much time in my home's main dining room since I'd returned to the fearmancer realm— the huge twelve-seater mahogany table had felt too intimidating for the solo meals I'd eaten before my mother had returned. Normally when I'd been here, I'd taken a plate into one of the cozier sitting rooms.

The space was appropriate for a baron-style meeting, though. I walked in under the glinting chandelier to find my mother sitting at the head of the table and Barons Nightwood and Killbrook next to her on opposite sides. Maggie and a young man who must have been assisting one of the other barons stood motionless near the wall behind them. A few of the other chairs were pulled a little out in the wake of the visitors we'd seen leaving. I counted eleven wine glasses around the table, most of them drained, the tang of alcohol giving the atmosphere an uncomfortably celebratory vibe.

The barons definitely didn't see any reason to celebrate my arrival with my nine companions. My mother frowned, Nightwood's expression hardened, and Killbrook pushed right to his feet as if he thought he'd be more intimidating standing up. I found it hard to worry much about the thin, sallow-faced man who'd acted like a coward in every dealing with his son. No, the first two were the ones really calling the shots.

"Persephone," Baron Bloodstone said with a faint edge in her voice. "When I asked you to come, I didn't think I needed to specify that the invitation was for you alone."

"I think all of the scions should know about and be able to comment on what the pentacle plans to do next," I said. "We were all affected by what happened after you tried to take over the town. We don't want to see our people in a position like that again."

Her lips drew into a thin smile. "With the operations we're planning, that shouldn't be a problem. We've learned from our missteps. And you can be assured the joymancers who attacked us won't get away with it unscathed."

I crossed my arms over my chest. "Are you planning to continue interfering with the Naries—working toward ruling over them like you were in town?"

"When one strategy doesn't have the desired outcome, you don't immediately scrap the entire initiative," Baron Nightwood said with a hint of a sneer.

Malcolm stepped up beside me. "Why is this an

initiative in the first place? The Naries weren't causing any problems. We were living our lives just fine. Who the hell is this supposed to be for?"

"It's for all of you," my mother said, her tone turning icier as her gaze slid to the Nightwood scion. "So you and the many families who've supported us for so long can have the power and freedom that should always have been ours. It shouldn't be difficult to see that."

"That's the way *you* see it," I said. "Please listen to us. We're the ones who'll be ruling in a decade or two from now—or sooner, in a couple cases. We're not interested in dealing with the stresses and the violence that we've already seen will come with that kind of power. That isn't the world we want to be running."

Declan came up at my other side. "I stand with the other scions. I *will* be baron in just a few months, and I don't agree with any of this. We have plenty of power and freedom without needing to become some kind of dictators over the Naries."

"It seems even my mother didn't totally agree," Connar spoke up from just behind us.

My mother's gaze slid over all of us. She had to realize how serious we must be to risk defying them to their faces. They hadn't been prepared for this kind of confrontation. But I didn't see any sign that our words were getting through—to her or the other two barons.

"I don't want us to fight about it," I said. "We're just here to talk—to be part of the conversation—to have a say in what's going to be *our* future. We're supposed to be preparing to lead and protect the entire fearmancer community, and we're practicing that responsibility right now."

Baron Killbrook's eyes narrowed. "I don't think you know your community all that well, then."

"Maybe you're the ones who don't know it," Jude tossed out. "There's a lot more to it than your cronies. The other families count too."

The disdainful curl of Nightwood's lips suggested he didn't agree. "*We* are the ones serving the community at the moment. These decisions are ours. And disloyalty isn't a good look on any of you."

"Who should we be loyal to first?" I asked quietly. "The three of you, or the hundreds of fearmancers who'll be affected by the next steps you take?"

My mother stood up then with a rasp of her chair legs against the floor. "I think you should assume those are one and the same."

I met her fierce gaze, restraining a flinch at the wounded fury it held. "After what I've seen with my own eyes, I can't assume that. I'm sorry. If you're willing to talk, we'll keep talking. If you aren't, and you insist on going forward… we will speak up about our concerns to the rest of the community."

"You will *not*—" my mother snapped, and a crackle of energy shot toward us just with those few words. Thankfully, our Guard had been, well, on guard, and their voices rang out at the same time. Whatever spell she'd cast to try to silence us, it sizzled away against the hasty shield.

"We're just asking for an honest conversation," I said, unwilling to let it go without trying one more time. At the clenching of my mother's jaw, my stomach sank, even though my hopes hadn't been that high to begin with. "All right. Then we'll go. Please, just think about what we've said."

But as I turned on my heel, my back prickling, I could summon even less hope that they'd really consider any argument we'd made. The battle lines had been drawn, and now all five of us scions stood on the opposite side from the barons.

CHAPTER TWO

Declan

It became clear that something momentous had happened within seconds of leaving my bedroom. When I came out into the common room to grab some breakfast, my few dormmates who were already up glanced at me and then quickly jerked their gazes away—not with the usual wary deference that came with my position, but something that felt much more anxious instead. A couple of them murmured to each other briefly before shooting me another look and vanishing into their rooms.

I decided the best course of action was pretending I hadn't even noticed. A soon-to-be baron shouldn't be fazed by a little gossip, even if their reactions niggled at me more than standard gossip would have. I had taken a fairly momentous stand against the remaining full barons yesterday. Some sort of backlash might have already begun.

More of those odd looks flicked my way as I descended the stairs and crossed the green. Even my professor for my Illusion seminar seemed to hesitate when I first came into the classroom. No one said anything directly to me, though, and I wasn't going to go begging for scraps of information—revealing that I was out of the loop. As soon as class was over, I'd see if any of my fellow scions were better informed.

In the end, I didn't need to reach out. I'd just taken out my phone as I left Killbrook Tower, meaning to text them, when my brother came jogging across the green with a family acquaintance I'd also invited into the Scions' Guard tagging at his heels. Noah's expression was tight enough to tell me *he'd* figured out what was up, and it definitely wasn't good.

"We'll go to the Guard room?" I suggested before he had to say anything.

He nodded. I didn't need to tell him it was better to keep a fraught conversation out of the public eye.

The three of us headed down to the basement room we'd set up for our meetings with the Guard. Noah held his calm well enough, but the second we passed through the doorway, he let out a frustrated huff of breath and spun around. "Show him, Anthony."

The other guy took a tablet out of his shoulder bag. He tapped on the screen and shot me an apologetic grimace, as if he thought I'd be angry at him for sharing the news. "A couple hours ago, your aunt sent around a video to, I guess, everyone whose contact information the barons could give her. Except for Noah, and we figured you too."

"Probably she skipped all of the scions, since she knows they'd support Declan," Noah muttered.

My heart was already sinking. "Let me see it."

Anthony handed me the tablet, and I started the video playing. It was Aunt Ambrosia, all right, standing haughtily at the Ashgrave point on the table of the pentacle where the barons held their meetings. She'd joined me there often enough over the years when she'd served as regent, but now she had an even more possessive air, her hands braced against the dark, polished wood.

"The time has come for me to step up and do what is right," she said in a sharply clipped voice. "I've served as regent to the Ashgrave barony since my sister's tragic death nearly two decades ago, and I've always supported my nephew in every way I can."

I had to restrain a harsh guffaw at the thought of all the ways she'd tried to undermine me—and occasionally outright murder me—in her bids for the barony over the years.

"Yesterday, Declan Ashgrave proved that he is a traitor to the pentacle and to all of us in the fearmancer community," my aunt went on. "He has set himself against the barons who are working so diligently to pave the way to a new era for you. We cannot let this treason stand unchallenged. So with heavy heart but great determination, I declare myself, Ambrosia Ashgrave, as the official Ashgrave baron."

I couldn't say I'd ever truly loved the idea of being

baron. It'd been more of a burden than a boon for as long as I could remember. All the same, I flinched at those last words.

That was my spot at the table. That was my role she was claiming. A role I might not have been overjoyed about, but that I'd worked my ass off to prepare for my entire life. And she thought she could just walk in and take my place like—

Maybe she could. The three remaining full barons joined her on the screen with solemn nods.

"We'll move forward with all the strength and commitment we owe you," Baron Nightwood said, and then the recording cut out.

I stared at it for several seconds longer, my hands tensed around the tablet. Noah muttered something obscene under his breath. Anthony shifted his weight nervously until I handed the tablet back to him.

Hell. No wonder people had been staring at me. They'd been gawking—yet afraid to openly gawk—at a supposedly displaced baron.

I drew in a breath and found I didn't know what to say. My innards had constricted from my throat down to my gut. What *could* I say if the barons were standing with Aunt Ambrosia? They had most of the blacksuits in their pocket. Who would give me a trial if I demanded one? Who would judge it fairly?

Nothing had really changed anyway, had it? The barons had been shutting me out of their decisions in every way they could for weeks. Now they were just making that separation official.

I'd spoken against them yesterday because it was time to—because someone needed to before they turned the community I meant to serve into something I hated. It didn't matter what my official title was. I could worry about reclaiming it later. For now, we still needed to fight in every possible way before they thrust us into a situation we couldn't return from.

"She can say whatever she wants," I said firmly. "It doesn't change what matters. We need to bring the rest of the Guard in, make our own plans for going forward, and when we've dealt with the most immediate problems, then I'll take her to task."

Noah gave me a sharp nod. "Do you want me to start rounding up the other members?"

"Let me check with the other scions first. They'll want to be a part of this discussion."

I sent a text to the whole group. We'd been waiting to see how the barons responded before we took any definite action—this was an awfully clear response.

I just heard, Malcolm said, with an angry emoji that expressed the fury I could imagine in his voice. *Definitely time to rally the troops. I'll be right down.*

I can be there in ten, Connar texted a moment later.

Rory's reply came shortly after. *What's going on? Jude and I are already on our way to talk to his uncle—we won't be back until the afternoon.*

She didn't know yet. I wavered and then wrote, *You don't need to worry about that right now. It's nothing urgent. We can hold off the rallying until you two are back.*

Forget that, she replied immediately. *You three know*

what you're doing. We don't want to give the barons any more chances to make headway than they've already had.

I balked at the idea automatically. Rory had spearheaded this cause—Rory had been the first of us to really defy the barons, to stand up for the Naries on campus. The Scions' Guard had been her idea. She should be here to have a say in directing them.

But I already knew how she wanted to handle the situation, didn't I? We'd hashed out our thoughts on pushing back against the barons an awful lot over the last few weeks. I was the one who'd been nearly baron for years; if anyone should be leading the charge, it was me. Rory deserved a break from that responsibility.

You're right, I said. *We'll fill you in as soon as you're back. Good luck with Mr. Killbrook.*

Let's hope we don't need luck.

Malcolm came through the door with his eyes flashing. "Assholes," he said without preamble. "Fuck them if they think they can screw you over like this."

"They won't," I said with all the confidence I could summon. "But first we've got to pull enough support to force the barons to back down. At least we've already got a start on that." I shot Anthony a genuine, if tight, smile.

Noah had a contact list of all our current recruits to the Guard. He paced the room as he reached out to each of them. A handful had already arrived, along with Connar, when my brother returned to me with an update. "There are a couple people in class right now, but they said they'll get down here as soon as possible. Everyone else is heading over."

"Perfect." I gave his shoulder a quick squeeze of gratitude. "We'll wait until everyone's here before we get started."

Malcolm and Connar had fallen into hushed conversation in the corner. From the tensing of Connar's stance, the Nightwood scion was filling him in on my aunt's machinations. One of the guys Malcolm had asked to come with us yesterday nodded to me on his way in and ambled over.

"This whole 'traitor' thing is about our talk with the barons, I'm guessing?"

"As far as I know, I haven't done anything else to offend them," I said dryly. The only small mystery was whether the barons had gone straight to Aunt Ambrosia or she'd found out about the confrontation and offered to jump in. Either seemed equally likely at this point.

The last few members hustled in, faces flushed as if they'd run straight from class. The video announcement must have given us all a greater sense of urgency. Malcolm and Connar joined me as I stepped into the middle of the rug to face our nearly twenty assembled classmates, but they looked to me, giving me the floor.

In a funny way, my aunt's declaration had set the stage for what felt like my first real act as a baron.

"We picked all of you because we trusted you to stand with us," I said to our Guard. "But now we're going to ask you to do more than just protect our well-being. The full barons are attempting to throw our community in an entirely new direction that, if they take things far enough, there'll be no coming back from. And as I'm sure most if not all of you have seen, they're also attempting to discredit and replace me as baron."

"What are the barons planning now?" a guy near the back of the bunch asked. "I thought they were backing off on the whole 'ruling the Naries' thing after what happened in town."

I shook my head. "We don't know the exact details of their plans, but we know they aren't giving up on that goal. They're absolutely set on revealing ourselves to the Naries and using our powers to control them—across the whole country, if they can manage that. All of the scions agree that a course of action like that will create far more problems than it's worth. We're hoping that you and people close to you feel the same way."

Cressida Warbury, who must have been in an awkward position with the way her parents had been fawning over the barons recently, stood up straighter, her arms folded over her chest. "Sure, I don't like it. But what can we do about it?"

I dragged in a breath. "First, I have to say that anything we decide to do will mean going against the will of the barons. It's not going to be easy, and you'll be putting yourselves and your families at risk. *We* don't want to be tyrants. If you don't feel ready to push back against the barons, you can leave the Guard, no hard feelings, no sanctions from us. I totally understand the need to protect yourself and the people you care about."

I paused, checking to make sure neither of my fellow scions were glowering in a way that might have suggested my words were a lie. Neither of them looked happy, but they waited for the response calmly enough. While a few of our classmates stirred on their feet, no one moved toward the door.

"We've got to do something," Victory piped up where she was standing next to Cressida. "We're *fearmancers*, for fuck's sake. We shouldn't be cowering away from a conflict, even if it's with our own barons. They're supposed to support us, not throw us into some epic mess that we don't even want."

I couldn't say I'd ever enjoyed Victory's company all that much, but her haughtiness served us well right now. At her words, other eyes in the crowd glinted with renewed defiance. Jaws firmed, and shoulders squared. No one so much as glanced toward the door after that.

"All right," I said, clasping my hands together. "Our first step is simple. We all reach out to people we know— family members, friends, teachers, whoever—that we've seen reason to believe disagree with these new policies. Spread the word that the scions are concerned that the barons may continue with similar plans against the Naries, and that the barons have refused to talk the issue through with us. If we see clear evidence that the barons are going through with those plans, we'll appreciate them being ready to make their own concerns known, as openly and clearly as they're comfortable doing. The more of us who speak out, the more obvious it'll become that this decision isn't for the good of the entire community, and the more likely others will reconsider their position too."

"If people are scared of saying anything on their own, let them know when the time comes, we'll arrange groups where they can speak together," Malcolm added. "We're all in this—no one is going to face the barons alone."

Anthony had stayed near the front of the group. His gaze slid over the three of us, his mouth slanting at an uncertain angle. "Even if we all protest, and our families too—if the barons won't even listen to the five of you, do you really think they'll listen to us?"

I could feel the attention of everyone in the room sharpening at that question. My stomach knotted. I offered the only honest answer I could.

"I don't know. But it's worth a try—there's always hope. And the last thing we'd want to do is skip ahead to the steps we'll have to take if they *don't* listen."

CHAPTER THREE

Rory

J ude rarely looked happier than when he was behind the wheel of his Mercedes, cruising at top speed along a highway. Even so, as we got closer to our destination, I noticed that his knuckles were starting to whiten where he gripped the wheel. He tapped his free foot restlessly, out of sync with the jazz music he'd tuned the radio to.

I turned down the volume a little so I wouldn't need to raise my voice. "How much have you seen of your uncle, anyway?"

Jude shrugged. "Not a lot. My 'father' never trusted him—obviously, or the baron wouldn't have gone to such extreme measures to manufacture himself a supposed heir. We had mind-numbing holiday visits a few times a year while their mother was still around, where hardly anyone really talked to each other. After she passed, their father started spending most of his time overseas traveling around… I think it's been three years since I last even saw the guy."

"But you think he's at least a bit less of a jerk than Baron Killbrook?"

"He at least wasn't enough of an asshole to get offended by the way the baron treated him. And I never saw any sign that he was actually scheming to get a seat at the table. Of course, it could turn out my impressions were totally off-base." He shot me a flash of a grin. "That's why it's a good thing I have a bodyguard along."

I rolled my eyes at him, but the truth was I *had* insisted on joining him on this trip partly to watch out for him. Jude was clever and quick and charming when he wanted to be, but his damaged magical abilities put him at a huge disadvantage compared to any member of a barony family. I intended to make sure his uncle treated him fairly —and that Jude didn't get any self-sacrificing ideas in his head like he had when we'd turned to the joymancers to interrupt the barons' takeover of the town off campus.

I'd also come along so any offer he made would carry more weight. We were essentially going to ask Hector Killbrook to commit treason against his brother. I had to imagine he'd be a lot more willing to consider the idea if he saw that the other scions supported the move too.

"Does he have kids of his own?" I asked. A family the barons could threaten would also factor into the man's decision.

Jude nodded. "A daughter… I think she's eight now? Hector is ten years younger than the baron, so his side of the family is a little behind on the whole heirs thing. The wife and the daughter didn't usually come along even when we were having the periodic dinners. I can't remember their names." He rubbed his forehead.

"Well, I guess don't mention that part. We'll just do our best." It was a weird balance between hoping the guy we were going to visit would be ambitious enough to like the idea of having some say in the barony but not so ambitious he'd screw Jude over to get at it.

Hector Killbrook might not have lived in a baron-style mansion, but the home we arrived at on the fringes of a small city wasn't that much smaller, with its own privacy wall and gate, gleaming white columns on either side of the massive oak door, and a castle-like air that was simply a smidge less foreboding than the Bloodstone residence. I decided I'd take that as a good sign.

Jude parked the Mercedes and then appeared to hesitate about leaving it, as if he thought there was some small chance he'd be able to conduct this meeting in the relative security of his car. He shook his lean frame and got out with a determined huff of breath.

He'd called ahead to make sure his uncle would be in when we arrived. A housekeeper opened the door and ushered us into a large sitting room that held a few loveseats and chairs, a card table, and a baby grand piano. The furnishings were stately and in a classic style as with most of the fearmancer residences I'd been in, but this family had gone for a lighter color scheme, the wood maple rather than mahogany or cherry, the fabrics pale earth tones. A softly sweet scent drifted from a delicate floral arrangement in a vase on a sideboard.

"Mr. Killbrook should be down in about ten minutes," the housekeeper said, and bustled off with no apparent worry about how we'd use the space unsupervised. I supposed she trusted that a couple of scions wouldn't trash the place.

Jude's gaze had lingered on the piano. "That's a nice one," he said with an eager flex of his fingers. "I wonder if any of them actually play or if it's just for show."

I smiled. Music was Jude's most secret passion, one he'd only really shared with me—which given his skill was a real shame. "You could check how well tuned it is," I suggested.

He raised an eyebrow at me. "Now you're just leading me into temptation." But after a moment he wandered over and tested a few of the keys.

The rich notes sounded good enough to my uneducated ears. Apparently they satisfied Jude too. He sat down on the bench and let his fingers fly into a classical piece I recognized but couldn't have named off the top of my head.

I doubted he'd have let himself indulge if he hadn't assumed we'd be alone for a little while, but he couldn't have been playing for more than a minute when the floor creaked in the hall outside. A slender man with flax-blond hair and a trim beard came to a stop on the threshold and leaned against the doorframe.

"That's a difficult piece," he said. "You play it well."

Jude's hands jarred to a stop over the keys. He swiveled

around and stood up with a hint of a flush coloring his cheeks. "Uncle Hector. I'm sorry—I thought we had a little time to kill."

"It's all right. Stella plays it but not anything all that complex yet. It's a pleasure hearing the instrument put to full use. I didn't know you'd taken up music lessons."

Stella must be his daughter. Jude shrugged, putting on his usual nonchalance, although his eyes gleamed with the compliment. "Just something to fill the time between my studies at the university."

Hector motioned to the nearby chairs, with a tip of his head to acknowledge me as well. "Why don't we all sit down, and you two tell me what this is about?"

I settled into an armchair next to Jude, watching the man carefully. He had a similar reserved demeanor to his baron brother, but it felt more relaxed. Baron Killbrook gave me a twitchy vibe. I couldn't tell yet whether that difference was necessarily good or bad.

Jude was eyeing the man with similar wariness. "How much do you know about what the barons are up to these days?" he asked.

Hector stiffened slightly at the question. "If this is business to do with the barony, I think you'd be better off taking it up with your father. My getting involved in those matters is just asking for trouble."

Jude and I exchanged a glance. That didn't sound like the comment of a man who was gunning for his family's power, but rather one who'd accepted it wasn't his and had no designs on it. Who knew how his attitude might change if he realized the barony was within his grasp, but I'd rather see him hesitant than over-eager.

"The thing is," Jude said, "I can't talk to my father about this. My father—and his cohorts—are the problem. We're hoping you might be willing to take on some of that trouble to help us, for the good of the community and all."

"We're afraid the policies they're working toward now will have a huge and horrible impact on every fearmancer, one that it'd be difficult to reverse," I added. "This isn't just politics anymore. It'll affect every part of our lives—yours and your family's too."

From the tightening of Hector's mouth, I suspected he knew at least the gist of what the barons were working toward. He focused on me. "Does your mother know you're off looking for allies to work against her?"

I swallowed hard. "She doesn't know I'm here, but she knows I disagree with the barons and that I'm going to work against their plans as much as I have to. All of the scions are in agreement. We're gathering support as quickly as we can. I don't know how much time we have before they completely overturn our world."

"I know you can't feel a whole lot of loyalty to—to my father," Jude said. "He's been an asshat to you for as long as I've been old enough to notice. I think having another Killbrook, someone who could have been baron, speak out against the policies he's supporting would make a significant difference. And you'd have all of the scions' support."

Hector rubbed his jaw. His expression had gone

pensive but not necessarily resistant. "You're the heir," he said to Jude. "Your word should matter more than mine. Anything I say, he'll most likely frame as bitterness from the one who didn't have a chance at the barony."

Jude looked down at his hands and back again. I saw him gathering his resolve in the tensing of his shoulders and the set of his mouth. We'd talked about how much he'd share from what he knew about his family's situation, and he'd been uncertain but willing to cross a few lines if the risk seemed worth it. Apparently he'd decided it was. I tensed too, restraining the urge to grasp his hand in an offer of support.

"He isn't going to be baron forever," he said quietly. "And, no matter what happens, at some point I'd be here asking you to step in as regent until my sister comes of age. I *can't* take the barony, and he'll age out before she's old enough to claim the spot."

Hector blinked at him. "Even if you don't want to be baron, you'll be old enough to act as regent by then."

"I *can't*. I'd rather not get into why right now, because it could have horrible consequences for me as well as my father. And even if that wasn't the case, with the injuries I took recently, I can barely cast anymore. I won't be able to protect her the way she'll need."

Jude's voice had turned raw with that last sentiment. I thought he was coming to terms with the loss of so much of his magical ability, but it obviously still ate at him.

Silence hung over the room for a moment. I cleared my throat. "Ideally what we'd like is for you to make a bid for the barony on the basis that Baron Killbrook is flouting fearmancer law—all the barons are, by making these huge decisions without any Stormhurst baron at all, not to mention the way they've displaced Declan Ashgrave. We're gathering families who'll back up that bid. But before we go forward, we'd ask that you make a magical agreement with us that if you do end up taking over the barony, you'll return it to Jude's sister—as regent and then stepping back completely—when she's old enough."

Jude leaned forward, his usual energy coming back. "You must have ideas you'd like to see put out there, policies you have opinions on. Just from talking to you now I can tell your approach has got to be better than the shit the current barons are getting us deeper and deeper into."

Hector inhaled sharply. "I'll have to give it some thought. This isn't the sort of decision anyone should make lightly. I'd say that applies to the two of you as well, but I get the impression you've already invested a lot in this matter." He stood up and nodded to Jude. "I have your current contact information now. I'll let you know if I'm ready to take part in this rebellion of yours."

That wasn't the definite yes we'd have hoped for, but it was a hell of a lot better than a no. Jude and I got up as well, Jude offering his hand to the other man for a brisk shake.

"It wasn't easy, coming here," he said, looking Hector in the eye. "I wouldn't be doing this if I didn't think it could make a huge difference in whether we end up in some kind of war with the Naries for who knows how long."

Hector grimaced. "Whatever I decide, I can assure you that's not something I want to see either. I don't know—some of these families—our *own* family…" He shook his head as he trailed off.

He led us back to the front door himself without speaking, but when we reached the front hall, he paused, and his voice dropped. "I appreciate the trust you put in me to reach out to me like this, Jude. I can offer, right now—I know a few of the people who've been the barons' most avid supporters in these new policies. And it might be useful for you to know that those mages have set off for Washington and other areas of major Nary political activity in the past couple of days. I don't think that's a coincidence."

A chill ran down my back. "You don't think they'd directly attack the Nary government, do you?"

"That seems over the top even after what we've already seen," Hector said. "But they're absolutely aiming to gain some influence there. How they're going to use that influence on the Naries who make the laws for *their* society… I'm not particularly looking forward to finding out."

CHAPTER FOUR

Rory

There was definitely still something a little strange in Malcolm's reaction to my presence. A few minutes ago when he'd caught me in the hall on my way back from visiting Hector Killbrook, he'd talked like his usual cool and cocky self. But as he'd led me down the stairs to the scion lounge, there'd been something almost anxious in his grip on my arm. After we'd sat together on the couch, he'd gazed at me for a beat longer than felt totally normal before he'd fished out his phone. But once he started playing the video he said one of the Guard had forwarded to him, any concern I had about that minor weirdness flew out the window.

My fingers clenched around the phone as I watched Declan's aunt declare him a traitor and herself baron in his place. If it'd been a more disposable device, I'd have hurled it across the room. I jerked toward Malcolm when it was over.

"Can she really do that? How the hell is that okay?"

"It's not," he said. "But as long as the barons are giving her legitimacy, it'll take a lot of people arguing the case to get anywhere. It doesn't help that Declan isn't old enough to completely claim the barony in the first place."

"He must feel awful." My heart wrenched at the thought. I knew how much of himself Declan had poured into the pentacle, how many sacrifices he'd made to preserve his role and shield Noah from having to take on the responsibilities and dangers that came with it. And now for this woman to simply snatch the title away from him with a few fancy words in a single video recording... Gah, I'd have liked to punch that self-satisfied smile off her face.

My thumb moved to rub the family heirloom ring my mother had given me for my birthday—one with a conducting pattern that could shape a little magic energy cast through it into a slicing projectile. Ambrosia Ashgrave was lucky she hadn't made this declaration right in front of me, or I might have been tempted to try out that power.

"He pulled himself together fast and didn't let it show that he was fazed, but I can't imagine he isn't stinging on the inside." Malcolm made a face. "You've seen how closed off he can get when he knows people are depending on him."

I had. Strange as it was to remember now, during the first few months I'd known Declan, I'd often found him detached, even cold. I just hadn't realized how tight a rein he kept on his emotions to avoid letting anything slip that could damage his standing. With the way he cared about his brother—the way he'd shown he cared about *me*—it was obvious he was anything but passionless.

"Did he say anything to you about how he's feeling?" I asked.

The Nightwood scion shook his head. "By the time I saw him after he'd gotten the news, he was already in full-speed-ahead professional mode. *I* was pissed off on his behalf, and he sort of swept the problem under the rug, saying we need to focus on the Nary situation first. Which maybe is true, but still." His hands clenched on his lap.

I handed him back his phone. "I have to talk to him. He might open up a little more if it's just me." I at least wanted to convince Declan he *could* talk to me if he thought it would help—and to comfort him as well as I could, whether he was willing to admit he needed it or not.

I texted Declan on my way up the stairs, but no immediate answer came. It was getting late, the lights dimmed in the halls and in my dorm common room when I stepped inside. Declan was typically an early riser, and he had to feel he had even more on his plate now. He might have already turned in for the night.

Standing in my bedroom, an idea tickled up through my head. I'd dropped in on the Ashgrave scion in his bedroom one night before. It was right under mine, just a short climb away. That should give him a little distraction.

A smile played with my lips as I went to the window. I pushed it open, bracing myself against the waft of cold night air that gusted over me. With casting words that were now much more practiced, I created an illusion of the wall beneath the window ledge to disguise me from anyone who happened to glance this way. We might not need to keep our closeness a total secret now, but it'd still look pretty odd for the Bloodstone scion to be climbing from one room to another.

Intensifying my concentration, I conjured a rope to dangle just past Declan's window. Then I scrambled out into the darkness.

In my hurry, I hadn't factored in just how different circumstances were now compared to that last time. Before, it'd been summer. Even at night, the air had been warm, the breeze pleasant rather than biting. Creeping toward the end of October, the New York autumn didn't cut me much of a break. I should have put on a thicker jacket.

And gloves. By the time I'd clambered down to Declan's window, my palms were aching from more than just the pressure of the rope, and my knuckles were stinging on the verge of numbness. The chill cut through my clothes.

Another difference: because it was this freaking cold, Declan didn't have his window open, of course. Suppressing a shiver as well as I could, I focused on the frame and mumbled a couple quick words to urge it upward.

The window slid open with a rasp. I swung inside as another shiver racked my body.

I landed a little better this time, with a light thump on

the desk below the window that didn't scatter any of Declan's possessions. Like before, that sound was enough to wake him up, though. As he sat up in bed, I twisted around to shove the window shut again. By the time I'd slid off the desk, he was there to meet me.

"Hey, are you all right?" he said, with so much concern that a jab of guilt ran through me. I was supposed to be here to comfort *him*. He tugged me into his arms, heedless of the fact that the cold clinging to my clothes would soak right through the undershirt and boxers he'd gone to bed in. "You're freezing. What happened?"

I let out a sheepish laugh. "I had the brilliant idea of recreating last term's stealthy entrance. It's definitely less brilliant in the middle of fall. I'm okay. I just... wanted to see you."

He kissed my cheek, his lips hot against my cool skin. "There are these things called doors, you know."

"But this was more fun. In theory."

"Hmm. Come here."

He pulled me with him over to the bed, a direction I wasn't going to object to. Then he tugged me right onto the bed, scooting over to make room and hauling the sheet and duvet over us the moment my ass hit the mattress. He wrapped his arms around me again, and I tucked my head under his chin, soaking up all the warmth I needed in what felt like an instant.

"There," he said. "Can't have my girlfriend turning into an ice cube."

A little tingle shot through me that had nothing to do with the temperature. For all the intimacies I'd shared with my four lovers, I couldn't remember any of them referring to me as their girlfriend before. But I was, wasn't I? And they were all my boyfriends. Hell, we'd made a commitment a few days ago to do whatever we could to stay together for the rest of our *lives*. If you really thought about it, we were practically engaged.

"Definitely not an ice cube now," I said, and nuzzled his neck, his cedarwood scent washing over me. Declan made an approving sound, one of his hands drifting lower on my back, but I tamped down on my desires. I hadn't come here to jump right into *that* either.

I raised my head so I could look him in the eyes. "Malcolm showed me the video. There's no way we're letting your aunt get away with this. You know that, right? You're Baron Ashgrave, case over."

One corner of his mouth quirked up, but his slanted smile was bittersweet. "So this wasn't just a casual visit."

"I needed to make sure you're okay. Just like you needed to stop me from freezing to death." I searched his face. "*Are* you okay? I know how hard you've worked for this. And… it's partly my fault it happened. If I hadn't suggested we confront the barons—"

"Hey," Declan said firmly, cutting me off. "We *all* decided to take that step together. I made the choice for myself. And it was the right choice."

He paused, his gaze slipping away from me with a momentary distance. "Maybe things will be harder for a little while, but if I hadn't stood up to the barons now, it probably would have been a hell of a lot harder down the road. I've spent so much time playing their games and biting my tongue when I wanted to argue… If I'm going to be baron, I have to be able to say what I really believe in. I don't deserve the position otherwise."

"You don't deserve to have someone try to rip it out from under you either," I muttered.

"No. But like you said, we won't let her get away with it." He stroked his fingers over my hair. "I'm not enjoying the situation, but at the same time, I can look on the bright side. It's giving me the chance to see who my real allies are—who will stand with us even when it looks like we're on the weaker side. I'm leading people in a way I never have before. I don't regret any of that. Maybe if I'd stood up to them sooner, we could have avoided things getting this bad."

I touched his cheek, wishing I could pass all the love I felt right into him. "You had a lot of responsibilities to balance. You were trying to find the way where the fewest people got hurt. I don't think you can blame yourself for that. I played along with my mother for a while too."

"I'm not going to dwell on it, but I don't want to go back to biting my tongue all the time either."

"Then I'll be right there making sure you don't have to."

"And that makes the difficult parts even more worthwhile." He gave me a softer smile and tipped his head to kiss me.

The press of his lips woke up all the longing I'd suppressed before. I teased my fingers into his silky hair and kissed him back. His tongue delved into my mouth with a hot swipe that left me shivering in a much more pleasant way.

"We don't have to be careful anymore, right?" I said, a little breathless, after. "It doesn't matter if the barons or whoever else finds out that we're together?"

"I'd still prefer not to broadcast my love life to the world at large, but no, I don't think we have to hold back in fear of the off-chance that someone might catch on." A glint lit in Declan's eyes. "I'll take that as my cue to add a little magical soundproofing to the room."

He said a casting word, and a tremor of magic flowed through the air around us. Then he ducked his head close to mine again, his lips brushing my cheek.

"The one thing I'm definitely never going to regret is being with you, Rory. You've made everything that was good in my life even brighter and everything that was a burden easier to bear. It would have been worth it even if we'd only had a short time together. If we get forever... I couldn't ask for a better miracle."

I choked up. "There'll be a way, and if anyone can find it, it'll be you. I love you."

"I love you too," he said, his mouth already seeking out mine, and then we were kissing and that said more than any words could have.

Between kisses, we stripped me of my clothes under the covers until I was down to my underwear like he was. Declan slowed, still claiming my mouth with as much intensity, but drawing out the swipe of his thumb over my breast, the trailing of his fingers down my side to my thighs, and finally the dip of his hand between my legs.

I whimpered as he stroked me through my panties and reached for the rigid length tenting his boxers. Our kisses turned sloppy as we teased each other. Through it all, a sensation I could only call joy radiated more and more sharply through me.

I was here, in this man's bed, without any secrets hanging over us, without any fear that being with me would destroy him or what he'd worked for. We could simply come together in love and passion in a moment where nothing mattered but the pleasure we were creating.

When I couldn't stand the hungry ache spreading from my core any longer, I tugged Declan's boxers down. He kissed my jaw and my neck in a heated path as he slid off my panties in turn. I gasped out my protective casting and drew his mouth back to mine, arching up and raising my knees to his waist as he dove into me with a perfect surge of bliss.

He rocked into me, and I embraced him in every way I could. With each thrust, we locked tighter together, our mouths melding and parting only to breathe, the friction between our bodies turning giddily searing. Declan lifted my hips off the mattress to find an even deeper angle. It only took a few more strokes of his cock to send me spiraling into my release.

I moaned and clutched him tighter. Declan kept up his rhythm as ecstasy swept through me, the pulse of our connection carrying it on and on, until I was shaking with the force of my orgasm. He let out a choked sound, burying himself in me as deep as he could get, and flooded me with that most intimate heat.

Even after he'd swayed to a stop, I kept holding him against me, reveling in the matching flow of our ragged breaths and the closeness that I could dream I'd never have to give up after all. The barons could attack us however they wanted, steal whatever they could from us, but no matter how bad things got, no matter what spells they cast, they couldn't truly destroy what we felt for each other. Not as long as we were all still living.

CHAPTER FIVE

Connar

The doctor stepped back from my brother's bedside with a long exhalation. He'd been absorbed in his healing casting for the better part of two hours, and the strain showed in the thin lines at the corners of his eyes and mouth. But when he turned to me, it was with a smile.

"I think you'll find the majority of the damage has been repaired now. He'll still need to take it easy as he gets his strength back, both physically and magically, but I've worked on his muscles as well so that the transition shouldn't be as hard as it could be. At this point, I'd give it a week or so, and if he notices any areas where he's still struggling without obvious progress, we can work on that."

"Thank you so much," I said. Words really couldn't express how grateful I was for the help the man had offered—even if the recent sessions had come with much less risk after my mother's death. Technically he was serving one of his soon-to-be barons now, rather than a traitor to an existing baron. I was beyond thankful that it'd turned out Holden could be healed at all from the injuries I'd dealt him years ago.

I could express my thanks in other ways, though. I pulled the cashier's check I'd had written up out of my pocket and held it out to him. A portion of my mother's holdings had gone to my father, of course, but the majority of her estate was considered part of the barony and so passed directly to her heirs. Since Holden was officially on record as being incapacitated, that meant it had all been transferred to me for the time being. Offering a generous payment only took a small portion of that.

The doctor's eyes widened at the sight of the number on the check, but he took it without argument, with a slight dip of his head. "It was an honor to be able to serve the Stormhursts, regardless of the reward. If I'd known of your brother's situation sooner…"

He wouldn't have been able to do anything, because my mother would have crushed anyone who questioned her judgment regarding her heirs. But I appreciated the sentiment all the same. "The late Baron Stormhurst kept the truth tightly under wraps, even from me," I said. "We won't forget how quickly you stepped up when called on."

I felt weirdly out of place, like a kid playing dress-up more than the near-baron he saw me as—and that I was trying to act as. Did I really deserve the respect indicated in that second bob of his head? Preparing to take over the barony was my role for now, and I had to do the best I could with it, but it was hard to feel comfortable with my new status.

"Holden should wake up in a few minutes," the doctor added before he left. "You might want to have a meal ready. I expect with all the work his body has been doing in healing, he'll be pretty hungry."

I walked him to the door of the apartment and then turned toward the kitchen. The place was pretty bland, nothing but the Ikea-esque furniture the rental had come with. I hadn't exactly had much time to decorate it into something homier. Maybe Holden would have his own ideas about that... if he ended up staying here. That was one of the many topics we'd need to discuss.

Since he'd recovered most of his capacity for speech a few days ago, I'd found out quite a bit about my twin brother's current tastes. Some of them had changed since we were young teens, before the vicious fight our parents had forced us into, but he still loved roast beef and mayo on rye. I assembled the sandwich with less art than our chef back home would have brought to it but with plenty of filling to make up for that and carried it into the bedroom just as Holden started to stir on the bed.

His gaze latched onto the sandwich the second he opened his eyes. He pushed himself into a sitting position. "Room service and everything. I can't say I mind."

It was still a little startling hearing such coherent sentences from his mouth when before he'd often had trouble getting out even a single word. I hadn't realized how much his voice had deepened over the years when he'd barely been able to use it.

"You need it," I said, handing him the plate. I sat in the stiff chair next to the bed as he dug in.

"Thanks," he said between bites. "You really don't need to wait on me like this. I should be practicing getting back up to speed with my independence as quickly as possible."

"I owe you a hell of a lot more than a sandwich, Holden."

He paused and lowered the remaining piece to the plate. His eyes, a darker shade of blue than my own, held mine, abruptly serious.

"I want us to put that to rest right now, forever. You know I don't hold what happened against you. I was *there*; I know you never wanted to hurt me. I was just about out of my mind at that point too. We were kids, and they were torturing us. That's all there is to it. Okay?"

This was the first time he'd managed to say quite that much all at once, without having to halt here and there to work through each thought. The absolution he was granting me seemed so generous my throat closed up for a second. "Okay," I said. "I just wish I'd realized sooner that I could help you."

He waved his free hand dismissively and went back to his sandwich. "*I* didn't even realize they hadn't actually brought doctors in to see me. How could you be expected to know? As soon as you found out, you did everything you could to get me away from them and have me healed, even knowing how furious Mom was going to be. That's more than enough right there."

He finished off the last few bites and licked the traces of crumbs and mayo off his fingers with a couple of quick swipes. I stood up to take the plate.

"You're feeling all right?" I asked. "The doctor said he thought this might be the last session you need."

Holden rolled his shoulders and shifted his legs under the sheet. "My head isn't at all muggy anymore. I don't feel like I'm ready to take up Olympic racing, but most of the aches in my legs are gone. It's a hell of a lot better than I was doing a week ago."

I hesitated for a second and then pushed the words out. "Maybe we should really talk then. About what happens now, with Mom gone and… everything." Over the last few days, I'd filled him in on the basics of our conflict with the other barons, but I hadn't wanted to push him to make any kind of decisions while he was still only partway through his recovery. I wasn't going to push him now either, but he should at least have a chance to give his opinion on how we went forward from here.

"I'm up for that," he said. "Why don't we take it to the living room? I should put these legs to work."

I gave him room to push out of the bed. He made his way across the room on his own two feet with slow steps and a wobble here and there. When he reached the walker the doctor had brought him, which Holden had left by the door, he grasped hold of it and let it support him the rest of the way to the boxy beige sofa.

I sat down at the opposite end and grappled with where to start. Maybe it made sense to focus on the most immediate considerations first.

"Since Mom isn't around to be pissed off or take anything out on us, you don't really need to stay hidden," I said. "You *can* stay here in the apartment as long as you want... but if you feel ready to enroll at Blood U, I can arrange a talk with the headmistress so we can figure out how the staff will want to handle that."

He'd had to put off his magical education for so long, I doubted he'd want to keep waiting to dive into his studies once he was up to it. Between the two of us, I'd always been a little more on the athletic side, but as kids and preteens we'd both been pretty rambunctious, more likely to be climbing trees or tossing a ball around in our free time than sitting in quiet contemplation. Holden's injuries had forced him onto a different path. He hadn't been able to do much with his body in the past six years, and I could already tell all that time when he'd relied on his books and his music to keep him sane had turned him into a more thoughtful and scholarly counterpart to me.

Putting proof to my suspicion, a smile crossed his lips at the idea of joining the school. "I'd like that," he said. "I'm not sure I could keep up with full classes yet, especially at the senior level, but maybe they'd be willing to start me out with individualized tutoring for at least the first little while."

"I'm sure they could arrange something like that. You *are* a Stormhurst, after all." I dropped my gaze. That statement led us to the much bigger aspect of our future we needed to consider. "And possibly the baron-in-training."

Even without raising my eyes, I felt Holden's attention

intent on me. "You earned the role," he said, simply and evenly. "It's yours. I'm not going to challenge you for it after all this time, Conn."

"I know you wouldn't. But I *didn't* earn it, not in any way that should have counted. Their way didn't prove anything about who'd really be a better leader." I forced myself to look at him again. "If anything, it proved the opposite. I had less control; I broke faster. You can see it as their fault, but you can't deny that."

Holden studied my expression. "You've been studying, honing your skills, and developing your connections with the other scions and all our peers for years now. Do you not *want* to be baron?"

I wasn't really sure. The thought of trying to rule alongside the current barons made my stomach knot. But if it could be Declan and Malcolm and Rory I was standing beside... There was something thrilling about that idea and the changes we might make, absolutely. That didn't change the facts, though.

"You'll have time to do all the same things once we get you into the university," I said. "Maybe you'd be better for the position than me because you experienced so blatantly how a baron can misuse their power. I don't want to shut you out just because I got first shot at it. Obviously we don't have to decide anything right away, but if you want a chance at the role, we can figure that out. I guess... I'll have to step up once I graduate anyway, since I'll do that first, and we'll see how that goes and how you feel once you're properly back in the community. I just want you to know the opportunity is there if you want it."

He was silent for a long moment. "All right. Thank you. I—I really don't know what I'd want at this point. I haven't even talked to anyone except the staff and occasionally you or Mom and Dad in years." He let out a self-deprecating laugh and raked his hand through his hair. "We'll see how I feel once I'm getting a handle on my magic and finding out how everyone else is going to adapt to my return. Their respect matters just as much as our personal preferences."

I bristled automatically. "Anyone who treats you like you don't deserve respect will have to answer to me."

Holden raised an eyebrow at me. "Which I'm sure will make them feel so much more respectful, watching my brother fight my battles for me."

Okay, he had a point there. I let out a breath. "First things first, I guess. Who knows what the pentacle of barons will even look like after this mess. But I do want you to be a part of the scion discussions and all that. You're just as much a scion as I am."

Holden inclined his head. "I can agree to that. I'm looking forward to seeing how the other guys have changed since I last saw them—and to finally meeting the Bloodstone scion." He gave me a crooked smile. "Let's hope the current barons don't burn everything down before we get any choices about our future at all."

CHAPTER SIX

Rory

The room we'd claimed for the Scions' Guard was crowded now, our numbers nearly doubled in just a few days. Looking at the classmates who'd gathered to support us and our cause, hope swelled in my chest even though we had a long way to go before we were anywhere close to victory.

Declan, Malcolm, and I had done most of the talking, Jude preferring to hang back with the knowledge that he wasn't officially a scion and Connar not being much of a talker in general. Malcolm finished the meeting off with a clap of his hands and a grin he aimed at the whole assembly.

"Keep up the good work, and make sure the people you've reached out to are prepared to speak up as soon as the barons' activities become public. If we all push back together, they can't dismiss us."

Someone toward the back of the group let out a whoop of encouragement, and a few others laughed—a little nervously, maybe, but the fact that they were here at all showed how committed they were. Associating with the scions right now was treacherous ground when our eventual victory was hardly a sure thing.

As our Guard filed out of the room, I touched Malcolm's arm. "You do know how to get them pumped up."

"Best part of the job," he said, shifting his hand so he could squeeze mine. His gaze lingered on me for a few seconds longer, and that uneasy vibe of intensity and uncertainty struck me again.

Something was bothering him, something he hadn't been able to overcome on his own. It didn't matter how much else we had to deal with right now—I couldn't see any good coming out of letting it fester any longer.

"Hold on a minute," I said to him, and he nodded, but his cocky smile looked a bit tense around the edges too. I saw the other scions off with a kiss here and a hug there while he hung back. When I turned to him, just the two of us left in the room, he sauntered closer with more of his usual self-assured air.

"And why exactly were you looking to get me alone, Glinda?" he said in a low voice, slipping one arm around my back. "Couldn't resist my impressive leadership skills?"

I gave him a pointed look. "They are very impressive, but I wanted to *talk*. You've been edgy about something all week. Something to do with me, it seems like. I think it's about time you told me what's going on."

His body tensed next to mine. He swallowed audibly, his attention sliding away from me for a moment. "It's nothing you've done. It might not be anything at all, so I've been trying not to think about it."

"Think about *what*?" I gave his chest a gentle shove. "After everything you've already put me through, it can't be that bad."

He met my eyes again, with enough turmoil in his dark brown gaze that my stomach sank. He thought it *could* be that bad. Shit.

"What?" I said again, my voice softening.

"Like I said, it could be nothing." He let out a ragged breath. "When I grabbed my sister to get her away from my parents, I went back to the house to pick up a few things. My mom was out, and I thought my dad would be holed up in his office working... but he had a guest over. Your mother was with him."

My mother hadn't told me about any one-on-one visits with the other barons, but then, I wouldn't necessarily have expected her to. "I guess that's not so surprising. It seems like they were always the closest friends out of the original pentacle."

Malcolm let out a dark chuckle. "Oh, they were being a lot more than friendly. It wasn't a business meeting or a platonic social call—they were hooking up. And from the way they were talking, it's an affair that's been going on for a long time. They were seeing each other while she was married."

"Oh." The thought made me slightly queasy. I disagreed with my mother on a lot of topics, but she had a good side too. I didn't want to add "cheater" to the list of her transgressions. I had wondered, having met my paternal grandparents, how much she'd actually respected my father if he was anything like them… Apparently she hadn't very much at all. "Well, that's unpleasant to know, but I can't say I'm totally shocked. Is that all you were worried about telling me?"

Malcolm studied my face for a moment as if he were looking for something else. "If they were involved before you were born… your father might not even really be your father."

I stared at him for a moment before the full implications of that statement sank in. Then my eyes widened even more. "You think—"

"I don't think anything," he said, quickly and firmly. "It's possible, that's all. And I—*I* don't fucking care, even if it's true, okay? I'm sure as hell never going to see you as a sister. If we're related by blood, I'll still want to be with you just as much as I did before. We just… won't take the risk of bringing kids into the equation, and then it doesn't really matter, right? You've got plenty of other options when it comes to providing Bloodstone heirs."

The corner of his mouth crooked up at a wry angle, but the intensity in his eyes hadn't faded. He was afraid that it'd matter more than that to me. I looked back at him, trying to wrap my head around the idea—that we might share a father, that we could theoretically be half-siblings—and how I'd feel if it were true.

Maybe that didn't even have to matter. "I don't think it's likely," I said. "She's said things about my father, at least once—about why she picked him, about balancing out my strengths, since she only has three… And I can't imagine her being careless about bringing *her* heirs into the world."

"On the other hand, the fact that you have more strengths than she does could indicate a particularly powerful partner. She can say whatever she wants about your father to deflect the idea."

True. I hugged myself and leaned into him instinctively. Malcolm's arm tightened around me, the tang of his aquatic cologne filling my nose.

I didn't want it to be true, because if I knew it was, maybe I wouldn't be able to look at him quite the same way. And the last thing I wanted was to give up the fire and devotion he offered up so easily now.

"There's no point in letting the possibility hang over us," I said. "There are spells that can identify a genetic connection, aren't there? That's why Lillian had me help with the spellwork to find my mother."

Malcolm nodded. "We'd need someone at least somewhat experienced with them doing the casting, if they're going by the two of us. Any connection less direct than parent to child or full sibling to full sibling is harder to confirm. It's in the physicality realm, so Connar *might* be able to pull it off without specific training."

But then we'd have to admit the problem to him. And if he couldn't, to someone completely outside the pentacle of scions. I wasn't eager to involve others either. I bit my lip.

"Before we go to that length, then, maybe I can talk to

my mother. I should be able to get a pretty good read on her at this point. If I can get a good enough answer out of her, then we won't need to worry about the rest."

"Or we could just… decide it's fine either way and not poke at the possibility any more than we already have."

I looked up at him. "Would you really not want to know for sure?"

His mouth twisted. "It's hard to say. If finding it out as a fact makes it impossible to ignore…" He ducked his head next to mine, tugging me even closer to him. "I've never denied that I can be selfish, Rory. I don't want to lose you."

A pang shot through my heart. Malcolm didn't often let himself express any kind of vulnerability. And I understood that emotion, because the same fear was coursing through me. I raised my hand to his cheek, struggling to put into words why I'd be willing to take that risk.

"I don't want to lose you either," I said. "And we could find out it's not true at all, or that if it is we can handle that. *I* want to know—I mean, we can't even be sure how official our relationship is ever going to be—but if we make it work… Maybe I'd want to have an heir with you if we can."

Malcolm made a rough sound in his throat, and then he was kissing me, so hard my legs wobbled. I gripped his shirt and kissed him back, and in that moment, at least, the ideas he'd raised didn't matter one bit.

"Okay," he said when he drew back. "You talk to your

mom if you find the chance, and after we see what she says, we'll figure out where to go from there."

It wasn't exactly a resolution, but it was a plan. I felt a little more settled for about five seconds, and then my phone rang.

It was Maggie—calling rather than texting like she usually did. My pulse stuttered as I answered. "Hey. What's up?"

"I'm not completely sure." Her voice had a slightly hushed quality, as if she were afraid of being overheard. "The blacksuits got in touch with your mother— something about 'joymancers' location'—and she and at least one of the other barons went off with a squad, looking pretty scary. I think they were looking for the mages who broke the wards around that town by campus. They figured some of the joymancers had stayed in the area to keep an eye on what we'd do next."

"And the blacksuits figured out where the joymancers are?" Oh, shit. My mother had been shaken up by the conflict with the joymancers. Their leaders had held her imprisoned for years—it was no wonder she wanted them to stay as far away from her as possible. And given the rage she harbored after her treatment at their hands, I had no doubt she'd go to awfully violent lengths to see them gone.

"I don't know if they'd found them or just had some promising leads," Maggie said. "I just didn't like the vibe I got from the group when they left. And the fact that your mother didn't ask me to come along—it didn't seem like it was just a fact-finding mission."

I shivered. "You must have plenty of connections

with the blacksuits after all your time working for Lillian. Do you think you can get any of them to find out where that squad was going?" If they had located joymancers nearby, maybe I could warn the other mages to get out of there before it turned into outright warfare. It was my fault they were in this part of the country at all; I'd asked them to come defend the Naries the barons were tormenting.

"It depends... I might be able to find the right angle to get it out of someone. Here, let me make a few calls. If I turn anything definite up, I'll let you know right away."

"Thanks. I know you're putting yourself in a precarious situation tipping me off like this."

Until recently, my secret second cousin and I had been at odds, her seeing me as just as bad as the Bloodstones her part of the family had told her about as she grew up. Now that we understood we both wanted a gentler approach to ruling, I couldn't have asked for a better ally on the inside.

"It's the least I can do," Maggie said. "Hopefully you'll hear from me soon."

When I hung up and turned back to Malcolm, he was frowning. He'd obviously caught enough to have a general idea what was going on. "The barons are out for joymancer blood?" he said.

"It sounds like it." What could we really do about that? I dragged in a breath. "We should get the others back here so we're ready if Maggie can find out where they're going."

Within ten minutes, the other scions had rejoined us, along with a few members of the Guard they'd been able to call on nearby. Just as Connar came into the room, Maggie texted me an address.

It's a motel, looks like about an hour away from you. Whatever you do with that information, be careful.

As if we were the ones in any danger. I looked up the motel's main phone number and dialed it as quickly as I could.

A busy signal beeped in response. I grimaced, hung up, and paced the room's mats for a minute before trying again. Still busy.

"I can't get through," I said to my companions. "The place isn't that far from here. Maybe we should go, see if there's anything we can do. The blacksuits might still only be surveilling the area."

Declan nodded, his jaw tight. "We should be able to stop them from noticing us if we're properly prepared. We'll take two cars, all of us go? If any sort of violence breaks out, I think we'll be better off having solid numbers."

"I'm in," Malcolm said. "Let's get going."

Jude drew back. "As much as I'd like to contribute, you all know I'm more of a liability than an asset at this point." He motioned to his chest, to the space where he could no longer contain much magic. "I'll keep an eye on things here and let you know if anything that seems useful comes up?"

"It's probably good to have someone stay back and keep watch." I bobbed up to give him a kiss before the rest of us hurried out to the garage.

I ended up in Declan's car, two of the Guard members

in the seat behind us. For all his usual reserve, the Ashgrave scion had no problem gunning the engine and racing down the highway with a quick casting to reflect the notice of any traffic cops we passed. I peered out the window with my hands clasped on my lap, my heart thudding hard. Every few minutes, I tried the motel's phone number again. It was busy a couple more times—and then it just rang until it went through to the answering machine.

"If they're fighting when we get there, should we risk intervening?" I asked. Taking the joymancers' side would be clear-cut treason, no questions about it, but the last thing I wanted to do was help the barons attempt to do away with them.

"I don't know," Declan said. "Better we wait and see what the situation is when we get there. Maybe we can deflect some of the fighting without being too obvious about it, but enough to give the joymancers time to get out of there."

That thought reassured me until we raced into view of the squat building just off the highway. It wouldn't have looked like anything all that striking—except three ambulances were parked out front along with several police cars, lights flashing all over. Another ambulance was just pulling away toward the nearest town.

My hopes plummeted. We were too late.

Declan slowed, and we parked at the far end of the lot outside the motel. A woman in a cleaning uniform was standing on the patchy grass nearby, dragging on a cigarette she held with a shaky hand.

"No rooms available right now," she said with a humorless laugh when we got out. "My God. I don't even know…" She gazed toward the building with a haunted expression.

"What happened?" I ventured.

She shook her head. "Fucking crazy. Everything seemed totally normal, and then there were these screams… By the time anyone got out to the rooms, it was all just blood, and more." Her face turned a little green. She sucked on her cigarette again. "Nine people staying here the last few days, came as the group of them, and all of them look like they got shredded. No one even saw who did it."

It hadn't been a battle then. It'd only been a slaughter. The barons and the blacksuits had descended on the joymancers and blasted through their defenses too quickly for them to fight back. And then they'd eviscerated them all without a second's hesitation.

CHAPTER SEVEN

Rory

I hadn't spoken to my mother since the day at our house when the other scions and I had confronted the barons. To say I was nervous meeting with her now was like saying the ocean is damp. But the staff office Ms. Grimsworth had let us borrow for this talk felt like at least somewhat neutral ground.

My mother didn't seem to see it the same way—or else she did, and that was why she cast a narrow gaze around the bookshelf-lined space with a disdainful curl of her lip. She'd have preferred an environment where she had the upper hand.

"Is this really necessary, Persephone?" she said. "Surely we could have met up for lunch or at one of our properties like we always have before. We may have our differences, but you're still my daughter."

True, but I didn't think I could stand to expose the

townspeople she'd lorded her power over to her presence, even if the memories of that horrible time had been magically wiped from their minds. Some part of them might react even if they couldn't consciously understand why. And I didn't trust her enough to risk venturing onto territory that was completely under her control.

Especially when I had more than one thing I needed to address today. I girded myself. "I thought it was the best option, considering the circumstances. And—I think you should know, I don't go by Persephone anymore. I know that's the name you gave me, but I grew up without knowing that. I've been Rory my entire life that I can remember. I'm a Bloodstone now, I'll never deny that, but I can't just become the person you expected me to be back then."

She blinked at me with a wince she couldn't quite suppress. "That's the name your jailors gave you."

"They didn't treat me like a prisoner," I said. "They never made me feel as if they thought there was anything wrong with me, even though they knew who and what I was. I disagree with plenty of things the joymancers have done, but they are people too, and some of them are good people. Even if it wasn't right for the ones who attacked us to take me in the first place, they made the best of a bad situation. I'm not going to forget that."

Her lips pursed in a thin line. Looking at her face-to-face, I saw even more than before how much I took after her in appearance. From our dark brown hair, though hers was silvered, to our height and our slim frames, anyone could have marked us as mother and daughter in an instant.

What had I gotten from my father? Where was there any confirmation in the mirror of who that man had been?

Questions I wasn't ready to ask quite yet, not when there was so much else hanging over this conversation. I'd stayed standing, not wanting to feel my mother looming over me, so she had her pick of the room's seats. Possibly unsurprisingly, she slipped behind the desk and dropped into the chair where the professor who normally would have used this space would have sat. I let myself sink into the chair opposite.

"You have a lot of opinions on many subjects," my mother said, picking up a pen that had been left on the desk. She tapped it against the wooden surface. "Perhaps you should consider that you have far from all the facts from which to draw your conclusions. You *didn't* grow up in this world. I did, even though I was torn from it for a time. I know our people. I know what we need. You should let me guide you. This resistance—it's not a good look."

"I'm not concerned about how it looks. And maybe I don't know everything about the community, but I know there are plenty of people who grew up in it who feel the same way I do. I know the fact that I didn't grow up here might let me see things from a broader perspective." I hesitated and then tried one last-ditch effort to appeal to her emotions, even though I doubted it would work. "You even said yourself that things have been moving too quickly for you to really think them through."

She tossed the pen back onto the desk with a dismissive flick of her fingers. "If I did, it was a moment of distraction and confusion—because of the horrors imposed on me by the people you say can be *good*."

My voice came out quiet but steady. "And what did you do to some of those people just yesterday? They weren't the same ones who kept you captive, were they? But you didn't show them any mercy."

My mother's gaze sharpened into close to a glare. "They came into our territory, attacked us, and destroyed what we were building. They deserved every wound we dealt them. Are you defending them too now?"

"I'm not saying you shouldn't have been angry with them, or that you shouldn't have taken steps to make them leave. I just think... taking them by surprise, with no ability to defend themselves, and going straight for the slaughter—we should be better than that. It wasn't even sinking to their level, because they didn't descend on any of us in our beds. It was sinking lower."

"They were vermin here, and we exterminated them," she snapped. "You have to take a firm hand if you want your enemies to know the consequences of meddling. We weren't going to risk any more casualties on our side than we'd already taken."

I could imagine other options that might not have risked fearmancer deaths without resorting to instant slaughter, but it was too late for those now, and my mother clearly wasn't in the mood to hear them. "And what are you going to do to the Naries you're targeting now? Did those kids in town the other day deserve to be slaughtered too—because they threw some rocks and dirt at us?"

Her shoulders stiffened. I'd seen how she'd reacted to the one little boy one of the blacksuits' crew had killed. She hadn't enjoyed witnessing *that* death any more than I had.

But she couldn't admit even that much. "They had to learn. They *will* learn. And you will see, once we remake the world for you, how much better it is for you after all."

"Why can't you explain it to me first?" I said. "Why can't we hold off on messing with their lives until we've all really talked about it—until you've given all of the fearmancers you're supposed to be serving a chance to say their piece without having to be afraid they'll be punished for it? If this plan is so great, you should be able to make a convincing case for it."

"You clearly won't believe that we belong at the top of the hierarchy until you've gotten to experience it for yourself." My mother pushed back the chair and stood up. "Is this all you brought me here for—to badger me about my decisions? I thought *you* were better than that, Persephone."

Her tone was so caustic in combination with the criticism and her insistence on using my birth name that I flinched. My hands balled at my sides. "I just want to talk about it instead of you insisting that you know what's best. You hardly know *me* at all."

There was something a little sad in the tight smile she gave me then. "Or maybe you don't fully understand yourself yet. You're a Bloodstone. I know what that means. I could keep showing you if you'd let me."

I didn't think Maggie would agree that the baron had sole ownership over how one could be a Bloodstone, but I wasn't going to reveal any of the secrets my cousin had told me. That comment did give me an opening into the one other topic I'd hoped I could bring up.

"Am I just a Bloodstone?" I said.

My mother paused, tipping her head to one side. "What do you mean?"

"I mean, I've heard rumors that you might have been... especially close with one of the other barons way back then."

I didn't need to spell it out any more than that. No more than a flicker of confusion crossed my mother's face before understanding dawned there instead. She let out a bark of a laugh and covered her mouth to contain the giggles that followed it.

"Oh, darling," she said. "I don't know who's been filling your head with ridiculous speculations, but I can assure you I took every care when it came to your conception. I valued your future ahead of my own happiness. Your father... was not everything I could have wanted in a partner, but he was an impressively strong master of insight, which has never been a great strength of mine. And clearly that line ran true alongside mine, considering that area of magic became not just one of your strengths but your specialty."

Her amusement at the idea convinced me with a trickle of relief. She didn't sound defensive or anxious about being exposed, only a little offended that I might have believed such an absurd idea. And when she put it that way, it did seem absurd. Persuasion was her greatest strength, and it was Baron Nightwood's too. If I'd gotten my heritage from the two of them, surely I'd have gravitated toward the same area no matter what my upbringing had been. I didn't even consider it my secondary strength—that would be Physicality.

"That's what I thought," I said, managing a little laugh of my own. "I just wanted to hear it from you, to be sure."

My mother's gaze rested on me for a moment, with a touch more warmth than had been there before. God, how I wished our conversations could be more like that brief exchange—that I could ask questions and get straight answers, and we could laugh together at the turns the discussion took.

If I'd just given in and gone along with her plans, maybe I could have had that. I'd bet that was what she was thinking right now: how much she'd given to me and why I was giving back so much less than that. I didn't know how to explain to her why I couldn't be who she wanted in any way she'd understand.

But damn it, what I wouldn't have given for a real *mom* again.

Then she shattered that moment of longing with a snap of her fingers. "I think this foolishness has gone on long enough. *Persephone, you will come with me now.*"

The persuasive spell rammed into the magical barrier around my mind with so much force I jerked back in my seat. If I'd only been relying on my own strength, I could tell it would have smashed straight through. But contrary to appearances, I wasn't alone. I had the combined strength of three other scions bolstering my shield—and they'd have felt the impact from where they'd been waiting for this talk to end a few rooms over, lending their power to protect me in the meantime.

A tingle of energy rushed over me as their castings wrapped around me to bolster my defenses even more. My mother frowned, her eyes turning piercing as she examined me. "You let others fight your battles for you. You should be better than that, too."

If I'd been "better," she'd have had me walking out the door with her already. I stared right back at her. "They're not fighting the battle for me; they're fighting it *with* me. Our pentacle stands together." Unlike hers, from what I'd seen.

Her jaw worked. I suspected she was tempted to try again, but she'd put a huge effort into that first casting when she'd thought she'd also had the advantage of surprise. I could almost see the gears turning in her head as she decided that no, it would make more sense to wait for a fresh opportunity.

"It doesn't matter what you think or how you behave," she said, "you're still my daughter." And with those words left hanging in the air, she stalked out of the office.

The moment she was gone, I slumped in my chair. The tension of the meeting had left me drained. But from their vantage point, the guys wouldn't know anything about how the conversation had gone, only that we'd fended off a spell. After a moment, I peeled myself out of the chair and made my own way to the doorway.

Ms. Grimsworth was just stepping out of her office at the far end of the hall. She looked me over with a solemn expression. "I gathered your conference is finished."

"Yes." I drew myself straighter, hoping my weariness with the conflict didn't show. "Thank you again for the use of the office."

"It was no trouble at all." The headmistress walked a little closer and stopped, folding her arms over her chest. For a second, with her strict expression, I thought *she* was going to chide me for my lack of daughterly respect.

"I know you haven't been happy with recent developments here on campus," she said instead. "Unfortunately I haven't always had final say. But I can tell you that I intend for you and your fellow scions to be able to count on this university as a secure place no matter what else is going on in your lives, and if there's anything I can do to make it more secure, I hope you'll tell me that."

My throat closed up at her offer, gratitude and apprehension mingling inside me. Gratitude that she was making that offer. Apprehension at what might be ahead of us that made her feel she needed to say it in the first place.

CHAPTER EIGHT

Rory

The last thing I expected to see when I walked into the common room was Cressida and our new Nary dormmate, Morgan, sitting at opposite ends of one of the sofas, having what looked like an at least somewhat friendly conversation.

"It's just been hard to wrap my head around, you know?" Morgan was saying, her hands twisting together on her lap. She startled a little at my arrival.

Cressida let out a light chuckle. "You don't have to worry about *her*. Rory has been championing the nonmagical students here basically since she arrived. Which hasn't always made her a whole lot of friends with the rest of us, but..." She offered me a crooked smile. "Some of us are starting to see her point. The way things have gotten is definitely beyond the pale."

It was one thing for Cressida to want to avoid having

to get into combative situations against the Naries in town, which was how she'd ended up on the Scions' Guard in the first place. I hadn't expected her to actually reach out to any of the Nary students and make an effort to get to know them. I had to admit I was a little impressed.

I came over and sat gingerly on a chair near Morgan. "Have you been holding up okay? I've done my best to at least get the other girls to hold off on harassing you while you're here in the dorm."

But I hadn't reached out to her directly—until the past week, I'd been too worried about keeping up a front of supporting my mother, and since I'd officially spoken up against her plans, I'd been so caught up in figuring out how to tackle the barons that I'd let other considerations slide. Now that the scions were openly opposing terrorizing the Naries for fun and power, we *could* take steps to make things more comfortable for them here on campus too.

"I'm surviving." Morgan's arms came up to hug herself. "I'm kind of terrified every time I have to leave the dorm. But… the weird thing is I do still love the actual program. I'm learning a lot when I can concentrate."

"What are you studying?" I asked. The only Nary disciplines Blood U offered that I was at all familiar with were the music and architecture programs, but I knew there was at least one more.

Morgan flexed her fingers. "Computer programming. Which makes it even more embarrassing that I can't seem to reach out to anyone back home… I can do pretty much whatever I want on the internet with my laptop, but whenever I try to send someone an email or anything, it's like I just freeze up."

I grimaced. "The mages who took your phones probably cast a spell on all of you to make sure you couldn't reveal what was going on here in any other way. I'm so sorry. We're trying to fix that. It's never been *great* here at the university, but the way things were before, no one would have thrown magic at you this openly."

"I guess we could…" Cressida slipped her hand into her purse and withdrew her phone with its pearly case. "The blacksuits never figured any of us would offer our own phones."

She gave me a questioning look, a worry line forming on her forehead. If Morgan *could* use our phones, then that would mean potentially letting her tell people beyond campus about magic and everything else that was going on here. I didn't like seeing the Naries cut off from their support systems, but I wasn't sure that kind of revelation would be a good thing in the long run. How would the barons respond to that information breach?

Morgan must have been able to guess the reason for my hesitation. "I won't say anything about magic or the craziness here," she said quickly, her face brightening with eagerness. "It'd be amazing just to let my family and friends know I'm okay and find out what's up with them. If it even works."

That was a big question, after all. If she started to say anything I thought might bring the barons' wrath down on her or the people close to her, we were right here. I could intervene. I nodded to Cressida. "We might as well try."

She unlocked the phone and handed it to the Nary girl. Morgan hovered her thumb over the touchscreen, her hand trembling. Her thumb twitched—and veered off just shy of tapping the phone icon. She tried again with the same result and lowered the phone with a rough laugh.

"It figures if I can't make myself do it with the computer, it applies to every phone too. Even if you dialed the number for me, I bet I wouldn't be able to make myself talk."

She was probably right. "We'll get it figured out as fast as we can," I said. "And in any case, the staff were never planning on keeping you all here away from the rest of the world *forever*. You'll get to make trips home for the holidays and all."

Just with their memories wiped of anything incriminating… unless it was into a world where the barons had already brought fearmancers into the light as humanity's new dictators, however exactly they were planning on doing that.

The uncomfortable thought was punctuated with the chime of a text alert on my own phone. Cressida's went off at the same moment. We glanced at each other with mutual understanding. Something was going on with the scions and their Guard. When I checked, Malcolm was calling us down to the Guard room.

"We've got to get going," I said to Morgan. "Just… hang in there as well as you can. And if there's something you think we might be able to help with, let me know."

Cressida stayed quiet as we headed down the stairs.

"You decided to make friends?" I said lightly after we'd passed the first two landings.

Her lips twisted. "I don't know. I figured… if we're going to all this work and taking all these risks to try to protect these people, maybe I should get a better idea of who exactly we're doing this for." She paused. "She wasn't actually *that* different to talk to than another mage."

How many Naries had she bothered to really talk to before? Maybe none. "They are still people like us," I said. "The only difference is the magic."

"I suppose." She flicked her braid back over her shoulder. "I'd still rather have magic than not."

I had to laugh. "Fair enough." I couldn't say that I wasn't glad I had my magic too.

We were among the first to reach the basement room. Malcolm motioned me over to where he was standing with one of the guys from his guard. He rested his hand on the small of my back, with a possessive sweep of his thumb and a gleam in his eyes that was much more his usual self than I'd been seeing in the past week. I'd told him what I'd heard from my mother as soon as I'd gotten out of that meeting, and his relief that no huge stumbling block existed in our relationship still radiated off him.

"It looks like the barons have made their first move," he said, with a nod toward the laptop his friend was holding. "Probably by way of the underlings they sent out to Washington, from what Jude's uncle said. There've been some very strange things happening in Nary politics today… Stranger than usual, anyway. I'm pretty sure they're stirring up trouble there."

My gut clenched. "Wonderful. I guess we'll go over the details once everyone is here?"

He'd made it clear his summons was urgent. More of the Guard trickled in by the minute, along with our fellow scions. Connar drew up the rear of the procession, with a guy who looked with a thinner, shaggier version of him walking a little stiffly beside him.

He'd mentioned his brother would be coming to the school to start his education, but I hadn't had the chance to meet Holden yet. The protectiveness with which the Stormhurst scion hovered near his twin sent a twinge of fondness through my chest.

There wasn't time for proper introductions at this exact second. Malcolm appeared to have judged that everyone important had turned up. He nudged his friend, who swiveled the laptop around. A news website with a video report was open on the screen.

"We have reason to believe that the barons have gotten their lackeys to start magically influencing major Nary political figures into pursuing extreme policies, most likely to purposely stir up conflict among the Naries," Malcolm said. "Several politicians announced major changes in approach today, things that their constituents are already expressing shock and horror over—things that are going to badly affect a lot of those people, as far as I can tell. All this appears to have come out of nowhere, too."

His friend started the video playing, and the tinny sound from the speakers carried through the room.

"There's a lot of confusion here in D.C. today as figures from both parties have come forward with proposals no one could have expected—but that they seem adamant about passing through Congress," a reporter said in dramatic tones. She listed several announcements including the rolling back of employment anti-discrimination policies, a huge increase in health care costs, and, most overtly strange, a motion to see actual soldiers patrolling high schools. Even though I'd been prepared for extremes, my eyebrows rose at that last one.

"When asked, none of the officers and representatives involved were willing to give an explanation for these sudden and significant shifts in their expected platform," the reporter went on. "We will continue to press for more details and share them as available. In the meantime, an outcry has already risen up across the country against the proposals."

The guy let the video play through a few clips of regular citizens talking about how the changes would shatter their lives, and then clicked it off. Declan, who'd come over to join us at the front of the room, looked to me.

"I'm not an expert on Nary politics by any stretch, but this sounds awfully extreme to be coming from the officials themselves," he said. "You'd have paid more attention to this sort of thing growing up the way you did, Rory. Would you agree?"

A hollow sensation had already formed in the pit of my stomach. "Yeah. For so many huge shifts in approach to all be coming out at once like this, and such significant changes from their previous policies... and when we *know* the barons intended to tackle the Naries from the top down—this has to be fearmancer interference, undermining the Nary leadership. I have no idea where exactly they think they're going to go with it, but it's obviously not anywhere good."

"So we have proof that they're meddling with the Nary government now," one of the Guard members said. "Where do we take it from here?"

The other scions would have a better idea of how *fearmancer* politics worked than I did. I glanced around at them. Declan frowned in thought.

"We'll figure out our most powerful talking points," he said. "Then we all need to contact at least one of the barons and express those objections. And not just us, because they're not going to give a lot of weight to the opinions of students, but all the people you've made overtures to in the last few days. If you think you can get your parents, other relatives, family friends who are more established—anyone from the older generations—to speak up now, let them know what's going on and do your best to encourage them if they're worried. Let them know they'll be far from alone."

"We're just going to talk," a guy said skeptically. "Do you really think that's going to accomplish anything? They haven't paid attention before."

"Do *you* really want to jump into full-out war with the barons and the families that are supporting them?" Jude asked with an arch of his eyebrows. "We didn't have specifics to argue against before. This is the first time we've been able to raise a real protest against their current actions. That's what we've had you reaching out to your friends and family for—so they're ready to speak up now."

"Exactly," I said. "We've only just started opposing them. I don't know if talking will be enough, but we're better off trying that first. I don't want to see anyone here getting hurt from the fallout if I can help it."

"*I* don't want to get into some kind of battle if we don't have to," Victory piped up. "Let's get going with the talking part. How are we going to approach this? We're going to need better arguments than that we don't like it."

"The barons don't care about the well-being of the Naries, so we can't use that angle," Declan said. "We'll want to focus on how it affects the people they're supposed to represent."

We shot ideas back and forth as a group for several minutes until we came up with what seemed like the most pointed criticism: the barons should be focused on improving our own society, not ruining the Naries', and getting a little extra power from scaring them openly wasn't worth all this distraction. That and the fact that none of us *wanted* to take control over the Naries on any scale, let alone a national one, I hoped would get through to them if they heard it from enough people. How long could they keep believing they were helping all of us if dozens of fearmancers were telling them the opposite?

Maybe I couldn't summon a lot of optimism, but I wasn't giving up on peaceful tactics just yet.

As the Guard headed out to start talking up the issue with their families and friends, I went over to properly meet the only member of Connar's family besides him who mattered all that much right now. Connar smiled when he saw me coming.

"Holden, this is our long-lost Bloodstone scion," he said, grasping my hand. "Rory, I'm glad you can finally get to meet my brother."

"So am I." I tipped my head to the other guy. "It's great that you can properly join us here at the university, even if I wish it wasn't in the middle of such a chaotic time."

Holden shrugged, the motion only slightly stiff. Connar had said he wasn't completely physically recovered yet. "If it wasn't for the chaos, you all might not have found out that I could be cured—or been in a position to arrange it. I can't resent that. I understand you helped find the doctor who was willing to work behind our mother's back. Thank you so much for that."

"Of course."

He glanced around the room. He had something of a detached air that I guessed came with having been set apart from his peers and the rest of fearmancer society for so long. "I'd like to be able to contribute more to your efforts, but I'm afraid I don't have any outside connections at all after all this time."

"That's not your fault," Connar said firmly.

"No, but I can still lament it." Holden gave his brother a mild smile.

I wasn't sure what to do with the subtle but awkward tension that had risen between them. Declan spared me from having to decide by herding us all toward the door.

"Let's take some time to regroup and discuss next steps in the scion lounge. I'll go grab lunch for all of us from the cafeteria."

Holden exclaimed over the lounge with the same distant vibe, and we all dug into the sandwiches Declan brought back. I didn't think any of us really wanted to *think* about what our next steps would have to be if putting vocal pressure on the barons didn't work, let alone talk about them. The silence started to grow heavy as we finished our meal—and then Jude glanced at his phone with a pleased cry.

"What?" I said with a holt of hope.

He grinned at us. "Some part of the tide is turning. My uncle saw the Nary news—he's just confirmed that he'll agree to our deal and campaign against Baron Killbrook."

Declan perked up. "That's a huge step in the right direction. With pressure from within the baronies themselves, and not just us scions, they really can't ignore how many of us disagree with the direction they've taken."

"It seems like something's going around," Malcolm said in a grimmer tone. He'd pulled out his own phone during Jude's announcement. "My father wants to arrange a parley with me, as soon as possible—alone."

CHAPTER NINE

Malcolm

I t was a strange sensation, both wanting someone with me and yet wanting them as far away from me as they could possibly get. I glanced over at Rory as I drove past the edge of town toward the meeting spot my father had picked. She sat tensed in the passenger seat, her expression so fierce with determination it sent a stutter of desire through my pulse despite everything ahead of us.

"You don't have to do this," I said. I'd expressed a similar sentiment to all of my fellow scions back in the lounge, but it was harder to accept Rory's insistence than it'd been with the guys. "The three of us can handle him— I can handle him myself if I have to."

She gave me a bemused look. "Are you suggesting you dump me on the side of the road? I think the ship has already sailed."

"I could bring you back to town. It'd only take a few

minutes." Declan and Connar in the car behind us would wonder what the hell I was doing, but I was okay with that if it got the woman beside me out of Baron Nightwood's attack range.

"Sorry," she said. "You're stuck with me. The more of us you have with you, the harder it'll be for him to hurt any of us. And maybe you *could* handle him on your own… but he is a baron, and your dad. It's… different when it's your own parent. Even when you haven't known them that long." A strain came into her voice as she must have thought of her own confrontations with her mother.

I wanted to tell her that she was wrong, that I didn't give any more of a shit what my dad did or said than any of the other barons, but that would have been a lie. If I'd been driving out to face Baron Killbrook or Declan's asshole aunt, I wouldn't have had this coil of dread clamped around my stomach.

I hadn't told him I was bringing company. Did Dad really think I was stupid or reckless enough to drive out to the middle of nowhere on his command with no backup whatsoever? It wasn't as if the other barons hadn't proven how willing they were to go on the offensive against their own heirs, and he'd never been more forgiving than the rest of them.

But before now, I'd never really stood up to him. I'd played the role of the avidly dedicated scion every time I'd been with him; I'd accepted his "lessons" and punishments without complaint, thinking I deserved them, that he was shaping me into someone stronger.

Maybe I *was* stronger because of all that. But then,

Rory had been raised by parents loving enough to leave her horrified by the way my and Connar's and Jude's parents treated us, and I wasn't sure I'd ever met anyone stronger than her. Maybe he'd just enjoyed exerting that kind of power over my sister and me.

It wouldn't be the worst thing I'd found out about him in the past few months.

"You just—you stay a little farther back," I said. "He's had it in for you practically from the moment you turned up. He probably blames you, at least in part, for me turning against him. If he's going to target any of us more than the others, it'll be you."

"We'll all be standing together," Rory said. A smile crossed her lips, sharper than usual. "And *I* can handle him. You focus on protecting yourself."

I wasn't sure she'd mind if she was forced to throw a few spells his way in self-defense. She'd been pissed off enough over the way he and the other barons had tried to sabotage her—she'd been even more upset when she'd seen how he'd retaliated after I'd stood up for her during her murder hearing.

I probably didn't need to worry like this anyway. Rory had the most composure out of any of us except maybe Declan. It wasn't as if she'd go in looking to provoke a fight.

When the location Dad had sent me came into sight, my heart sank. It was an abandoned farm with an ancient For Sale sign that was faded from the weather posted near the road. The windows on the house were boarded up, and the roof of the big barn sagged. My father's car was parked outside the barn. The door stood a few feet ajar.

He was waiting for me in there. And the only reason for him to lower himself to setting foot in a decrepit place like that was if he wanted to make sure no one outside could witness any magic he cast my way. He might as well have thrown the first shot before I'd even set eyes on him.

Rory might not have automatically thought through Baron Nightwood's choice of setting to the obvious conclusions, but Declan and Connar had clearly recognized the implicit threat the same way I had. When they got out of Declan's car, parked next to mine several feet from my father's, they both eyed the building with blatant wariness, Declan's shoulders stiffening, Connar flexing his muscles as if the barn would be intimidated by his posturing.

I didn't really want to bring any of them in there to face my prick of a dad, but fucking hell, I was glad to have them with me all the same. Poor Jude back on campus was probably pissed that he wasn't here too, even though he'd automatically bowed out the way he had for anything that would require much use of magic ever since his own supposed father had messed him up.

"Ready?" I said to my three colleagues—friends and lover. They all nodded. There was nothing for it but to march right in as if I wasn't at all fazed.

I'd rather die than let the old man see he'd shaken me even slightly. He didn't deserve the satisfaction.

Dad would have been monitoring the area around the barn with a spell. He couldn't be surprised when the four of us walked in rather than me alone. Still, he made a show of turning to face us where he was standing by a few scruffy bales of hay at the far end of the gaping space and lifting his eyebrows with the perfect mix of astonishment and admonition. A smell like dank dead grass trickled into my nose. I restrained a grimace.

"I asked to have a private conversation, Malcolm," Dad said in his cool voice. The wind made the bowed-in roof creak overhead.

"This is my pentacle," I said. "Whatever you say to me, they'll end up hearing it anyway. I'm just streamlining the process."

If he made anything of the fact that one of my theoretical pentacle wasn't with us, he didn't show it. Instead, he let out a sigh. "It was bad enough that you roped several of your fellow students into this backlash against us. Now you're putting out calls for support farther abroad? Do you think they'll respect you as baron after you've shown how little *you* respect the barons you have now?"

I resisted the urge to grit my teeth. "I think they'll respect the fact that I cared about what they want and encouraged them to say their piece instead of expecting them to fall in line just because I said so."

"Is that how this looks to you?" He chuckled dryly, but a weird light came into his eyes, something almost manic. "How I raised a son this ignorant… We've done all this for *you*, you idiots."

"How can it be for us when we're telling you in every

possible way that we don't want it, and you're ignoring us?" I demanded.

He shook his head. "You have no idea—how many generations of our family have dreamed of reaching this point, how long we've gathered support among the families that matter, all building up to when I could offer you the world. And you can't think of anything better to do than throw that generosity back in my face."

My temper started to fray. "I don't care how long you've been hoping for this or how hard you worked. I don't want to be a fucking Nary overlord. I had all the power I needed already. Don't pass your greed off on me and try to make it out as if it's for my benefit."

"That—that attitude." He waved a finger at me. His gaze slid to the others as if he thought he could sway them against me. "You have no idea what could be possible. What you're shutting yourselves off from."

Rory's voice rang out, pure and beautiful and oh dear God why couldn't she have hung back like I'd asked her to?

"We've seen exactly what you're doing. Dozens of people have told you they don't want this either. Is it really so hard to understand that not everyone feels the same way you do?"

"You." Dad's voice took on a cuttingly cold edge. "Your mother might not see it, but I have from the start. Those superior assholes got their claws into you too deep for anyone at that university to pry them out. We should have tossed you back to the joymancers, and you'd see what sort of kindness you'd get there."

"The reason they hate me is because fearmancers like you behave like monsters," Rory shot back.

I held up my hand for her to stand down. A prickling ache was forming at the base of my throat. I had to force my words past it.

"None of this matters. We've heard it all. You just refuse to hear *us*. Well, I'm done. I'm done with taking your shit. I'm done with being your whipping boy. You thought you were so smart with all your sadistic little tests, but all they taught me was that you'd rather put your heirs through hell than have to justify what you believe."

"Malcolm," Dad said, wielding my name like a warning.

I hurtled onward. "You cheat, and you screw people over, and you throw the fearmancers you say you're working so hard for to the wolves when it suits you. I'm more worthy of the Nightwood name already than you ever were or will be. My only regret is that it took me this long to figure that out."

"You little bastard," he snapped. "We waited so long, and now you're ruining everything."

He lunged forward so abruptly that I didn't think any of us was prepared for it. We'd anticipated a magical assault, not a physical one. As a casting word tumbled from my lips to build a different sort of shield, I registered the dagger my father had whipped from his sleeve, the runes etched on its gleaming blade, and realized that even the four of us might not be strong enough to fend that weapon off with only a second's notice.

Did he mean to cut me down completely or just to

stab me into submission before patching me back together like he had more than once before? I was recoiling, my arms coming up to deflect him as much as my magical defenses might, when Rory spat out a casting word and thrust her hand forward.

A fiery gleam flashed off her ring and condensed into a tiny scythe of a blade that whipped through the air. Her aim had been true. The conjured blade sliced straight through my father's thumb where he gripped the dagger, severing it below the main joint.

The dagger wobbled and slipped in his hand with the spurt of blood. The blade swung to the side just shy of my chest, and I hurled another casting word to shove Dad backward. Connar was there too, heaving my father away from me with his bodily force on top of my magic. Dad reeled back and tripped over the misshapen bales of hay.

He sprang back to his feet in an instant, smacking his bleeding hand against his chest as he passed the dagger to his weaker side. Blood soaked into his shirt. He looked down at the wound and then at me with that unsettling light blazing in his eyes.

"You cut off my fucking *thumb*."

Technically Rory had done that, but I had brought her along, and I wasn't going to correct him if he hadn't followed every spell cast at him in the heat of the moment.

"Come at me like that again and I'll cut off worse," I retorted. Adrenaline thrummed through my body, heady but piercing enough to make my muscles quiver. My stomach flipped with a queasy lurch. I'd had enough.

A few casting words spilled from Dad's lips. My

colleagues' voices rose at the same time to deflect the spells. He started at us again, and I met him with a slap of magic that locked his legs in place. As he snarled the words to free himself, the three beside me added their own strength to the spell. It'd hold him for at least a few minutes.

"Let's go," I said, turning on my heel. I stalked out without another glance at my father, ignoring the insults he hurled after me. Passing his car, I tossed out a spell to sever the rubber on the tires so they'd be deflated by the time he did make his way out of the barn, if he got it into his head to chase after us.

Not that he wouldn't know where I was whenever he decided to finish the fight he'd started here. It wasn't a question of if; it was only how soon. And next time, we might be up against not just him but all the other barons and their supporters as well.

CHAPTER TEN

Rory

Malcolm got into the car steadily enough, but his knuckles whitened as soon as he'd gripped the steering wheel. He didn't even bother snapping on his seatbelt before starting the engine. I watched him as he jerked the car around toward the road, feeling as much as seeing the tension strung all through his body. It laced the air with an electric prickling.

My thumb moved to my heirloom ring. I'd spoken a casting word to activate its powers without thinking, only knowing that the Nightwood scion's life could be at stake and that I couldn't stand to see another of my lovers brought low by his own parents. All that blood afterward... Baron Nightwood was *definitely* going to be gunning for me after this. And maybe for Malcolm even more, since I'd been there for him, acting in his defense.

I couldn't say I regretted the spell, though. Hell, the

baron could probably find some fearmancer doctor who could magic his thumb back on. Whatever he'd been going to do to his son, I doubted it'd have been as easily cured.

For several minutes, neither of us spoke. The roar of the car's engine, too loud to be totally comfortable, filled the space. Malcolm's hands shifted on the wheel, his shoulders flexing. His throat bobbed with an audible swallow. The forest now beside us whipped by even faster as he pressed harder on the gas.

I tapped a quick message to Connar on my phone. *We're okay. We'll see you back on campus.* Then I turned to Malcolm. "Pull over."

His head jerked toward me and then back to face the road. "What? Why?"

"Because you're obviously upset, and I think it'd be better if we talked about it when you're *not* hurtling more than a ton of steel down a highway."

"Who says we have to talk about it?"

"I do," I said firmly. "Pull over. Please?"

His mouth twitched. For a second, I thought he was going to keep arguing. Then he eased off the gas and drove the car onto the gravel shoulder with a rattle against the undercarriage. When the engine cut out, the silence was momentarily deafening.

Malcolm dropped his hands to his lap. "There isn't really much to say. He's an asshole. And possibly a little insane about this whole taking over the world thing. I'm glad I got to see just how far around the bend he's gone, and I'm glad we got out of there when we did." He glanced over at me. "Thank you for that trick with the ring, even if I hate to think how he's going to try to pay you back for it."

"He deserved worse," I couldn't help muttering, but I wanted to focus on Malcolm, not his dad. I reached over to grasp one of his hands. "You didn't expect him to come at you like that. Even if you didn't trust him and you were prepared for some kind of fight, it makes sense to be shaken up."

He let out a ragged breath. His fingers squeezed tight around mine. "I don't care what happens to him. I wish I'd stopped caring a lot sooner. I just…" He hesitated, his jaw clenching and his gaze scudding away from me. "I'm a Nightwood too. I've got his blood running through my veins; I'm the man he and my mother raised me to be. I can see everything that's wrong with them *now*, but what if—"

I waited after he cut himself off, and then gently prodded, "What if?"

His voice dropped. "I've been wrong too, before. I've hurt people—I hurt *you*—because I got too caught up in my own ideas of what was right and what needed to happen. What if I start sliding that way once I'm baron and I have all that power? I could end up like him twenty, thirty years down the road."

Every particle of my body resisted that suggestion. "No, you couldn't," I said, tugging his hand until he looked at me again. "Just the fact that you're thinking about it and wanting to be on guard means you can't go down the exact same path. Do you really think you'd ever be okay with treating your kids the way he treated you and your sister?"

Malcolm's flinch said enough. "Hell, no. If I start with the torture tests, you're welcome to slit my throat with that ring."

"I don't think that'll be necessary." I scooted closer so I could lean my head against his shoulder. "Even if you don't totally trust your own judgment, you trust mine, right? I wouldn't be here with you right now if I saw any chance you'd turn out like your father. Everyone makes mistakes. It's how you make up for them that shows who you are as a person."

"Rory…" He cupped my cheek and tipped my face to bring his mouth to mine. His kiss was as determined as ever and yet also urgent in a way I hadn't felt before, as if he still thought he had to make the most of it before I might change my mind and pull away.

An ache shot through my heart. I eased back from the kiss, staying close, a rush of my own determination coming over me.

"Push back your seat."

Something in my tone must have convinced him without any further discussion. He gripped the control and shoved the seat as far as it would go. As soon as it had clicked into place, I clambered over to straddle his lap, my head bowing over him. He reached to steady me automatically with one hand resting on my waist and the other coming up to tease into my hair, guiding it back from my face. His dark brown eyes searched mine, already lit with hunger.

"*I* trust you," I said. "I'm yours. Do whatever you want with me."

His fingers tensed against my side. With a rough sound, he pulled me to him. Our mouths collided, my core settling even more firmly against his groin, and my breath stuttered with the kiss. He was devouring me, as if he could claim me in every possible way from now through the end of time with the press of his lips and the sweep of his tongue.

One hand stayed tangled in my hair, the shift of his fingertips sending sparks through my scalp. The other tugged off my jacket and tossed it onto the other seat. In a swift movement, he tipped the seat back so he was nearly lying down, bringing me with him. As he kissed me even harder, he rocked my hips against him, each motion rubbing my sex against the growing bulge of his erection with a flare of desire that shot straight through my belly.

The rumble of an approaching car made him draw back with a muttered curse. He tossed out a quick casting word, presumably to hide us from view. Then he took advantage of our temporary separation to tug my blouse up over my head. The cool air tingled over my mostly bare torso. I leaned closer to him, grasping the bottom of his sweater. He helped me strip him of that before pulling me flush against him again, the heat of his solid chest radiating into my skin.

"You're everything I could possibly want, Rory," he said hoarsely. "And I don't just mean like this. I want you in my bed, and I want us fighting our battles side-by-side. I want you telling off any jackasses around, even if the jackass happens to be me. I want you standing at that table of the pentacle with me, making sure we don't forget anyone who matters. I want all of it, always."

My throat closed up with emotion. I kissed him with all the tenderness I had in me.

"I want that too," I murmured against his lips. "Always."

"I'm so fucking glad I can do this without those worries about your goddamned parentage in my head."

He captured my mouth again with all his usual passion, his hand gliding up my back to undo my bra. As soon as it had slipped off me, he was stroking my breasts. The swivel of his thumb over my nipple made me whimper. He urged me a little higher on him so he could bring the other nipple to his mouth, and a flick of his tongue sent pleasure racing through me.

Malcolm's other hand delved between my legs to massage my clit through my pants. The heady throb of need spread through me with every pulse of pressure. I might have been on top, but there was no doubt that he was in charge, working me over with devoted intentness.

For a while I rode on the waves of bliss as he sent me soaring higher and higher. The throb turned into a sharper ache, and his touch became as torturous as it was pleasurable. With a growl of impatience, I ground against his groin and reached for the zipper of his slacks.

Malcolm chuckled. "All in good time," he said, but his words were taut with his own hunger. He kissed me again, hard, and tugged my pants down first, pausing to tease his fingers over my panties. I couldn't suppress a moan.

As I kicked my pants the rest of the way off, he took the opportunity to flip us over, pinning me beneath him. The heat of his body flooded me as I melted into the leather seat. He brought his lips to my neck, my shoulder, and then my collarbone while he worked me over even more intimately through the thin fabric. Finally, at the choked sound of longing that slipped from my throat, he pulled my panties off too and freed himself from his slacks.

I touched my opening to cast the protective spell, and the sight seemed to fan the flames of his desire even hotter. He resumed his teasing in the most potent way, stroking the head of his cock from my clit down over my opening and back again, leaving me a little more wanting and wet each time. He brought his mouth down to my breasts again and tested his teeth against the peaks with a light nip —and then a sharper one.

A gasp escaped me with an arch of my hips, my whole body quivering with anticipation. "Malcolm," I said like a plea.

He nuzzled the side of my neck with another nibble of my skin. "What do you want?" he asked slyly.

"You. Inside me. *Now*. Please."

His eyes blazed at the words. He didn't make me wait any longer. With a single powerful stroke, he thrust all the way into me. The force of the penetration burned through me with bliss and knocked the air from my lungs.

He lifted me up to lock our hips perfectly together as he plunged into me again and again. The rest of our coupling became a haze of crashing mouths and sweat-slick skin. I gripped his shoulder, his side, twisted my fingers into the short curls of his golden hair. With every thrust, I bucked into him in turn, chasing the release I could feel swelling from within.

"You're mine," Malcolm mumbled against my cheek, his pace speeding up. "And I'm yours. Always yours. They can't *ever* change that."

I hummed my agreement, too lost in the surge of pleasure to form words. He bit down on my shoulder, and with that the wave tumbled over me, carrying me high and far in a wash of ecstasy.

Malcolm groaned as I clenched around him. He pulled me even closer, thrusting harder. I felt the catch in his chest when he hit his own peak, like an echo between our bodies.

He gathered me beneath him on the curve of the car seat and brushed a kiss to my dampened forehead. The gentleness of the gesture made my heart ache all over again, but in a much more joyful way. I touched his face and drew him closer to me.

"I guess we should get back to campus before the guys start to worry," he said after a moment with a regretful tone.

I snuggled into his embrace. The cocoon of lust and heat that we'd built around ourselves had settled into a perfect warmth, one I had no desire to break just yet.

"I told them not to worry," I said. "I think we can take a little more time."

Because Lord only knew when we could be sure of having another pocket of peace like this.

CHAPTER ELEVEN

Rory

When I came back to my bedroom after my morning shower, raised voices were carrying through my closed window. I leaned close to the glass, peering to make out the source.

At the edge of my view, a bunch of students were standing around just beyond the green. After a moment, I could tell it was five of them surrounding the other two—two guys I knew from the Scions' Guard.

"Fucking traitors!" one of the five was shouting. "When the barons are done putting the Naries in their place, what do you think they're going to do with you?"

"Why wait for that?" another said. "We can get started on their punishment right now."

He crackled his knuckles and spoke a quieter word that must have been in casting. One of their two targets jerked up his hand with a mumbled response that appeared to deflect most of the effect, but not enough to prevent a wince.

My hands balled into fists. Some of our classmates didn't think anyone should speak out against the barons? Let them find out what happened to anyone who harassed those who stood with the scions.

I pulled on my jacket and shoes in a rush. As I hurried downstairs, my hand rested on my purse, but it didn't look like a big enough deal to warrant calling in the other scions just yet. My defense would have more impact if it was obvious to the assholes out there that just one scion could subdue five of them no problem.

When I reached the green, I was met with a yelp and a hiss of pain. No one was bothering with talking anymore. I hustled around Ashgrave Hall.

Several spectators had gathered around the conflict, a few of them calling out encouragement—to which side, I couldn't tell. A girl who was also on the Scions' Guard had joined the two guys. Both they and the five who'd ganged up on them were snapping out casting words as quickly as they could.

Magical energy crackled between them, lighting sparks here and flames there. Shields thrown up shuddered and cracked before being rebuilt.

Up close, I recognized a few of the harassers from the gala the barons had held a few weeks ago to reward their supporters and butter up new ones. The Scions' Guard hadn't done anything overtly against the barons on campus, but word about the calls and complaints we'd prompted must have spread to the barons' allies, and those families were encouraging the students in our midst to take action.

"Hey!" I said sharply as I reached the edge of the growing crowd. The spectators startled and parted in my wake. The bullies tossed out a couple more spells before they appeared to realize who was approaching. With lips pressed tight and eyes narrowed, they fell back a step from their targets, who lowered their hands as well.

"If you have a problem with the Scions' Guard, then you take it up with the scions," I said, putting my hands on my hips with as intense a Bloodstone glower as I could muster. "We're the ones calling the shots. And if you feel so strongly about whatever the hell your problem is that you're going to attack your fellow fearmancers, I sure hope you've got the guts to say it to me too."

A couple of the attackers faltered, one with a swipe across her mouth as she averted her eyes, another outright taking off. The other three stared back at me defiantly.

"I don't see any point in talking to traitors, no matter what their family is," one of them sneered.

"And what exactly makes any of us a traitor?" I asked, stepping closer. "I don't remember hearing that telling the barons what we think of their plans is against the law. How are they supposed to serve all fearmancers if no one's allowed to say what they want unless it's what the barons are already planning?"

The guy opened his mouth and closed it again, clearly not having any argument to that.

"You've done more than just tell them things," said the girl next to him.

"Like what?" I asked. "I've been here the whole time. I think I'd know if anyone acting in my name did something actually criminal."

"Well… You've been insulting them behind their backs. Riling people up against them who might have been just fine with everything that's going on."

I barely restrained myself from rolling my eyes at her. At least this gave me a chance to appeal to the wider audience still gathering around us.

I pitched my voice a little louder. "Do you honestly think that we could convince people to push back against the barons if they didn't *really* feel it was necessary? Almost everyone is scared of them, for good reason. All we're trying to do is make sure everyone who's scared but worried about what they're doing can say so together with others who feel the same way, so they have safety in numbers. And anyone who's been too scared until now should know that if they decide to speak up too, all of us scions will stand with them."

"You're trying to keep us low down in the shadows like we've been lurking around beneath the Naries for so long," piped up someone from the fringes of the crowd. "Maybe it doesn't matter to you because you're already as high as you can get, but the rest of us don't want to throw away the chance at that power."

I frowned in their general direction. "Unfortunately, you can't take that power without dragging everyone else along with you. And how much enjoyment are you going to get out of it when you have to spend all your time making sure the Naries don't fight back? It's a heck of a lot easier to lord it over them when there's way more of us than them here on campus. Did you ever think about how many more there are in the entire country?"

A muttering spread through the gathering, sounding both irritated and unsettled. More unsettled, I hoped.

The guy who'd first argued with me gave an indignant sniff. "Well, we'll support our actual leaders, and you can keep on being traitors. I know who'll come out ahead."

He turned to stalk away, and the others followed him. The three members of the Guard they'd been harassing shot me sheepish smiles.

"Sorry," the one guy said. "I didn't know how to talk them down."

"It's fine." They'd probably only backed away from fighting with me because they were nervous of my powers as a Bloodstone. "Has this sort of thing happened before?"

"I heard a couple of people with Guard badges got snipe-attacked with some painful spells last night on their way back to the dorms," the girl said. "And there's been a lot of... talk. Classes aren't super fun right now." She brushed off her arms, one sleeve of her jacket deformed where a spell had melted a splotch of fabric.

I guessed that was to be expected. They didn't look surprised by it. "Stay on your guard, then," I said. "Ah, no pun intended. And if you need backup from any of us scions, all you have to do is say so."

The second guy gave me a little salute, and they headed off to whatever business they'd been involved in before our classmates had interrupted them.

I'd have liked to think that incident and the one the

girl had mentioned were isolated pockets of resentment. But as the day went on, I couldn't help noticing the looks cut my way in class, the glares when certain students thought I wouldn't notice them followed by a jolt of fear when I did. And if they were displaying even that much hostility toward *me*, they weren't going to hold back with the regular students who'd signed on to the Guard.

The tensions came to a head faster than I could have anticipated. In the late afternoon, when a bunch of classes were letting out, I came out of Nightwood Tower to find a swarm of students forming on the green.

Declan, who'd been in the same seminar as me, scanned the assembly with a deepening frown. "I don't like the look of this. I'd better alert the others."

As he tapped out a text, a pattern in behavior emerged. Some of the students ahead of us walked straight through the crowd without interference. Those who were wearing their Scions' Guard badge, though, found their ways blocked by their classmates. At least a few dozen people were closing in on us, their expressions stormy. One of them snapped out a spell at a Guard member near him, who blocked it only to be shoved to his knees by another spell cast from behind.

"That's enough!" I said, loud enough for my voice to carry. "We're all fearmancers here. We want what's best for the community."

"Yeah," someone shouted back. "And we're going to make sure we get it without a bunch of stuck-up heirs screwing us over."

"Oh, really?" Malcolm strolled up at the other end of

the green, his tone cocky but his eyes blazing. "And you think ganging up on people you disagree with and pummeling them into submission would make you right? If your ideas are so great, why do you have to stomp on the opposition rather than convincing us?"

"Hey." Declan lifted his arms to catch people's attention and then spread his hands. "We'd love to hear why the moves the barons are making are so important to you. Maybe you *can* convince us. I'm a lot more likely to think you have something useful to say if you actually say it instead of beating up on everyone else."

"Who the hell cares what you think?" another voice rang out. "You got kicked out of the barony before you even had it. Traitor!"

"Traitors!" a cry went up from several directions at once. Magic flashed through the crowd. I murmured my defenses even stronger around me and flung out more magic toward the members of the Guard I could spot. My spells shuddered with the impact of the searing energy thrown at them.

We scions were strong together, and we'd picked our Guard well, but we were outnumbered at least three to one here. Unfortunately I didn't think our classmates were going to pick up on the analogy that they could overpower us the same way all those Naries might overthrow any rule we ended up imposing on them.

A quiver of my own fear was just passing through me with the cries and grunts ringing out when several dark figures marched onto the green from the back doors of Killbrook Hall.

"What the hell is going on here?" hollered the blacksuit in the lead, coming to an abrupt halt at the edge of the crowd. He motioned to his colleagues, and their casting words flew out together. A momentary dizziness swept over me and everyone else I could see, bringing the fighting to a halt.

I stiffened as I eyed the blacksuits, rubbing my head. Had the barons sent a force to *officially* bully us into submission? I wouldn't put it past them. They'd used the law enforcement officers to collect the Naries' phones and cast that anti-communications spell on them just a couple weeks ago.

"We're bringing down the traitors, like they deserve," said someone in the crowd.

"I don't see any traitors here. I see a bunch of unruly school *children*." The disdain in the blacksuit's voice came through loud and clear. He swept his arm toward the mass of students. "All of you except the scions, out of here, now. You've created enough of a disturbance as it is."

That didn't sound totally antagonistic. On the other hand, maybe they didn't want any witnesses for whatever they were about to do with us.

I waited until most of our classmates had dispersed in their various directions, and then walked over to meet the blacksuits, braced for some new attack. Declan came with me, Malcolm and Connar, who'd emerged from Ashgrave Hall, joining us. Jude was nowhere in sight, but he had been bowing out of any confrontation likely to involve magic.

I stopped several feet from the blacksuits and looked

them over. "Thank you," I said warily. "Things were getting pretty... riled up. We haven't instigated anything against the students who support the barons."

The lead blacksuit grimaced. "No, from what I've seen it's the barons doing most of the instigating." He tipped his head toward his colleagues. There were eleven blacksuits in total now, clustered around him. "Which is why we're here. The way the situation has escalated, and the talk we've heard from the barons recently... I gather Baron Nightwood outright attacked the four of you yesterday. I can't think of any clearer indication that they're not in their right minds. It was time to draw the line. We don't feel comfortable following their orders any longer."

Declan's eyebrows rose. "You've defected."

"We prefer to think of it as a temporary hiatus from duty," said a woman next to the leader in a dry tone.

The leader nodded. "We understand that you're spearheading efforts to encourage people to speak up and show their disapproval of the recent plans involving the Naries. Standing together so no one feels they're an isolated target. That approach seems rather wise. We were hoping we could stand with you here too rather than facing whatever penalties might be waiting if we simply go it alone."

All these blacksuits had not just defected but come to support our cause. The tension gripping me fell away. I found myself smiling at them. "Of course. Obviously we could use a little policing around here if we want to avoid being mobbed by our own classmates. Have you talked to Ms. Grimsworth?"

"We've been granted accommodations in the staff area," the man said. "Although I'm thinking we should operate on a rotation of some sort. Perhaps set up regular posts in the dorm areas to keep an eye on things?"

"And someone on the green wouldn't be a bad idea," Malcolm put in. "It's the people we've brought on for our Guard who'll be more at risk than us."

"Excellent. We'll draw up a schedule and consult with you to finalize the details."

We exchanged contact information, and the blacksuits filed back into Killbrook Hall. I couldn't help letting out a little laugh of relief as my fellow scions and I headed down to the scion lounge to find Jude. "I guess those phone calls made some kind of difference even if it wasn't the way we were expecting."

My good mood lasted until we stepped into the lounge and found Jude staring at a laptop with an unusually grim expression. He glanced up at us and motioned us over.

"You dealt with the mess outside?" he said.

"Some blacksuits who aren't too happy with the barons arrived and lent us a hand," Malcolm said. "What's going on?"

"I'm starting to think our dear classmates weren't acting of their own accord, but that the barons might have nudged their families to encourage a distraction. Things for the Naries are not looking good."

My stomach sank. "What do you mean?"

He made a face at the computer. "I got suspicious about the timing, so I went looking for more news reports.

The Naries have been forming mass protests to rally against the policies the barons are arranging. And I'm going to guess that it's not normal for police to open fire on thousands of peaceful protesters?"

"What? No!" I dropped onto the sofa beside him. At the sight of the photograph on the screen of dozens of bodies draped in cloth and blood spattered on the pavement around them, I brought my hand to my mouth in shock.

Jude sucked in a rough breath. "Over seven hundred dead across three different rallies," he said. "The mages the barons sent out into the world aren't just working their magic on politicians, I'm going to guess. They want to strew around as much chaos as they possibly can." He looked at me, his dark green gaze painfully bleak. "The barons don't give a shit what any of us say. What the hell can we do to stop them now?"

CHAPTER TWELVE

Jude

I went to sleep with queasiness gripping my stomach and woke up feeling just as sick. Looking at my reflection as I went through the motions of shaving, the realization came over me that the problem wasn't that I had no idea what to do to make anything in this shitstorm any better. The problem was that I did, and it was the last thing I'd ever have wanted to do.

But it might be the only thing I could actually contribute right now, given that my current magical feebleness made me useless in almost every other way we might tackle the barons. At least it wouldn't necessarily mean throwing myself into mortal danger, so I should be able to convince Rory and the guys to get on board. I wasn't going to put her through the same stress as when I'd snuck off to New York to deal with the joymancers.

She wanted me with her, feebleness and all, and I sure as hell wasn't going to toss that love away.

I ordered up some breakfast from a place that did delivery in town, because I'd be damned if I didn't hold up my end in every non-magical way I could, and sent out a call for the scions to join me for waffles and bacon in the lounge.

"You didn't have to," Rory said as she came in, but seeing her face light up at the sweet scent of warmed maple syrup told me that yes, I absolutely had. We all dug in without much talk, although as tasty as the offerings were, I found it difficult to swallow each bite.

Which Mr. Insight naturally noticed no matter how carefully I tried to disguise my nerves. "Did you want to get us all together for some other reason?" Declan asked after he'd popped his last bite of bacon into his mouth. He contemplated me as he chewed in that way that made me feel like he might be reading my mind even though he hadn't spoken a single casting word.

I leaned back in my chair, striking what I intended to be a casual pose. "Actually, there is. I have an idea for upending the barons' current solidarity."

Rory gave me a curious look. "I'm all for that. What are you thinking?"

"Well…" I twirled my fork in my hand. "We were hoping that losing Connar's mother would throw the pentacle off, right? But it hasn't really, because there's still the three of them who've been tight since the old days— and Declan's aunt who'll grovel at the snap of their fingers. But what if we could break apart even that trio?"

"That should at least slow them down," Malcolm said. "But it's not like they'd listen to anything we tried to tell them anyway, even if it's true."

Rory grimaced. "Yeah. I'm not sure my mother would even react all that much if I told her how the other barons treated me when I was first here... Either she wouldn't believe me now that she doesn't trust me, or she'd think it was my fault, just like she blames me for turning against her now."

"Except there's something we absolutely *can* prove, and that has nothing to do with any of our loyalties, only theirs." I inhaled slowly, squaring my shoulders. "I can reveal that Baron Killbrook has passed off a false heir for almost twenty years."

Rory stared at me. "However angry they get about that, they'll take it out on you too."

I shrugged. "Not if I've got the four of you backing me up. We'll have to arrange the reveal carefully, so I can be sure of getting away from them safely, but you've managed to fend off any further attacks my fake father might have wanted to stage here on campus. I can live under lockdown for a while if it screws up their little coalition."

"It would help your uncle's bid for power too, wouldn't it?" Connar said tentatively. "Even if the barons wanted to brush off what Baron Killbrook did, it's a huge crime. Their supporters wouldn't be happy about it—some of them might even push for him to be replaced."

"Which makes it an even more obvious move to make." My not-actual uncle had made some noise about wanting a say in current affairs since Rory and I had gone back out to meet him and confirm our agreement, but it didn't seem to have shaken the barons up much. With this, I could give him real ammunition.

And I just wouldn't think about how much disdain he might look at me with after he found out the truth. Our magical deal wasn't dependent on me being a Killbrook by birth.

Rory was still watching me, her face paled but not outright resistant. "Are you sure about this?" she said. "Once that information is out… it's probably going to spread. Everyone will know."

"So let them know," I said. "Like you've always said, *I* didn't do anything wrong. He's the traitor. Let them all chew on that. If it makes life here a little more annoying for the next year and a half before I graduate, oh well. After that, I never have to see any of these people again if I don't want to."

The corner of her mouth twitched upward at my tone. I was putting on a whole lot more bravado than I actually felt—but to tell the truth, the twist in my chest wasn't anywhere near as fraught as when I'd told the guys around me the truth.

The four people in this room had accepted me as I was, regardless of my name and talent. I really didn't give a shit what the barons thought about it.

But I would very strongly prefer not to get killed in the process of telling them.

I leaned forward, bracing my elbows on the arms of the chair. "I had a few ideas for how we do the reveal. We'll definitely want them all together for maximum impact. If we can find out when their next meeting at the Fortress of the Pentacle is…"

* * *

We let Connar drive, seeing as he was the only one of us who hadn't gotten into a direct spat with the remaining barons, so the arrival of his car might not provoke as much hostility as any of the rest of ours. As much as I generally enjoyed being behind the wheel of my Mercedes, I couldn't say I minded. I was too distracted by thoughts of the impending confrontation to have immersed myself in the journey.

Rory turned where she was perched between Declan and me in the back seat and touched the dragon charm pendant she'd lent me for approximately the millionth time. It felt like a sort of good luck charm at this point, considering the spell she'd had it imbued with before had been instrumental in saving Connar's ass from his parents' machinations. Hopefully it'd prove just as useful this time around.

"With the four of you casting on it, I'm sure the spell won't have worn off in the two minutes since you last checked it," I teased.

Rory wrinkled her nose at me. "It's not just about whether the spell lasts but whether it'll be powerful enough in the moment."

"I return to my initial point about that spell being the work of four scions. I can't imagine it could be much *more* powerful than it already is."

She let out a huff of a sigh. "You can't blame me for worrying. One of the people we're about to send you off to face tried to *kill* you just a few weeks ago." She paused, her jaw tightening before she added, "Are you completely sure you have enough energy right now to activate it?"

I understood her hesitation in bringing up that topic, but it was a reasonable concern given my current state. I took a deep breath and focused on the quiver of magical power that lingered in my chest.

There wasn't a whole lot of it. My capacity for containing fearful energy had expanded since I'd first woken up in the infirmary, but only to the extent that when before I couldn't sustain any kind of illusion for more than an instant, now I could have created a small one that would last perhaps ten seconds before I exhausted my stores. Not exactly an immense improvement.

But all I needed to do to set off the spell that should ensure my escape was utter a single word with enough magic to set off the much greater magic my lover and my friends had poured into this piece of glass. Not a problem.

"I've got everything I need," I said. "And if I get into trouble anyway, I'm counting on the bunch of you to do your scion thing and get me the hell out."

I winked at her, but my gut had tightened at the same time. The four of them had been able to stand off against a single baron at a time in the past. This would be four against four. We were definitely going to need all the advantages, surprise and otherwise, that we could get.

"I still say we should have brought more company," Malcolm muttered from the seat in front of me.

"Then we'd have risked the barons refusing to come out at all, since we'd have looked like a much greater threat," Declan reminded him in his mild tone. "They'll be startled by the news, and more focused on Baron Killbrook than on us. They might not even try to stop us from leaving."

Ha. But my fake father almost certainly would. Or at least, he'd want to strike me down and into as many tiny pieces as he could manage.

The drone of the engine faded as Connar eased on the gas. Just ahead, the gloomy stone structure where the barons did their business loomed over the fields. My heart started thumping twice as fast.

I was doing this. No second-guessing, no hesitations. That was more likely to get me killed than anything else.

"It feels like forever since I've been out here," Connar said. I didn't think I had either since we'd all gotten busy with our studies at the university. The times when we'd roamed around the fields entertaining ourselves while our parents held their meetings might as well have been another lifetime ago.

The intel we'd gotten from Rory's cousin was correct. The barons' cars formed a line at the far end of the parking lot. Connar took a U-turn in the lot and parked right at the foot of the road for a speedy getaway, as planned.

Rory was already typing on her phone, telling her mother that we had something important to tell the barons and promising we came peacefully. We didn't expect them to believe that second part, but it was better than starting off on the offensive. After a few back-and-forths, she glanced at me. "They're coming down."

"That's my cue." I couldn't help delaying for one moment, though, to draw her into a kiss. If this did go wrong, I'd like the taste and warmth of her lips to be one of the last sensations I'd gotten to experience.

Rory kissed me back with her fingers gripping my shirt as if she wasn't totally ready to let me go either. "We're right here," she said when I drew back. "Just get to the car as fast as you can when you're done, and we'll handle the rest."

I nodded, my throat too constricted in that moment to allow speech, and ducked out of the car. The others swiveled around to watch as I headed across the lot to the thin path that led to the fortress's entrance.

I stopped partway along that path, knowing I'd have to get fairly close to the barons but not wanting to overdo things. Making this statement was going to be hard enough without having them in arm's reach.

The barons emerged a moment later, a couple of their loyal blacksuits with them as if they needed even more backup to face one maimed mage. Declan's awful aunt was there too, her nose in the air as if she thought colluding with this bunch made her special or her claim on the barony legitimate. I ignored her and my false father, focusing on Barons Nightwood and Bloodstone in the middle of the pack.

"You have some message to deliver?" Rory's mother said imperiously.

"I do." I resisted the urge to clasp my hand around the

dragon charm as if that would help the spell on it work better. I'd be more likely to break my fingers that way. The damp breeze ruffled my hair, and I flicked it back from my eyes. "I thought you'd want to know about a major crime that's been committed against you."

At the edge of my vision, Baron Killbrook shifted his weight, but he had to still be hoping I was too concerned about my own safety to mention this particular crime. I needed to time this right if I was going to get it and the proof out before he realized.

"That would certainly be of interest if it's true," Baron Nightwood said in a bored tone that suggested he doubted it was. "What crime is that?"

"I think it's easiest if I show you. Does one of you have a knife of some sort?"

Nightwood's eyebrows arched. "A knife? What kind of fools do you take us for?"

I gave him a pointed look. "The kind who could surely defend themselves against a nineteen-year-old mage who's lost most of his magical capability if I *was* planning on stabbing you, which I'm not."

"I don't know—" Baron Killbrook started, but Bloodstone interrupted him with a snap of her fingers.

"Let's just get on with this."

Declan's aunt produced a pen knife from her purse, small enough that I couldn't have done much damage with it even if I'd been aiming to carve up the people in front of me. "Good enough?" she asked.

"Perfect. I'm not even asking to get close to you."

Nightwood let out an exasperated sigh as Ambrosia

tossed it to me, but his eyes were fixed on me as avidly as everyone else's when I snatched the weapon out of the air. I flicked the blade open, my pulse thundering right inside my skull now.

Just spit it out and get it over with.

With one quick movement, I swiped the knife across the heel of my hand, deep enough that blood immediately welled up to coat the blade. I tossed it back toward them and pointed to the man who'd set himself up as my father.

"Baron Killbrook has lied to everyone for my entire life. I'm not his son, just a kid he arranged his wife to have when he couldn't manage it himself. Test my blood, and you'll see it."

Killbrook was jerking forward before I'd even finished speaking, his face blanched with fury. "Why you—"

I didn't wait to find out how he'd attack me or how the other barons would react to my announcement. "Dragon," I snapped out with a jolt of magic trained at the pendant resting against my sternum.

The trigger word set off the spell the scions had embedded there. The energy I'd sent into the glass figure exploded a hundredfold in both directions. It flung me backward to land on my ass in the middle of the parking lot—and shoved the barons, including Killbrook, in the opposite direction toward the Fortress.

My tailbone jarred against the pavement, and pain shot up my spine. My palms scraped the ground, the hand I'd cut throbbing. I blanked all that out and focused all my attention into hurling myself to my feet and racing the last short distance to the waiting car.

Rory had flung the door open. "Jude!" Baron Killbrook's voice rang out, harsh with rage, as I leapt inside. Then Connar slammed his foot on the gas, and we were rocketing away from the barons and the horrible secret I'd just laid bare.

CHAPTER THIRTEEN

Rory

Maggie's voice rose up from my phone's speakers with a faint crackle of static. "There's definitely a lot more tension in the pentacle right now, but they seem to have decided to deflect and deny for the time being. I don't think they want the wild card of Baron Killbrook's brother interfering with their plans, especially when he's already expressed that he doesn't agree with what they're doing to the Naries."

Jude sat back with a huff where the five of us were poised around my phone on the scion lounge coffee table. His hands clasped together over the bandage that was wrapped around the wound he'd sliced into himself yesterday. "That figures. I threw the proof in their faces, but obviously nothing means more to them than their campaign for world domination."

His tone was dry, but the comment wasn't much of an

exaggeration. The Nary news had been full of more reports of key politicians in the White House pushing forward the divisive policies already announced and even revealing new ones. More protests were breaking out in the wake of that news and the violence that had been dealt out at the earlier rallies. Just an hour ago, I'd watched images of cops beating down civilians who'd been holding nothing more than Bristol board signs.

If the barons had wanted to sow chaos and destruction in the Nary world, they were doing it awfully effectively.

"They can't keep it secret," I said to Maggie. "We passed on word to Hector Killbrook so he'd have that information as a point of leverage."

"Oh, people are talking about it." My cousin sighed. "But the barons are redirecting them to other subjects or implying that Baron Killbrook didn't even know, so he didn't actually commit any crime. I don't for a second think they believe that themselves—they're being much too hostile with him when they're in relative private—but it serves their purposes for now."

Malcolm made a face. "And when it serves their purposes to get rid of him, they can announce that they found new evidence proving he did know all along."

"Don't the barons care at all about how many people are telling them they're not happy with the new direction they're taking?" I asked. Both my mother and Baron Nightwood had insisted they were doing this for the good of the community—how much of the community needed to tell them they didn't see any good in it before they'd listen?

"They're not happy about the calls that keep coming in… but I think most of those are from people they don't see as particularly important anyway. They've got a lot of allies among the established fearmancer families, some of whom are celebrating the news about the Naries. It hasn't been pleasant to watch."

My stomach knotted. "No, I guess not. Are you sure you're still safe there? No one suspects that you've been helping us on the side?"

"Not as far as I can tell. The way your mother talks to me, it's obvious she assumes I was on Lillian's side when it came to screwing you over. I've kept quiet about a lot in the time I've been here. You don't need to worry about me."

Maybe not, but if any of the barons caught on to her duplicity, I hated to think what would happen to her. "Just be careful," I said.

After I'd ended the call, I looked around at the guys. None of their expressions showed any more hope than I felt.

"Well," I said. "We've played an awful lot of our cards, and it's shaken things up, but not enough to stop them. What's left?"

"My 'uncle' did tell me that a few members of major families have contacted him since word got out, telling him they'd support his bid against Baron Killbrook," Jude said. "Apparently they've had enough dealings with my parents to know it's more likely that my fake father created this scheme than that my mother went behind his back. It sounds like they're still nervous about speaking up publicly, though."

Declan's mouth pulled tight. "We knew phone calls might not be enough. Maybe we need to stage a protest of our own. Get together all the supporters who are willing and confront the barons—refuse to leave until they listen."

Malcolm nodded. "A lot of their supporters are off screwing with the Nary politicians. With us involved in the confrontation too, it should be a comparable stand-off. And if we can get those prominent families involved with the promise of plenty of backup, that will strengthen our point."

Connar's hands had clenched on his lap. "And if they still refuse to listen to all of us—then what?"

I hugged myself. "I don't want it to come to this—but if we have enough power on our side, we might be able to force the issue. Restrain them with magic until they agree to call back the agents they've sent to meddle with the Naries?"

"They'd be awfully pissed off about that," Jude said. "And they could go back on their word the second we left. We can't hold them hostage forever. Well." He touched his chest. "I can't hold anyone anywhere at all."

"We've proven we can overpower them, though," Declan said, his eyes going distant with thought. "It would be a big gamble—we'd risk far more retaliation than we've faced for anything we've done so far, going on the offensive at that extreme. But the situation might not come to that, and if it does, it might be the best gamble we can make."

The thought of throwing spells at the barons—at my mother—out of more than self-defense sent a twinge of queasiness through me, but what choice did we really have? How could *we* consider ourselves the future leaders of the fearmancers if we weren't willing to take a risk like that when so much was at stake?

"We should have the Guard start reaching out to their contacts," I said. "Find out when people would be able to gather and how many seem willing to as long as we've got good numbers. Make sure they know we scions will be there, and the potential new Killbrook baron too. Once we have a solid sense of what we're working with, I'll touch base with Maggie and figure out when the barons will be in a place we can easily confront them."

"The Fortress has too many permanent protections," Malcolm said. "We'd never get in there in the first place if we showed up with a crowd. But they've been meeting other places too."

Jude sprang up. "Since I can't pitch in much with the actual confrontation, I'll get on with wrangling the Guard. I'll remind them all that *I* looked death in the face yesterday with just the four of you, so really, taking a stand with a bigger crowd is barely anything." He winked at us with what seemed like genuine good humor despite the tension I could still see in his stance and headed out.

Malcolm rolled his eyes at Jude's back, but he was smiling at the same time. "I'll start talking people up and pitching the idea too. It might need a little more finesse than he can typically offer."

I could touch base with Cressida and Victory the next

time I saw them. Maybe Victory's family would be willing to stand with us too. She'd said her father would let the barons know of his disapproval, although whether he'd actually done that in the end, I wasn't sure. The Blighthavens had generally enjoyed good favor with their rulers, which they had to be hesitant to lose even if they disagreed with them this once.

Declan and Connar got up as I did. Connar drew in a breath as if to speak and then stopped, rubbing his hand across his mouth. I paused, taking in the shadow that had crossed his face.

"Are you all right?" I asked. "Do you think this is a bad idea after all?"

The Stormhurst scion gave me a pained smile. "I'm not sure what I think should really matter all that much."

"What are you talking about?" Declan said. "You're as close to full baron as I am now—closer if we consider my aunt's claim. You've got just as much say as the rest of us. If you're concerned about something, I definitely want to hear it."

Connar exhaled slowly. He looked away from us for a moment before he continued. "It's just, as Holden continues recovering and I'm spending more time with him… I'm starting to think I should hand over my position as scion to him. He hasn't wanted to intrude on our dynamic that much, but if I made it official—"

I blinked at him in confusion. "Why would you hand it over? You're the one who's been training for it and working with us all this time. Not that you should shut him out, but you've got at least as much right to take on the barony as he does."

"Do I?" His head dipped. "I think my history proves I'm unfit to rule. I was weaker than him when our parents were testing us—I wasn't strong enough to stand up to Malcolm when he was attacking Rory at first, even though I thought it was wrong—I couldn't defend myself when my mother cast that spell on me. My brother's the kind of guy who could be trapped in a few rooms with barely any human contact for years, and he still managed to keep his mind sharp by reading and learning all kinds of things… He'll catch up fast."

"Hey." Declan grasped Connar's arm. "None of those things makes you unfit. In the first instance you were only fourteen, and you don't know that Holden would have handled the latter two incidents any better than you did. You *did* stand up for Rory—you've helped protect all of us more times than I can count."

"What does it even matter?" I found myself saying. "Even if he'd make a good baron too—why can't you two stand at the table together? Isn't the insistence on only letting one heir from each family have a say part of what makes fearmancer politics so brutal in the first place?"

Declan and Connar both stared at me. Then Declan chuckled. "You know… you're right. I've been so stuck in the standard assumptions that I never really thought of it that way. Not that I have any intention of sharing with my aunt—"

I snorted. "She's proven *herself* unfit."

"But in general, adjusting that policy would make a lot

of things easier." His expression turned even more pensive than before.

Connar shifted his weight on his feet. "I'm still not sure I'd really be all that useful in the pentacle if Holden could simply take it himself."

I studied his face. "Is that what you really want? If you don't like the idea of being baron just in itself…"

"I don't know. I never had much chance to think about whether I *wanted* it before. All I know for sure is I want to do what's best for all of you. We were sitting there talking a few minutes ago, and I had no idea what to offer to the strategy or anything else."

"Not all of us need to be focused on planning," Declan said. He paused and then tugged Connar toward the door. "You've offered plenty of other things that maybe meant more than you realized. Come with me?" His gaze shifted to include me too.

Connar didn't resist. Declan led us up out of Ashgrave Hall into the bright sunlight of a temperate fall day. I tipped my face back for a moment to soak in the thin warmth before following him across the green and on toward the lake.

When he set off down the path that led through the east woods alongside the shore, I got an inkling of where he was taking us, if not exactly what he hoped to prove with it. He veered off the path in the right spot to head up to the clearing at the edge of the cliff, where I'd first gotten to know Connar all those months ago.

Even though the Stormhurst scion was obviously still in turmoil, Connar's posture relaxed as we stepped out onto the rocky ground with its sparse grass and the sparkling stretch of the lake ahead of us. I eased closer to him and took his hand. His love for this spot and his need to separate himself from the brutality of campus politics had been what had first drawn me to him.

Declan turned to face us. "You don't always say a lot," he said to Connar, "and maybe sometimes people— including myself—have underestimated you because of that. But you *see* a lot. You pay attention, you recognize things in people, and you have the courage to act on what you see even if it goes against the status quo—even if you're not perfect at it. You recognized what Rory was really going through before any of the rest of us did, didn't you?"

Connar squeezed my hand. "As much as I screwed that up afterward."

"It still meant something, having that time when you were on my side," I said. "And you made up for what happened after."

"It's not just that," Declan said. "It was up here... You realized how much I wanted Rory, how much she meant to me, before I was totally willing to admit it to myself. And even though you could have ignored that so all her attention would be on you, you encouraged me to act on it. You kept the secret, even though it could have ruined me. I'm not sure I've ever properly thanked you for that."

"I never would have wanted to do anything else," Connar said, sounding puzzled.

"Exactly. And that's what you bring to the table of the pentacle. That's something we need among the barons."

Connar didn't look completely convinced, but he didn't argue either. I touched his cheek, bringing his gaze to me. "I can't imagine ruling without you there. We can go to your brother and make it clear we want him included among the scions too, but not to replace you. We're stronger when you're standing with us too."

His throat worked. Then he traced his fingers along my jaw and leaned in to kiss me, the gentle press of his lips answer enough.

Declan came over to join us, kissing the side of my neck. Enveloped by the two of them, sheltered from the cool breeze drifting off the lake, I felt just how much we *were* together, in every way. I kissed Connar harder, reaching back to caress my fingers into Declan's hair at the same time. A familiar pulse of desire woke up low in my belly.

Connar could certainly pick up on that. I ran my hand down his chest, tracing the sculpted muscle there, and he drew back with a faint groan. With a quick casting word, he conjured a bubble of warmer air around us.

Even with the added warmth, it was a little chilly for shedding *all* our clothes. I settled for letting my hands roam over his body through his shirt, and he slipped his hands under my sweater. Declan continued to mark my neck with his mouth. He stroked his fingers up my back, provoking a quiver of hunger.

I reached down to discover the evidence of Connar's arousal straining against his fly. A shaky breath escaped him. "We were supposed to be organizing our big coup."

"And we'll do that," I said. "We can keep this short and sweet."

He made a rough sound of agreement and brought his mouth back to mine. As I fumbled with the zipper of his slacks, Declan helpfully tugged up my skirt. Connar's hand delved lower, easing aside my panties to dip past my slit. I gasped, gripping his erection at the jolt of pleasure.

Connar lifted me against him like he had weeks before, but this time it wasn't just us. He didn't need to hold me up by only his power. As he eased me down onto him, his hard length filling me with that delicious burn I couldn't imagine ever having my fill of, Declan steadied me from behind.

The Ashgrave scion kissed a lingering path along my shoulder while his hands cupped my breasts. Each stroke of his fingers made me tremble with delight.

Connar grasped my hips and rocked me against him, and I gave myself over to their combined attentions and the bliss that was flooding through me. In a moment like this, I had to believe that the strength and passion we generated together could overcome every enemy and challenge ahead of us. Because I didn't want to live in a world where it couldn't.

CHAPTER FOURTEEN

Rory

The shiny office building in front of us didn't look as if it'd be the site of what might become a huge historic moment for the fearmancer community. Nothing about it stood out amid the other buildings on the downtown street, a business district array of similar mirrored fronts mixed with marble plating and older concrete. I tuned out the rumble of traffic passing behind me as I peered up at it.

Maggie had informed me by text late last night that the barons planned to convene for a meeting that would include a couple of their allies in the offices here around noon. It was currently a quarter past twelve. And we had arrived in cars parked wherever we could find spots on the surrounding streets and were now gathering here: the four of us scions, Declan and Connar's brothers, and some fifty classmates and outside supporters who'd agreed to join us for this confrontation. Even a few of the blacksuits who'd defected to the university had come along, uniforms and all.

Hector Killbrook had met up with the four of us as soon as we'd reached the building. He peered up at it too, his narrow face brooding but determined. Then he glanced at me. We hadn't had a chance to talk in person since the latest revelations.

"You know," he said, "if Jude had told me the full story when you two came to meet me, it wouldn't have affected whether I trusted him or you. I wouldn't hold him responsible for my brother's decisions." His gaze returned to the building as his mouth twisted. "I'm very familiar with just how far Edmund can take his preoccupation with power—and his paranoias about those who might want to usurp it."

"I'm sorry we had to ask you to prove him right," I couldn't help saying.

He shrugged. "That's his own doing too, even if he won't see it that way. You all deserve better than this. Before I even came into my magic, my brother made me wish I wasn't second in line with all the horror he held for my position. I've stayed as far away as I can from that part of the Killbrook legacy. Maybe I stayed too far and let things go on that I might have been able to sway if I'd intervened sooner."

"You're here now," Declan said. "We wouldn't ask for more than that. I know as well as anyone what a burden being within arm's reach of a barony but not owning it can be." He tipped his head toward the doors as the last few members of our massive delegation joined us. "We'd better head in there before they have any more chance to notice something's developing."

I squared my shoulders and strode ahead with my colleagues and Hector. We were the ones asking the mages of less standing to take this risk; we should lead the way.

The offices owned by Baron Nightwood filled the fourth floor of the building. We ignored the elevator, which would have required several trips to fit all of us, in favor of the stairs. The sensation of marching up those flights felt like an echo of my many climbs of Ashgrave Hall, waiting to find out what I might have to deal with in my dorm next.

Thankfully I'd never had to encounter four hostile barons there.

The moment we stepped into the office, it was obvious the barons were waiting for us—with plenty of advance preparation. They were standing in a tense row at the far end of the main room near the doors to the inner workspaces, the desks between us and them empty of employees, several other regular mages and close to twenty blacksuits positioned around them. My heart plummeted even as I stepped forward with the others to make room for our entire contingent to enter.

Someone must have tipped them off about our plans. Someone we'd thought was on our side, or else they wouldn't have known about those plans.

I spotted Maggie at the back of the stand-off, her mouth tight and her arms folded over her chest. She was clearly distressed, even if she was making a good effort at hiding it.

Could she have been responsible for this turnaround? I didn't want to think so—I couldn't see what she'd gain from betraying us after the hopes she'd shared with me, and those under the forced honesty of a persuasion spell. It would have been hard for her to warn me if she hadn't known until the blacksuits had arrived.

There really was no way of knowing who'd thrown us under the bus. It could have been anyone we or our Guard had reached out to who'd decided they were better off currying extra favor with the current barons than supporting their future leaders. Did it even make that much of a difference? Would we have backed down and called the whole thing off if we'd known?

No. We still had to say our piece. The other tactics we'd been prepared to implement would just be a hell of a lot harder to pull off now.

"This is quite the militia you've gathered," Baron Nightwood said in a sneering tone.

Beside him, my mother stood stiffly, her dark eyes smoldering with offence as she looked at me. Despite everything she'd argued for and done since she'd returned, guilt pinched my gut.

"It isn't a militia," Declan said. "These are the people you're meant to serve—dozens of them. It's important enough to them to prevent the conflict with the Naries that you've been preparing for that they're all willing to stand here and tell you so to your faces. We're hoping that you care enough about *all* your people not to dismiss this many of them because other families only care about what they get for themselves."

"If you see us as powerful enough that you needed to summon half the blacksuits in the state to protect you from us, maybe we're worth listening to?" Malcolm said, cuttingly dry.

"We don't want any dominion over the Naries," someone piped up from behind us. "We don't want to see them killing each other, and we don't want to have to fight them to keep them in line."

"And we support Hector Killbrook's bid for the barony," said a voice I recognized as Victory's father's. Mr. and Mrs. Blighthaven had shown up at the last minute when we'd been getting ready to set off. "Why should we tolerate a criminal in the pentacle?"

"Baron Killbrook hasn't been convicted of any wrongdoing," Nightwood said, although at the same time I thought my mother suppressed a grimace. "And we stand as your leaders because you trust our families to make the decisions that are best for all of you. This has never been a democracy. If problems arise from our activities, we'll deal with those as we move forward, just as we dealt with the joymancers' recent assault."

By slaughtering them all, I thought but didn't say. Plenty of our supporters might be just fine with that turn of events. Better to focus on how their interests were at risk.

"Once we reveal ourselves to the Naries on a larger scale, we won't be able to go back on that decision if it turns out to be more trouble than it's worth," I said. "We can't wipe the memories of the entire country."

"You have no idea what plans we have in place to make it a smooth transition," Baron Killbrook snapped. "We're not going to be bullied by scared children."

Nightwood definitely bit back a wince at that tone-deaf comment, insulting every adult on our side of the room.

Killbrook's brother drew himself up even straighter. "I'm far from a child, and there are plenty of people here with more life experience than either of us. And for a transition this big, where every fearmancer's life will be irrevocably changed, all of us *should* have a say."

Someone else on our side spoke up. "You can hardly keep claiming it's about giving us more freedom when you're forcing the decision on us!"

"Why don't we all sit down and have an actual discussion about this instead of your continual dismissals?" Hector went on. "If your plan is solid enough, then you should be able to address our concerns, and then this conflict can be over. If there are weak areas you haven't thought of, surely you'd want to know that before going forward? What would be the harm in talking it out?"

"Yeah!" Cressida dared to say from where she'd ended up near me. Murmurs of agreement rose up all across our side of the room.

"Our plans require a series of intricate operations," my mother said. "We've already faced more challenges than we should have because we couldn't count on all of our colleagues handling that information in a responsible way. Why should we trust that none of you will turn full traitor too? We were brought up for this role, we were born to lead you, and we will *not* have our authority questioned."

Nightwood gestured to the blacksuits around them. "And that's all we need to say on the matter. Please see these people out of the building so we can continue with our business."

No. We couldn't let them turn us away that easily. My pulse skipped a beat, but I raised my voice. "Stand firm! We deserve to be heard."

Hushed casting words filled the air all around me, and energy thrummed through the room. The blacksuits halted a couple feet away from us where we'd conjured a magical barrier together. They exchanged a glance and threw out their own casting words in unison.

Their spells sent shudders into our crowd that raised the hairs on my skin. Baron Nightwood scowled and took a step forward. He and the other barons added their own barrage of spells, and I felt our defenses cracking.

"More!" Declan called out, with another casting of his own. The voices on both sides blended into a garbled mess of potent syllables. The floor quivered beneath our feet with the force of our opponents' onslaught.

For all our numbers, the barons and their allies were some of the strongest mages around. And they'd had the benefit of advance preparation, thanks to whoever had tipped them off. As the barrier protecting us frayed even further, lashes of magic slipping through it to scrape at my limbs, another spell triggered over us. A thunderclap boomed, and a wallop of energy smacked us to the ground.

As I fell to my hands and knees, my ears rang so hard I couldn't make out any other sound. Then the blacksuits were on us, shouting spells I could only decipher from the movements of their lips, hauling people to their feet and toward the door, directing others with what looked like magical compulsion to march out on their own.

So much for forcing the barons to listen. We could barely keep ourselves in the room. But even as I scrambled for the right words to maintain our attempted siege, our allies were fighting back. Some of them with magic, three here and four there shoving back or freezing a blacksuit with combined spells—some of them physically tackling the officers to the ground.

The barons launched into renewed castings of their own. A fresh wave of magic rammed into us, sending those who'd started to recover toppling again. But Baron Killbrook didn't appear to be satisfied with that. Taking advantage of the chaos, he strode straight toward his brother, his hands jerking up as his mouth formed a casting that I suspected he intended to use to end any question of who would be baron once and for all.

Hector saw him in time and spat out a casting of his own that propelled the spell to the side. A gouge sliced into the floor just a foot from where he was heaving himself to his feet. The baron's lips curled into a snarl, and he flung himself at his brother.

Sparks flared and whirled around them. A blacksuit

charged at me, and I yanked my attention away to hurl a spell at her that knocked her onto her ass. As Connar spoke a casting word to pin her in place, Baron Nightwood whipped the dagger he'd brandished at our last meeting from his suit jacket and pitched it toward his son with magically driven aim and speed.

"Malcolm!" I yelled. It was too late for my warning to do much good, but thankfully he'd spotted it the second I had. He jerked himself out of the way with a split-second casting that only managed to send the dagger slightly off course. It still sliced straight through his sleeve where he hadn't moved quite fast enough, deep enough that a gush of red blood bloomed on the fabric.

It would have killed him if he'd been any slower.

An ache clutched my stomach. I whirled around to see Declan's aunt barking casting words, her vicious eyes turned his way. The Killbrooks had fallen to the ground with spasms of their bodies as they tried to fend off each other's attacks and make their own. Our attempt at a delegation had turned into a war zone in no time at all.

Hector Killbrook flinched with a crackling sound and a whiff of burning flesh. Baron Killbrook lurched toward him, his teeth bared as his lips moved to form another casting—and his brother spoke sharp and harsh to stop him at the last second.

The baron slammed back against the floor. A spurt of blood colored the tiles with the collapse of his skull. Hector stumbled backward, looking as sick as the sight made me feel. He'd won his part of the battle, but I didn't think he was happy about how.

For all our efforts, the blacksuits were still pushing us back. Their persuasion spells had sent several of our allies out of the room, and now the officers were simply blasting everyone at the front of the line. Bodies slumped unconscious all around us.

We weren't going to win the entire war, that much was clear. Declan caught my gaze with the same sense of desperation ringing through me and nodded.

"Fall back!" he said. "We've seen just how little we can trust our current barons."

We shouted out more defensive spells to cover our retreat, the four of us scions letting the less powerful mages exit first. My mother extended her hand toward us, and I flinched in anticipation of a spell. But that wasn't what she was doing at all.

"Persephone," she said. "Please. It doesn't have to be like this. You were meant to stand with me. Let me show you the future we're going to make."

Her plea and the rawness of her voice tugged at me. I wanted to believe I could still change her mind. I wanted to believe I could still make a difference through peaceful means.

But her colleagues had just tried to slaughter the men I loved, and she hadn't done a thing to stop them, even if she hadn't attacked me herself. I'd tried appealing to whatever compassion she had in her so many times before —and her need for power had always defeated me.

"I'll listen to you when you're ready to listen to all of us," I said.

Malcolm grasped my arm. The last of us retreated,

hustling down the stairs with magical barriers thrown up behind us to protect our backs. Every step reverberated through my body with a growing sense of finality.

There was no going back from this—for any of us.

CHAPTER FIFTEEN

Rory

"We left too many people behind," I said as Malcolm's car raced on toward campus. We'd taken off in a hurry, not wanting to risk the barons themselves or their loyal blacksuits catching us in our escape. My gut was twisted with the memory of the bodies that had been lying limp in the office—most if not all of them only unconscious, I hoped, but even so, they'd be facing harsher punishments once they woke up.

"They knew they were getting into something dangerous," Malcolm said. "They were willing to take that risk. If we'd stayed back to try to get them out, we'd *all* be in some blacksuit detention center—or worse."

My gaze lingered on the bloody sleeve of his wool jacket. Connar and I had managed to stop the bleeding with our amateur healing efforts, but the wound had to still be hurting him. *He* could have faced a much worse fate. He could be dead right now.

"The barons really don't care about anything except this plan now, do they?" A hollow sensation spread through my chest. They didn't care about their people, or about their heirs—would they slaughter us all in the end like they had the joymancers, just to make sure we wouldn't stand in their way? Was ruling over the Naries so important they didn't mind if the hearts of their baronies passed to someone who'd been born outside the family— or were most of them counting on the younger siblings falling in line once we were out of the way?

Maybe that was why my mother had held back with me: not because I meant all that much to her but because I was the only remaining thread in the Bloodstone line.

"We're not worth anything to them if they can't order us around," Malcolm muttered.

"The blacksuits and their other allies there witnessed how they treated us—how they treated the fearmancers who stood up with us," Declan said from the back. "The violence all started on the barons' side. Anyone can see they're getting out of control after that. I wish it had gone better, but I think in some ways we did prove our point."

"Now what?" Connar asked, his voice strained. "They'll be even more prepared for us next time. If they won't back down, what else *can* we do?"

"Let's get back to campus and regroup," I said. "And then… then hopefully we'll be able to come up with a better idea. There are only two barons from the original pentacle left. How long can they keep people's faith when their own group is falling apart?"

No one attempted to answer that hypothetical question. I suspected we were all afraid the answer was, "A hell of a lot longer than we'd like to think."

Several other cars pulled into the campus garage with ours as our Guard and some of our other allies also came to regroup. Victory's parents had driven her; Hector Killbrook had gone with a couple of his colleagues. The man now first in line for the Killbrook barony still looked sallow as he got out of the car. Blood flecked the collar of his shirt, and his jacket lapels were charred. A burn mark someone had done a hasty and incomplete healing spell on darkened the pale skin that showed there.

Holden and Noah moved to join us as we left the garage, Declan clasping his younger brother's shoulder with tightened lips. I couldn't imagine how worried he'd been for Noah during the fight.

I assumed we'd gather in the Guard room to take stock. But as we crossed the grounds toward Killbrook Hall, a mass of students surged off the green to meet us, a few professors in their midst.

"Traitors!" the yell went up like it had before. "You don't belong here. We don't want people who'll attack the barons messing things up for the rest of us."

I halted with the other scions around me, abruptly exhausted. The few blacksuits who'd joined us for the confrontation stepped forward to break up the crowd, but a couple of the students flung spells at them defiantly.

Were we going to have to fight all over again just to

get back to the closest thing some of us had to a home right now?

"There will clearly need to be sanctions placed on all those students who participated in this embarrassing spectacle against our leaders," Professor Crowford was saying when the front door of Killbrook Hall flew open.

Ms. Grimsworth strode out, flanked by several of the other professors—including Viceport, who was my current mentor, and Razeden, who'd supported me more than once—and the rest of the blacksuits who'd defected. The oncoming crowd quieted as the headmistress approached.

Ms. Grimsworth came to a stop and clapped her hands with an air of absolute authority, made more rather than less imposing by the fierceness in her normally prim expression and the strands of hair that had come loose from her tightly coiled bun.

"Enough is enough," she said. "I will not have my school turning into a warzone—and it's clear which side has instigated the conflict. From this point onward, I declare Bloodstone University a safe haven for anyone who disagrees with the barons' attacks on the Naries and needs protection from retaliation. Anyone who attempts to instigate further violence will be escorted off campus and blocked by the wards. You may leave of your own accord or force the issue, but I will not let this savagery continue any further."

Faced with a few dozen of us, including the scions, on one side and the ultimate authority over the university on the other, our accusers faltered. Mutters passed between them as they stirred restlessly. Professor Crowford looked as if he'd swallowed his tongue.

Hector Killbrook appeared to shake himself out of the semi-daze he'd been in since his fatal skirmish with his brother. He stepped to the front of our group with his shoulders squared. His voice came out firm.

"As acting Baron Killbrook, I support the headmistress's declaration. This isn't a time when I expect any of you can focus on classes. If you want to stand with us, you can stay and we'll discuss how. If you'd rather support the other barons, who are acting more and more irresponsibly and beyond the law, I suggest you take the opportunity to leave now and rejoin your families until this dispute is settled."

Many of the students started to move toward the garage to get their cars and make good on that suggestion. The professors in the bunch glanced toward Ms. Grimsworth.

"Helene," Crowford said with a note of protest in his voice.

She fixed him with a steely stare. "I know where your loyalties lie. I'm not going to punish you for them, but your teaching skills will not be required until this situation is resolved."

His mouth twisted, and he marched past her to Killbrook Hall, I hoped to collect his necessary things from his apartment in the staff quarters before he left campus too. The headmistress turned to the blacksuits with her.

"A few of you can handle the adjustments to the wards, I assume?" she said.

The man next to her nodded and gestured to a couple of his colleagues to accompany him. As they jogged ahead of him down the road toward the edge of campus, he swiveled to face us scions again.

"Miss Bloodstone, Mr. Nightwood, and Mr. Ashgrave, if you'd accompany us, please? With your help, we should be able to attune the wards so it's at least more difficult for your parents and aunt to breach the university's defenses, if they should choose to try."

"Of course," I said. My heart beat faster as we moved to join them, but it wasn't all anxiety now. We were in an awful situation, and I didn't see the way through it yet, but our allies were more willing to stand up than ever. I didn't know whether we could win this war, but we'd at least make the barons work for any victory they claimed.

By the evening, the campus wasn't so much less populated as differently populated. While dozens of students had left, many of the older members of the families who agreed with us had arrived, either wanting to be part of our planning or feeling the campus was safer from the barons' possible vengeance than their own homes—or both. Several more blacksuits had arrived, at least a couple of whom I thought I recognized from our confrontation with the barons. Apparently our leaders' show of force had turned some people against them instead of into more avid supporters.

We had at least one mage in our midst who didn't fully support our cause. After I spoke with Hector about the evidence that someone in on our plans had revealed them to our opponents, the new baron asked several of the blacksuits to question those who'd stayed on campus with a spell to compel their honesty. It wasn't long before they turned up a friend of one of our Guard members, who blanched as the confession spilled from his lips.

"My family has really been struggling," the young man stammered in an attempt to defend himself. "I thought I could get a favor from the barons if I helped them a little —I didn't mean for anyone to get hurt."

I wasn't sure how much I believed that, but I was just glad to see him escorted off the grounds.

As daylight dwindled, Ms. Grimsworth called all of the Nary students onto the green with many of us looking on. Regret colored her voice as she spoke to them.

"You've undergone a lot of turmoil during the past few weeks, and all of that under my watch. I apologize for not intervening sooner. The situation has become untenable. Unfortunately, the spells that were cast on you are keyed to the mages who performed them, and we don't have them with us to undo that magic. But while I can't let you return home with what you know, I'm making it clear to all the magical students on campus that attacks on our scholarship students will not be tolerated. For now, you can at least relax and know you won't be harmed any further."

There was no mistaking the relief, if wary, that passed over most of the nonmagical students' faces. They drifted back to their dorms more like people and less like panicked prey. Watching them made me think of the Nary student I *had* managed to get out of here before the chaos had reached its peak.

How was Shelby doing with all the chaos that was now happening in her own world? The city where she was now living for her new orchestra job wasn't a huge one, so I didn't think there'd have been violence there, but I couldn't be sure of that.

Hey! I texted to her. *Just wondering how you're doing with all the craziness that's been happening lately. Have there been any protests near you?*

My worries eased when her reply came just a moment later. *Nothing around here, but it's scary seeing that stuff on TV. Thankfully my family's nowhere near the worst of it either. I can't believe the White House is really going to go through with some of those policies.*

I know, I wrote back. *It's ridiculous. Hopefully things will get resolved soon. You stay safe!*

You too!

At least she had her music and her orchestra performances to distract her. I'd feel better if I knew how the hell we were going to resolve the conflict already, though.

As I put away my phone, Ms. Grimsworth motioned us scions over, and several members of our Guard came with us. A couple blacksuits flanked the headmistress.

"Our colleagues have adjusted the wards around

campus not just to repel those we've removed but also to alert us if any magic is used on them," she said. "We want to be prepared if the barons attempt to break through those wards. There'll be a sound like a fire alarm that should carry right across the grounds."

"Good to know," I said. Then we'd just have to worry about stopping the barons and their allies from managing to break through, if they made that attempt. My stomach knotted at the thought of another battle.

"We'd like to gather everyone together to discuss our own strategies moving forward," Declan said. "I assume it's no problem for us to make use of the gymnasiums?"

The headmistress made a weary gesture with her hand. "Make whatever use of the university buildings you see fit to. The sooner we come out of this mess, the happier I'll be."

It didn't take long to put out the call. Within the hour, we'd gathered all of our allies who'd come to the university in the larger gym in the Stormhurst Building.

"We can't simply hide away here forever," Mrs. Blighthaven jumped in as soon as Declan had thanked everyone for joining us. "That won't change anything that's happening."

"Do any of us really want to go up against the barons in a full-out fight, though, especially after they've shown no mercy before?" another woman said.

"Technically, we should have the greater balance of power." Malcolm motioned to our cluster of barony families that had grouped together at the head of the room. "Barons Nightwood and Bloodstone may not want to acknowledge them, but we have the only qualified Baron Killbrook as well as the rightful soon-to-be Barons Ashgrave and Stormhurst too."

Declan nodded. "Some of you here would have supported the current barons in the past, but you've recognized their growing instability and flouting of the law. We need you to reach out to any friends and colleagues you think you could get to recognize that too. If we draw away enough of their support, they won't be able to keep this effort up."

"We can't let the situation with the Naries escalate in the meantime." The new Baron Killbrook scanned the crowd in front of us. "We know that several fearmancers have taken assignments in Washington and other areas of major political activity to instigate anger and violence among the Naries. We can challenge those goals directly. I'd like to hear from volunteers willing to head to those areas and work magic to counteract the effects of our opponents' spells. Cut off the barons' plans at the root, and they'll have to reconsider."

A bunch of the older mages in the room stepped forward with offers of support, including Victory's parents. I guessed there wasn't much for those of us school-aged to do other than continue our regular efforts. We'd already tried pretty much everything we could think of.

Declan stepped to the side to discuss something with his brother in hushed tones. "I think I may have a way to strip away my aunt's political power," he said when he returned to us. "I'm going to consult with the blacksuits and see if we can put that in motion quickly."

That would leave my mother and Malcolm's father running the show alone. I glanced at the Nightwood scion, but he just grimaced. "I don't know if anything short of death is going to force my dad to back down now." His gaze slid toward the doorway. "I think I'd better bring Agnes onto campus. At this point, the grounds are more secure than the apartment I set up for her. You all can survive a few hours without me?"

Jude rolled his eyes. "Just make sure *you* survive stepping outside the wards."

"We'll be fine," Connar said, clapping his friend on the back. "Even with the protections we put in place at the apartment building, she'll definitely be better off here with us now that Ms. Grimsworth has given us the campus."

We'd have all the heirs together in one place then— well, all except one. I glanced at my phone as if Maggie might have texted me without me realizing it. I hadn't heard from her since the confrontation, and that didn't seem like good news. I knew for sure now that she hadn't been the one who'd tipped off the barons. Had they realized she'd given away their location to us? What would they be doing to her if they had?

Even if they hadn't figured it out yet, she'd taken enough risks for us. I didn't want her death on my conscience too.

"I'm going to tell Maggie to come here," I said to the guys. "She's helped us a lot, and maybe she could help us more if she stays out there… but I don't think it's fair to leave her in the line of fire. Sooner or later, the barons are going to realize that she's leaking information to us, and I don't think she'd survive that."

"She's your family," Malcolm said to me before he headed off. "You do what you think is right."

"And hey, the more the merrier!" Jude gave me a tight but genuine smile.

I tapped out the message on my phone. *Things have gotten too dangerous. I'd rather have you here with us than out there and vulnerable. Come to campus as soon as you can, please.*

Now I just had to hope that she saw the message in time to accept my plea.

CHAPTER SIXTEEN

Declan

Every time I tried to loosen my grip on the steering wheel, my fingers started to clench again a few seconds later. My chest was clenched up too and had been since the moment we'd set off.

"It's going to be fine," Noah said, stretching out his long legs from the seat beside me. "You'll be right there, and we'll have plenty of cover from our 'friends' in the back."

"If there's anything to cover the two of you from," muttered one of the blacksuits sitting behind us.

There were three of them back there, although they'd cast spells that made it nearly impossible to make them out unless you knew the signs to look for. A defector who'd joined us on campus had convinced two of her colleagues who were still officially on duty but unofficially on the fence about their loyalties to join us for this trip. The other woman had stayed pensively quiet since we'd picked them up; the man seemed to be making a show of his skepticism.

I ignored the attitude. He'd see soon enough what I knew Aunt Ambrosia was capable of.

"I'm basically using you as bait," I said to my brother. "You would have been totally justified in telling me off."

"You're using yourself as bait too," Noah replied. "The whole plan makes sense. I'm not some little kid—I can make my own decision about it. Which you let me do. You're not the bad guy here." He paused, and his eyes gleamed briefly. "I can't wait to see the look on her stupid face when she realizes how epically she's screwed up."

"Let's not get ahead of ourselves." I had no doubt that our aunt would try *something* during this meeting. I never would have expected a gambit like this to have worked in the past, when the balance of authority had been in my favor. Now, with the other barons supporting her bid for the Ashgrave barony and crushing anyone who stood up to them, she'd have much less fear of potential consequences. How could she resist the opportunity?

But whether we'd come out on top during this confrontation was yet to be determined.

She didn't know we were coming. No one knew about this little mission except the blacksuits with us and my fellow scions. I hadn't wanted any risk of her being ready with accomplices to displace the blame for whatever move she decided to make.

Unfortunately, that also meant we were approaching her at her home. I didn't like the idea that my cousins, who were only kids, might see this, but for any official business she went out on, she'd be much more likely to have professional company. She'd always made a fuss about Sunday family brunch, with lots of passive-aggressive posturing when my side of the family had stopped joining hers here for it... after the second time I'd come down with a mysterious illness the night after, despite my father's and my best attempts at checking over my food. I was counting on her not skipping this one tradition no matter how busy she'd been playing baron.

Because of the spells hiding the blacksuits, to her eyes it'd look like just her two nephews dropping by for a visit. When we reached the tall steel gate, I idled in view of the security camera for a minute before it whirred open. I'd been gambling that her recognition of the opportunity we'd presented her with would override any concerns she had about facing us.

I drove up the drive and parked where it widened in front of the big stone mansion, modeled closely after the baron homes. There was a garage off to the right, but I needed the car out in the open for the blacksuits to act as witnesses. That also meant we had to stay out here and wait for her to come to us. Setting foot in that building not only cut us off from our backup but also opened us up to more potential traps than I wanted to worry about. She'd be dangerous enough out here.

The two of us got out of the car. I left the driver's side

door open as if for making a quick departure but really so the blacksuits could hear the conversation more easily. I'd have liked to leave a back door open so they could exit with more speed, but I couldn't think of a way to do that without raising suspicions.

I leaned against the hood of the car, facing the front entrance. Noah stood near me, shuffling his feet, more with anticipation than nerves from his expression. I raised an eyebrow at him, and he schooled his demeanor to be more serious.

Ringing the doorbell wasn't necessary. Aunt Ambrosia would have been aware of our unexpected arrival from the moment her staff had spotted us on the camera at the gate. Still, she took her time making an appearance. We'd been waiting at least five minutes when the door finally opened and she stepped out.

She stayed on the doorstep, eyeing us with her head held high. Neither of us had ever attacked her in any way, but people who were inclined to be underhanded tended to assume everyone else was willing to resort to the same tactics. She didn't trust us.

I wouldn't be surprised if she'd already notified the other barons of our visit. She probably also had her husband and a staff member or two watching from the windows to magically intervene if she seemed to be in danger. She just liked the appearance of handling us on her own.

"Boys," she said in the flat voice that came out when no one she wanted to impress was in the vicinity. "To what do I owe the pleasure?"

"I thought we had a few things to discuss," I said. "Seeing as you've stolen my barony, and effectively Noah's too if I'd wanted to hand it over to him."

She sniffed and crossed her arms over her chest. "You tossed your barony away when you turned your back on the pentacle and started encouraging those who would overthrow it."

"No one we've been talking with wants to overthrow the barons," Noah put in. "They just want the barons to *listen* to them instead of turning our whole world upside down without caring what we think about that."

I offered her a tense smile. "And I think we've made that very clear in past discussions. Meanwhile, the barons have made it clear they can't even hear criticism without resorting to violence."

"I recall plenty of violence on both sides yesterday," Aunt Ambrosia said haughtily. "Disturbing a business meeting you weren't invited to was an act of aggression all on its own."

And declaring me a traitor while claiming my seat wasn't?

I bit back that accusation and the rancor that rose up with it. Our aunt didn't give a crap what I thought of her. All that mattered to her was having that seat and lording it over us. She'd had her eyes on it from the moment our mother had died.

Would she have been this villainous if Mom had lived? It was hard to imagine her having much love for her sister but still being willing to sabotage that woman's children at every turn. Maybe she'd always held these ambitions and only dared to act on them when the most obvious obstacle had been removed.

It didn't really matter. Her vicious greed would bring about her undoing now. We just needed to draw it out.

"You should enjoy this while it lasts, I suppose," I said, adjusting my stance against the car into an even more nonchalant pose. Jude would have enjoyed playing this role. I tried to channel his careless air. "Because it isn't going to last long. We've already got plans in motion to take our rightful place. We just wanted to give you the chance to do the right thing and step aside before the situation needs to become even more fraught. It'll make you look better when this is all over."

She sputtered a laugh. "That's a lot of confidence from a young man no one has any interest in following anymore. Did you come all the way out here to make empty threats?"

Noah raised his chin. "It's not a threat. It's just a fact. We came here to be *generous*."

"And you really thought I'd capitulate and go along with this request of yours simply because you so generously asked?"

"No," I said. "Not really." Words I'd wanted to throw at her for years started to bubble up my throat. I let them come, part of me still balking at letting my anger show openly and part of me reveling in the release. "You've never been that smart, have you? But you're smart enough to know we've got a better claim than you do, and that it's only a matter of time before we prove that. How long did you really think this gambit of yours could last?"

"I have the support of the barons who—"

I barreled right over her. "It isn't long before the two currently empty seats will be filled by people who support me. Baron Nightwood has never liked you all that much, and Baron Bloodstone barely knows you. Do you really believe you can count on their loyalty when they have another, better option? What have you ever contributed to the pentacle other than backstabbing and simpering anyway?"

Aunt Ambrosia's hands closed at her sides. Of course she understood the tenuousness of her situation—but she didn't enjoy being reminded of it either. Especially by the people who made it so tenuous. Of course, there was an incredibly simple solution right in front of her if she decided to take it.

Go ahead, I dared her silently. *Show me how angry* I'm *making* you.

She descended one of the front steps with a brief movement of her lips that I suspected was a casting. The tickle of magic that brushed the edges of my awareness a moment later confirmed it. She was checking us for magical defenses. We purposely hadn't built any protections around ourselves. By all appearances, we were easy targets. Vulnerable.

Tempting.

"I'm not sure why you assume you're better," she said, studying us. "I have far more experience. I can stand with Barons Nightwood and Bloodstone as equals, not a junior. And there are plenty of ways I've proven I'm much wiser than you are."

Noah snorted. "This from the woman who couldn't manage to get one over on my brother even when he was a little kid. What makes you think you stand a chance against him now?"

Her eyes flashed. "Do you imagine you've seen my full power? I've always treaded carefully out of respect."

I couldn't restrain a guffaw. Maybe I didn't want to. It felt good letting everything I'd bottled up for so long pour out. "*Respect*? Are you kidding me? You've done everything you could do to undermine me at every turn, when your one job as regent was to support me. If you fuck up your job as baron even half as much, you'll be the worst thing that ever happened to the pentacle."

Aunt Ambrosia's voice came out as caustic as mine had been. "You should have known better than to speak to me like that. The tables have turned in the last few weeks. I'm the one who can demand respect now. You've come to my home to insult and berate me. When I tell this story later, no one will question why I felt it necessary to defend myself by whatever means necessary."

She'd barely spoken the last words when she thrust out her hand and spat a casting word. Magic blazed through the air—and Noah and I flung ourselves backward around the sides of the car.

We hadn't built up magical defenses around *ourselves*, but she hadn't tested the object behind us. A split-second after we stumbled through the magical barrier, the spell she'd hurled at us crashed into it with a searing crackle. The impact rang through the air and down into my bones, pinching my nerves. If that thing had actually hit *us*, we'd have been scattered on the driveway in tiny pieces.

As the blacksuits who'd helped us cast that shield had no doubt felt as well. Aunt Ambrosia only had time to take another step forward when the back doors of the car whipped open, and the three blacksuits charged out, the illusion spell that had hidden them dropping away. The baron usurper stared at them in horror.

"Ambrosia Ashgrave," said the previously-skeptical man in a clipped tone. "You're under arrest by the power of the blacksuits for an unprovoked assault on two minors of a barony family. I'm afraid we'll have to take you into custody." He raised his phone to his ear to call for the backup he'd asked to stay on patrol nearby.

"But I— They were—" Her mouth snapped shut as she must have realized there was no justifying what they'd witnessed. In the next instant, she was whirling toward the house, as if by fleeing there she could somehow escape her fate.

The other two blacksuits were on her in an instant, the woman who hadn't defected clicking the cuffs that would restrain Aunt Ambrosia's magic around her wrists. "Your time as baron is over," she said. "Don't make this harder than it needs to be."

Watching the woman who'd spent so much of my life trying to destroy me sag with defeat wasn't the triumphant moment she probably assumed it was. Queasiness filled my gut. I didn't enjoy seeing her humiliated. If she could have simply heeded our warning and backed down, I'd have preferred that outcome. But this was the woman she'd always been—and we'd stripped away one more piece of the current pentacle's power.

I glanced across the car to my brother. "I think our work here is done. Let's get back to campus."

CHAPTER SEVENTEEN

Rory

Less than a month ago, the sight of Maggie Duskland coming out of my dorm room would have made me stiffen up with wariness. Now, a smile sprang to my lips at the visual confirmation that my cousin had made it away from the barons and onto campus safely. She'd taken over one of the bedrooms that a few of my former dormmates had vacated after Ms. Grimsworth's announcement.

"Where are you off to?" I asked.

She smiled back a little wearily, and her voice came out more harried than it'd been the last few times we'd talked while she was still acting as my mother's assistant. "I offered to consult with Hector Killbrook on a few subjects that came up while I was working with the barons. Things that might help him enforce his own claim on the barony.

Might as well put everything I learned during that time to use."

"Of course. Just make sure you take some time to rest now that you're here too. You've done tons for us already."

"I'm just glad I ended up on the right side," she said, her smile softening.

She headed downstairs, and I went into the common room to find Morgan sitting with a bunch of Nary friends on the sofas. The sight warmed me and saddened me at the same time. On one hand, it was a relief that the nonmagical students felt comfortable gathering here now that the more antagonistic students had left and Ms. Grimsworth had banned any further torment. On the other hand, they were gathering so they could exchange horrified murmurs over the latest news from beyond campus.

There were more protests and more violent acts of retaliation happening all across the country. The news reports I'd watched on their computers showed reporters giving shocked commentary on the developments and ordinary people explaining how the proposed policies would screw them over. Some of our older allies had headed out yesterday, but if they'd managed to interfere with the persuasion spells the barons' lackeys were casting, the effects weren't yet clear.

"Is there anything particularly new or is the news all just as horrible as usual?" I asked with a grimace, coming up to the sofa near Morgan.

"The usual horrible, as far as I can tell. Which is still pretty horrible." She shuddered as she looked at the screen.

The Naries around her glanced at me with wisps of fear that I couldn't blame them for. Even if I'd never terrorized them myself, they'd suffered plenty at the hands of my fearmancer classmates.

"We're keeping an eye on the political situation too," I said. "And we're finding as many ways as we can to try to set things right. I'll let you know when we've made concrete progress." And hopefully that wouldn't take much longer.

While I went over to the kitchen to grab some lunch, the Naries started up their hushed discussion again. After several minutes, most of them left to go back to whatever else they were occupying themselves with these days. Morgan meandered over to the table where I'd sat down with my sandwich. She hesitated behind one of the chairs, her hands fidgeting along the top, and finally opened her mouth.

"I know we don't really know each other all that well or anything, but—you're the closest thing I have to a friend on campus who can actually *leave* campus right now. Would you mind if I asked you a pretty small favor?"

Even if I'd been inclined to balk, her awkwardness about the request would have won me over. "What do you need? I'd be happy to help if I can." It was the least I could offer after everything she'd been through here that I hadn't been able to protect her or her friends from.

"Well, I..." She made a face at the chair before looking at me again. "It's going to sound silly. I have this tradition. Every year my favorite horror author puts out a new book in the fall, and I always get it to read around

Halloween. It's almost that time, but I haven't been able to get to a bookstore or anything. I wouldn't want you to go out of your way, but if you're going into town to grab groceries or whatever else sometime and you wouldn't mind stopping by the bookstore there… He's a pretty popular author so they'll probably have it. I can give you the money for it, of course."

She was already turning back toward the sofa to grab her purse when I made a dismissive motion. "I think I can afford a book. Consider it a thank you gift for trusting me even though so many of my classmates have been assholes. Just write down the name and the title so I can make sure I get the right one."

It felt good having a mission I knew I could fulfill with minimal trouble, but my spirits dampened when I emerged from the forest path at the edge of town. Nothing nearby looked suspicious, but my hackles rose instinctively as I set off through the streets. The barons must have heard of Ms. Grimsworth's declaration by now. Between that and the arrest of Declan's aunt, my mother and Malcolm's dad had to be furious. Nowhere beyond the school's wards was all that safe.

On top of that, in every person I passed I saw echoes of the trauma the townspeople had been through that the blacksuits had wiped from their conscious memories. One woman's gaze lingered on me for a few beats longer than was natural, a flicker of anxiety passing from her into me.

A young man flinched and did a double-take when our paths crossed. The wounds we'd dealt were still there, just buried under uncertainty they'd never be able to shake.

I said a few casting words under my breath to draw a temporary shield against magic around me as well as bolster my tighter mental shields. I couldn't do much to soothe the townspeople's lingering discomfort, but I could make myself as secure as possible out here.

The bookstore had a display at the end of one of the aisles with the novel Morgan had asked for. Easy enough. I grabbed it and brought it up to the counter, pretending not to notice the nervous twitch of the shopkeeper's cheek as she rang it up.

I walked back to campus laden down by that and the groceries I'd picked up for both myself and some of the Naries I'd asked, whom I'd realized might be getting tired of the cafeteria food. At least I hadn't come under attack during my venture beyond the wards. A little tension bled away as the campus buildings came into view at the other end of the path. I stepped out onto the field beyond the forest and paused at the sight of Jude hustling toward the garage, too intent on his goal to notice me.

He paused several feet shy of the entrance, his body tensed. Then a woman emerged—a woman with wavy red hair an even darker shade than Jude's, her belly rounded with pregnancy.

His mother, I realized. She lit up with a wobbly smile when she saw him, as if she wasn't any more sure of his welcome than he appeared to be sure how to give it. She walked toward him tentatively and reached to take his hands. After a few exchanges, she tugged him closer and gave him the tightest hug she was capable of at her size.

I started to feel weird about watching, but as I pushed myself onward, Jude stepped back and happened to glance my way. He waved me over, his posture much more relaxed than it'd been when I'd first spotted him.

The tightening of his mother's expression when she saw me suggested she recognized who I was—and that she hadn't had the best experiences with Bloodstones in the past. But it was only a fleeting reaction, and then she was giving me a little bob of her head as Jude introduced us.

"Rory, meet my mother. Mom, this is Rory Bloodstone. And also my girlfriend." His grin widened as he said that last bit.

"It's a pleasure to meet you," Mrs. Killbrook said in a soft voice, and offered me her hand.

The woman had just lost her husband a couple days ago—in a confrontation that had been kind of my fault. I grappled with my words for a second before saying, "The same to you. And I'm sorry for your loss."

"Yes. Well." Her gaze dropped for a second, too many conflicting emotions for me to follow washing over her face. Her hand came to rest on her belly.

"She decided she was better off with us, now that— now that 'Dad' is gone," Jude said, a bit of strain creeping into his voice.

His mother clasped his hand again. "You're my family. I *should* be here. Maybe I should have come sooner…" She rubbed her face. "We have a lot to talk through, obviously."

Jude turned on the cheer again. "And thankfully we have all kinds of time, seeing as I'm not good for a whole lot these days other than talking. Come on—let's find someplace you can get off your feet."

I shot him a smile before he turned away, even though the self-deprecating comment pained me. Jude might not be using his diminished magical ability as an excuse to go off on suicide missions anymore, but I didn't think remarks like that were all in good humor. The loss might never stop rankling him.

And seeing him walking his mother toward Killbrook Hall sent a different sort of twinge through my chest. Baron Killbrook had been the main villain in Jude's life, but I knew he'd had plenty of frustrations with his mother too—for going along with the baron's plans, for keeping the secret of his parentage from Jude, for letting her husband treat him as if he were unworthy for so long.

But in the midst of tragedy, they were coming together. Maybe he'd find some kind of peace in this. Was I ever going to have any kind of peace with my birth mother?

My throat constricted with an ache that ran down through my chest. I continued on toward the dorm building, but after I'd handed Morgan's book over to her and put away the food, I went into my bedroom, cast a silencing spell around the space to ensure my voice didn't travel, and got out my phone.

For a few minutes, I just looked at the device in my hand. What were the chances this would make any difference? I'd tried to talk to her so many times.

But what could it hurt to try again? In spite of everything, she *was* my mother. The only parent of any kind I had who was still living. I didn't really want to lose her.

As I made the call, my fingers closed around the glass dragon charm that the mother I'd already lost had given me. The silence of the room around me seemed to expand with each ring on the other end. The points on the charm dug into my palm.

There was a click, and my mother said in an even voice, "Persephone. I wasn't expecting to hear from you after all this."

"Mom," I started, and didn't know what to say next. What *could* I say, really, when I'd turned my back on her the last time we'd seen each other? When she still refused to call me by the name I'd claimed as my own?

"Well? I assume there's a reason for this call." A hint of her obvious anger bled through.

I swallowed hard. "I just wanted to talk to you. I—I don't want to fight. I *never* wanted us to have to fight."

"Then you've made some very odd choices."

"You've made some choices that hurt people I care about." I paused and dragged in a breath. Making accusations didn't feel like the right direction. "I know you don't feel totally right about this situation. I know you weren't happy seeing that little boy killed in town because the mages on patrol got overzealous. Don't you think that's going to happen again, over and over, if we try to maintain control like that over so many more Naries?"

"A baron doesn't let her personal sensitivities sway her

judgment when it comes to serving her people," my mother said. "A lesson you clearly haven't learned yet. Along with the lesson that a Bloodstone always stands with her own kind."

"If you'd meet me halfway, I'd be happy to stand with you," I couldn't help saying, my voice dipping with the words. "I want to learn all the things you can teach me. If we could have just focused on that…"

"I tried." A ragged note came into my mother's tone. "But the most important thing you need to understand is what we deserve as fearmancers, what we owe ourselves and each other, and you've made it clear you don't understand that at all. That you don't *want* to understand it." She paused, and some of the anger faded. "If you'd come back—I'm not turning you away, Persephone. This is your choice. I can still show you. We can still build this future together."

The offer held enough hope that my stomach twisted. I closed my eyes. "It's not the future I want. I'd come and see what we could work out… if you and Baron Nightwood agreed to back off on setting the Naries at each other's throats until we've come up with a plan we can all support. That's all I've ever wanted; I swear it."

She sighed. "It's too late for that now. The balls are already in motion. If we pull back now, we may never regain that momentum. Can't you simply *trust* me?"

No, I couldn't. I never had, though I wouldn't dig the knife deeper by saying that. "I have to trust my own judgment too, Mom. And it's telling me that what you're doing is going to hurt so many more people than it helps.

Why is this plan so important to you that *you'd* put it over our family?"

"That's what you refuse to accept," she said, her voice going taut. "This is for you, not against you. Do you have any idea— I watched for so long, as my father and my grandmother did before me. We saw how our people make themselves smaller to fit our lives around these feeble beings who are capable of so much less than we are. I made promises to those people that I would change things. My imprisonment set back those plans for far too long. I have to make good on them now."

"No, you don't," I protested. "There are plenty of people who don't want any of it. You're allowed to change your mind."

"I keep my promises. I know what loyalty is." I heard her swallow. "I wouldn't deserve to be baron if I went back on everything I meant to achieve for us now out of weakness."

I couldn't help trying one more time. "It's not weakness; it's recognizing that sometimes what seemed like a good idea in theory isn't working out in practice. Haven't you seen—the actions you and the other barons have been taking are already destroying your own pentacle! If you ignore that, you're not being strong. You're ignoring what's true. If you can't acknowledge that, how do you deserve to rule anyone?"

My mother's tone turned icy in an instant. "If that's the way you still see things, there's no point in continuing this conversation. I *will* show you, on a larger scale. I'll force you to see how weak the feebs are, how ridiculous it is that we have to hide from them. And then you'd better be prepared to earn my forgiveness for turning your back on our family."

She disconnected the call without giving me a chance to respond, leaving me clutching the phone as the dial tone droned in my ear, not sure whether I'd just made things even worse than they'd been before.

CHAPTER EIGHTEEN

Malcolm

Shadow might have been able to pick up on the tensions around campus through my emotions, but he didn't let that get in the way of playtime. My wolf familiar bounded around the field, eagerly awaiting the next toss of the conjured ball I'd given to Agnes for her to join in the game.

My sister laughed and flung the shimmering sphere across the grass. As soon as it bounced on the ground, it leapt up in the shape of a rabbit. With an eager pant, Shadow sprang after it. He pounced, only to have the image dissolve under his feet, but he looked around as if determined that he'd catch one sooner or later rather than resentful.

I nudged Agnes's arm. "We should let him get some real hunting in now. He'll come around for more attention when he's gotten his fill."

"All right," she said with a hint of a pout, but her lips curved back into a smile as she watched me direct Shadow toward the woods. He loped off between the trees like a living representation of his name. The brilliant autumn leaves overhead rustled with a passing breeze that licked cool over our faces.

Agnes's gaze turned distant. "I'll be able to have a familiar soon. You got Shadow as soon as your magic came, didn't you?"

"About a month after, so pretty much." I glanced at her. "It's a big decision, even if you go with a smaller animal. They live longer than they regularly would because of the magical connection, and it's not something you can easily break, so you want to be sure of your choice."

"I know." She lifted her head, the fading sunlight making her hair gleam gold, looking more confident than I ever remembered seeing her back home. Just a matter of days away from our parents had changed her that much. "I've had lots of time to think about it while I wait for my magic to kick in. Nightwoods usually get their powers close to their birthday, don't they?"

"For me it took two weeks," I said. "Mom and Dad weren't surprised by that. I don't think you have to worry."

"It still feels like ages. Assuming I even make it past my fifteenth birthday without Mom and Dad killing me for running off on them."

She said that last bit dryly, but she kicked at the grass at the same moment, a little of the familiar nervous hunch coming back into her shoulders. The damage they'd already done couldn't be completely healed in a week or two of freedom.

"They won't," I said smoothly. "Because they're going to want to kill me even more, and they've got to keep at least one of us around."

A giggle tumbled out of her before she could catch it. She clapped her hand over her mouth. "I'm sorry. I shouldn't laugh about that. You're going to be in a lot of trouble for helping me leave… and everything else, aren't you?"

I shrugged. "If they get the chance to do anything about it. At this point, I'm perfectly happy to never go home until the barony passes to me."

"Do you really think we can manage that? How long can we actually hold out here?"

That was a good question, one I'd hoped she wouldn't be thoughtful enough to ask. But my sister was clearly sharper than I'd given her much credit for when she'd been living under my parents' thumb. It was hard to grow up in their presence without learning to consider all the angles and potential consequences. I'd certainly had those habits beaten into me.

"I don't know," I said. "Dad and Baron Bloodstone must have their hands full keeping their allies happy and sure of them now that it's down to just him and her. We might be okay here for a while."

"But they've also got to be incredibly pissed off at all of us for defying them. They won't want to let us get away with it."

"No." I grimaced. "And our current living situation is

obviously just temporary. But we're going to keep fighting their plans, and if we can stop them before they see those through to the end, then we'll be in a much better position. We'll have proven that they can't ignore the laws and charge ahead despite people's protests. We'll have the majority of the pentacle on our side. But to get there… it might take a lot more fighting. I'm not sure how far we'll have to go to manage to push them back."

"Yeah." Her eyes flashed, and she pulled her posture straight again. "I know you got me out of the house because you wanted me to be safer, but I realize things are going to get dangerous if we're really going to make a difference. Even more than they already are. That's okay. You—you always took the worst of it because Dad expected more from you. I shouldn't get to take it easy while you keep sticking your neck out for both of us and everyone else here. Maybe I'm not going to be baron, but I don't want to see our community ruined either."

Her words stirred up the thoughts I'd been having ever since Connar and Declan had brought their brothers in as nearly joint-scions—ever since the five of us who'd originally made up that pentacle had started discussing how we'd change things if we got the chance. It'd been hard to picture how Agnes would fit into that dynamic when I hadn't spent much time with her since I'd started classes at Blood U. But looking at her now, listening to her, I had no qualms about bringing the idea up.

"You know," I said, "the other scions and I have been talking about making some changes about how the pentacle will work in the future. To make things more balanced, and to try to cut out the infighting that keeps happening within our families, and just to give us all more freedom."

Agnes gave me a curious look. "What kind of changes?"

"Well… that we might share the spots at the table and rule together with other heirs rather than one baron having all the authority. Connar and Holden could stand together, Declan and his brother, Rory and her cousin, we'd have to see how the Killbrook situation works out— and you and I could work together."

Her look turned into a stare. For a few seconds, she stood there speechless. When she found her voice, it came out hushed. "You'd actually—you'd want to share the barony with me?"

Her startled awe brought a crooked smile to my face, full of affection that she respected me enough to see me as the ultimate authority and regret that I hadn't stepped in more to help her see how much she could offer.

"You'd have some catching up to do on policies and how to present yourself and all that," I said. "Although I'm sure simply living with our parents gave you a decent grounding. And who knows when we'll be in the position to take over anyway. But yeah. Having all the responsibility isn't a piece of cake, you know. You'd be helping me as much as I'm doing you any favors."

"Anything I can do to help. Then or now. That would —wow." She drew in a breath and appeared to compose herself. Yeah, the Nightwood instincts hadn't passed her by. "It'd be an honor to take on those responsibilities."

I gave her a light cuff to the shoulder. "Keep on like that, and you're off to a good start. Ready to grab some dinner?"

We headed back toward the green and Killbrook Hall, where even the seniors had taken to eating most of their meals in the junior cafeteria now that any trip beyond the boundaries of campus was a risk. I'd never eaten much there to begin with, always taking advantage of the family chef's willingness to send regular meals, and I had to admit I'd been shunning it for no good reason. Ms. Grimsworth knew how to pick her cooks.

There was less variety than usual on offer now that some of the staff had left with the announcement that the university was a safe zone for dissenters, but I could live with that. Tonight we were choosing between filet mignon and shrimp linguine. I asked for a steak and Agnes for the pasta, and when we had our plates we picked one of the emptier tables to sit at. Other than a bunch of juniors chattering in one corner and a cluster of girls who looked intent in their current conversation, it was mostly Naries in the place right now.

I'd only taken my first bite when a tall, slightly pudgy guy with a leaf pin on his collar came over and stopped by the seat beside Agnes. From the width of his shoulders and the sparse but visible five o'clock shadow creeping across his jaw, I figured he had to be about my age, but the meekness of his posture made him seem younger. He stood there for a moment, just blinking and apparently working up the courage to speak.

"You're one of the—what they call the scions, right?"

he said in a throaty voice much deeper than I'd have expected given his shyness.

"I am," I said, resisting the urge to raise a questioning eyebrow or make any other move that would set him more off-balance. I might not have any desire to see the Naries hurt, but that didn't mean I wanted to be hassled by them either. Still, I could play nice. It wasn't their fault they were stuck in this awful situation.

"Well, I—" He gripped the back of the chair so tightly his knuckles blanched. "I had an idea. For making it harder for the people you're trying to stop to mess with our politicians and all. This girl in my program said that's what's going on and that the rest of you are hoping to get in their way."

I hadn't realized the nonmagical students were picking up on that many details—but after seeing how so many of the fearmancers here had treated them when they'd been given free rein, maybe it wasn't hard to guess what was going on in the wider world. Or maybe Rory had been sharing more than I'd ever have felt comfortable doing.

She would have wanted me to find out more, even if I couldn't figure out how this timid kid could possibly challenge the most powerful fearmancers out there. I studied him as I cut off another piece of my steak. "What's the idea? And what would you need to pull it off?"

A more determined energy came over him at my interest. He pulled out the chair and let himself sit down, bracing his elbows on the table. His eyes gleamed with unexpected intensity.

"It'd be a little tricky, because whatever magic those

people in the black clothes put on us, none of us can interact with the world outside the school, even over the computer. But I'm sure I could talk one of you through the steps if you're willing to be patient and listen. The— the mages or whatever you call yourselves who went off to mess with people, they couldn't control the *entire* government or FBI or whatever, right?"

"Not in any sustained way," I said. Even the powerful family members who'd gone out on their mission from the barons would have trouble consistently controlling more than a small group to keep up the policy proposals and so on. They'd have to keep meeting with them face to face to renew those spells. The wider-spread chaos, like the violence at the riots, they'd have incited in the moment with the effects quickly fading afterward.

"Okay. So, I was thinking." The guy clasped his hands together, looking almost excited now. "I got accepted here because of the computer skills I could show off in public, but I've messed around a lot on my own in private too. I've broken into a whole lot of government servers just to see if I could. If you know the right tricks— Anyway, everyone's still awfully on guard against terrorists right now."

"Terrorists," I repeated, still not sure where he was going with this.

He nodded emphatically. "With enough time, we could get in wherever we need to and set up profiles for the people you want out of the picture on the watch lists and so on. Put in all kinds of red flags that'll bring the establishment down on their asses. Maybe they could escape getting arrested with their magic, but it'd at least interfere with them getting access to any important political figures. It'd keep them on their toes and distracted. At least, I think it would. It seems worth a try."

It was my turn to blink at him. My stomach grumbled, annoyed that I'd delayed filling it, but what this guy was saying... I didn't totally understand how he'd be able to do it, but he didn't appear to have any doubts that it was possible.

If we could sic the entire upper levels of Nary law enforcement on the pricks who were meddling with them, the barons would have a hell of a time seeing the rest of their plan through.

It sounded a lot more efficient than our own plans so far had been. And it'd come from this wimp of a Nary—who wasn't coming across as so wimpy now.

"You know," I said slowly. "I think you're right. It's absolutely worth a try. Let me get through my dinner fast, and I'll take you to talk this through with the rest of the scions."

CHAPTER NINETEEN

Rory

"**P**erfect!" Brandon leaned over to check Declan's progress on the tricked-out laptop he'd lent the Ashgrave scion. They'd been poised side-by-side on the sofa in the Scions' Guard room for the better part of four hours, painstakingly working through layers of computer defenses I wouldn't have had a clue what to do with myself.

To be fair, neither did Declan. He was just following orders, with a bemused expression most of the time.

The Nary guy consulted the tablet he'd been working on, tapped away on his portable keyboard, and then showed Declan the next lines of code he needed to enter. It'd taken a little trial and error to figure out how he could communicate everything necessary around the blacksuits' spell, but they'd gotten into a good rhythm by now.

I sipped the espresso I'd made in the scion lounge in

an attempt to keep myself awake for as long as it took to see this scheme through. The hot liquid flooded my mouth.

Maggie had taken a few members of the Guard off to the side to go over some of the defensive strategies she'd learned from her time working with the blacksuits. Over on the mats, Connar was talking Holden through some Physicality techniques to help bring him up to speed with his magic use. Jude and Noah had just left on a snack run. Malcolm was sitting with his sister, filling her in on some of what we'd been through in our conflict with the barons before now. None of us was offering anything particularly useful, but we all wanted to feel at least somewhat a part of this potentially game-changing development.

As I drifted from one end of the sofa to the other, doing my best not to distract the two guys in their work, Agnes leaned back in her chair with a yawn. At something Malcolm said, she made a face, but a moment later she got up and left, presumably to catch some sleep. The Nightwood scion ambled over to join me.

"I found a good one, didn't I?" he said with a satisfied smile, his gaze lingering on the computer screens.

I eased back from the sofa, keeping my voice low. "He didn't know what he could be getting into, coming to you out of all of us," I teased.

"Hey, I was perfectly amiable. I listened to him and brought him in, didn't I?"

"And it looks like we should all be very grateful for that." I knuckled his side playfully with my free hand.

"Hard to think of people like him as feeble when he can pull off something like this, huh?"

"It is," Malcolm said, more seriously than I'd expected. "I guess I didn't really think about all the things they could be experts in that I don't have much of a clue about." He let out a light laugh. "All the better for us. I doubt any of my dad's or your mother's lackeys are experienced in computer programming."

"They won't know what hit them. I just hope it hits them hard enough to force them to back down—or at least slow down."

"One step at a time. We're making progress." He paused. "Maybe there are other ways we could get the Naries involved. Obviously they can't fight the barons and the rest directly, but—there could be other approaches they'd think of that we haven't."

That wasn't an admission I'd ever expected to hear Malcolm Nightwood make. "Absolutely. Why don't we see how this gambit plays out… We can always hope we won't *need* any other approaches."

Malcolm's snort showed exactly how likely he thought that was. "Always the optimist," he said with obvious affection, and stroked his fingers over my hair to tip my head so he could kiss me on the temple.

Jude and Noah and the Guard member who'd joined them for extra protection returned right then with four bulging grocery bags between them. Brandon claimed his pack of Twizzlers without so much as glancing up from his tablet. Noah dropped Declan's requested bag of barbeque chips on the sofa beside him. The rest of the loot they spread out on the table near Maggie and her companions.

I grabbed a cupcake from its plastic tray, needing some sugar to cut through the coffee bitterness. One of the guys from the Guard who'd been talking with Maggie nabbed another. I couldn't remember his name off the top of my head, but I knew his mother was one of the mages who'd volunteered to travel down to Washington to interfere with the mages who were enacting the barons' plan.

"Have you heard anything from your mom?" I asked him.

He chewed and swallowed the big bite he'd just taken and shook his head. "I think they're being pretty cautious —better if the other fearmancers don't realize anyone's trying to disrupt their spells. Last I heard they were experimenting with different shielding techniques from a distance."

"That sounds like a reasonable start, at least."

"Yeah." He glanced toward the sofa. "Are you sure *that* is a good idea?"

The note of disdain in his voice made me stiffen. Beside me, Malcolm raised his head with a wary expression, but he gave me room to handle the question.

"Why wouldn't it be?" I said, keeping my voice even. Maggie leaned over to grab a handful of Doritos, watching both of us too.

A flicker of anxiety tickled my chest as the guy groped for his answer. He could tell he might have stepped wrong. "Well, you know—taking a Nary's advice, when he doesn't know anything about the politics and everything involved."

"I don't know," I said. "I think he knows more about the Nary side of politics than any of us do, and it's Nary politics the fearmancers are mostly screwing up right now. I'd listen to him over any of us."

"But, I mean, I'm not sure any strategy they'd think of would be of much use against the mages out there in the first place."

"We'll find that out, won't we?" I tilted my head toward Brandon. "He didn't have to offer us anything at all. Most of the people on campus have been awful to him and his friends for most of the term. But he still reached out when he thought he could help. The least we can do is listen and give him a chance to show what he's capable of."

The guy opened his mouth and then closed it again with a slanted smile. "You know what—you're totally right. Forget I said anything."

I thought I could still read some doubt in his tone, but that was fine. If Brandon knew what he was doing, which as far as I could tell was true, the results of his efforts would erase those doubts soon enough. A couple of the other Guard members glanced over at the sofa with hints of skepticism too, which only made me more hopeful that the Nary guy's scheme would pan out.

It wasn't enough for fearmancers to realize it was cruel to torment those among us without magic. They needed to respect them as people if things in this community were really going to change.

Brandon gave a muffled shout around the licorice stick

he had dangling from his mouth. He pointed to Declan's screen as he tugged the candy from his lips. "There we go! We're in."

Declan let out a weary laugh and swiped his hand across his forehead. "You did all the real work. I was just your proxy. What's next?"

The rest of us gathered around the sofa. Brandon peered at the laptop, telling Declan where to click and a couple more commands to type. Then he glanced back at us. "You've got the info on the people we want to target?"

"Right here." Malcolm brandished his phone. "I'll transfer the folder over."

All of us heirs had spent the first couple hours while we'd waited working out which fearmancers the barons would have sent out and gathering as much basic information on them as we could. Photographs had been harder to come by, but some of our allies had been able to help with their personal pictures from social gatherings. For a supposed criminal's profile, I didn't think anyone would expect a particularly professional-looking portrait.

We all stayed clustered behind the sofa as Brandon told Declan how to set up the first few records. Holden stepped right up to the front of our group, studying their activities with avid concentration, but Connar hung farther back. He never seemed to trust himself to have much input when it came to situations that were more about mental strength than bodily power.

Maybe the insecurities that had gripped him the other day had risen back up, despite our interlude with Declan on the cliffside. As I gulped down the last of my cupcake, I moved to join him. The Stormhurst scion slung a companionable arm around my waist, and I happily leaned into him.

"Pretty amazing what you can do without any magic at all," he said.

"It is." I nudged for him to follow me farther back in the room while the others stayed by the sofa, so we could talk in relative privacy. "How have you been holding up?"

"Me?" Connar said with a rough laugh. "I should be asking you that. I'm the only one who hasn't had to deal with hostile family members at all—thanks to your mom, weirdly enough."

"I know, but still, this is an awful situation for all of us. And you have the pressure of your inheritance hanging over you."

He shrugged, but his mouth twisted a little. "I'm still figuring out how I want to handle that. It won't really matter until we've tackled all the problems the barons are currently making anyway, right?"

"Of course." I looked up at him, taking in the perfect contrast between the chiseled planes of his face and the soft gleam of affection that came into his eyes as he gazed back at me. I'd never felt the need to discuss how my feelings for the guys intersected with our political positions except with Jude, because of the position he didn't really have. That might have been a mistake. I wanted Connar to pursue whatever role made *him* happy, not what he thought I expected or even required.

I nestled as close to him as I could while still holding his gaze. "You know it doesn't matter to *me* one way or another whether you end up taking the title of baron or not, or how much you're involved in the pentacle, don't you?"

His arms tightened around me. "Rory, you're allowed to care about that stuff. It wouldn't be surprising for you to want partners who'll stand on equal footing with you."

"You don't have to be a baron to be my equal. I love *you*, the way you are. And if the way you are doesn't really want that pressure and responsibility after all, then I'll support whatever you decide to do instead just as much as I'll speak up for you as baron. I've been encouraging you because I don't want you to give up over worries that you're not qualified, not because it makes any difference to whether I want to be with you. Okay?"

A smile crossed his face, small but so bright it lit me up in turn. Without any hesitation about the others in the room who might glance over, he dipped his head and kissed me hard. I kissed him back, letting the heat of his answer radiate through me.

"Okay," he murmured when he drew back. "And not that I can imagine *you* giving up the barony, but just for the record, everything you just said is just as true for my feelings about you."

I enjoyed his embrace for a moment longer before reluctantly peeling myself away. We drifted to the refreshments table where I took a handful of chips and then back to the sofa to check what progress had been made.

The code on the screens looked about the same to me as it had when I'd last considered it. As I scanned the lines for clues to their function, a thread of uneasiness trickled into my chest. Not my own—someone else's passing into me, as if I'd unnerved them.

I glanced around, but no one in the room was even looking at me now. Brandon was too focused on the work for me to think he'd be nervous about me standing there. I didn't think I was acting at all threatening anyway. Even the guy I'd had that brief argument with seemed absorbed in watching the scheme come together.

Maybe someone not even here had simply thought about something I'd said or done a little while back and that had provoked some kind of discomfort. The benefit we got from generating fear lingered, even if it made *me* uncomfortable to think that I'd unsettled someone that much.

The sensation didn't fade, though. If anything, it expanded. Mostly all I caught were little flickers of nerves, but here and there a sharper prickling of fear ran through me. What the hell was going on?

I couldn't just stand around ignoring it. Maybe something really was wrong elsewhere on campus, even if it didn't appear to be affecting any of the other scions. I hesitated and then leaned toward Maggie to whisper, "I'm going up to the dorm for a minute. Just need to check something."

She considered my expression. "Is everything okay?"

"I'm not sure. I'll let you all know if it isn't, as soon as I figure that out."

I hurried up the stairs, nudging the door open on each landing to check the hall for any signs of a disturbance.

The flow of fear continued to rise and ebb behind my collarbone. My store of magical energy thrummed with it.

I didn't see anything unusual. Most of the halls were empty and quiet, dimmed in recognition of the late hour. I came into my own dorm even more confused than before.

The common room was empty other than Morgan perched in one of the armchairs with her legs drawn up. She had the book I'd bought for her open against her knees. At the swing of the door, she flinched—and another jolt of energy with the same flavor as before tingled into me. Huh.

When I hesitated just past the threshold, a flush colored her cheeks. She tucked the book close to her chest. "Not your fault that you startled me. I just got caught up in the story. It's a really creepy one. That's why I'm reading out here. It feels a little brighter and less spooky even with no one else around."

"Don't worry about it," I said with a laugh, but a quiver of a suspicion rose up in the back of my head. I crossed the room as if I'd only meant to head to the kitchen anyway. "You go ahead and keep reading."

She rolled her shoulders and swiped her hand across her mouth as if suppressing a yawn. "I really should get to bed soon. But I'm almost at the end of this chapter... Hey, is Brandon doing his thing? I'm so glad I told him to talk to you guys."

I grinned at her. "Yes, he's been a lot of help. We'll have to wait and see how it all pans out, but he obviously knows his stuff."

"Oh, yeah." The color in her cheeks came back. Between that and her tone, I wondered if she didn't have a bit of a crush on the guy.

I poked around in the fridge while she went back to her book. Within a matter of seconds, that quiet but distinctive trickle of fear returned, seeping into my chest. It *did* feel just like the jolt I'd gotten when I'd startled Morgan—but then, different people's fear didn't usually feel all that different, so that didn't necessarily mean anything.

After a few minutes during which I nibbled on an apple, Morgan closed the book and gave a little shudder. "So good," she said. "Hopefully my dreams don't get too crazy after that. Good night!"

"'Night."

I watched her head into her bedroom. No nervousness was prickling into me now. I waited, polishing off the apple, but the sensation didn't return.

Interesting. It did make sense, just not in a way I'd considered before. The book had been scaring her, and I'd gotten the book for her, so technically I'd brought about that fear. It never would have occurred to me that fearmancer magic worked that way, but I had all the evidence I needed to believe it now.

There were too many other things going on for me to give that fact much immediate attention, but I filed it away for later. Maybe I could make something useful out of it when I didn't have a civil war to prevent.

As I tossed the apple core in the garbage, Maggie came

in. "The coast is clear?" she said with an arch of her eyebrow.

"Everything's fine," I said. "There wasn't really anything to be nervous about. Are they already finished downstairs?"

She shook her head. "It looks like it's going to be a while longer, and your Nary friend says there isn't anything for the rest of us to do. I figured I'm better off getting some sleep while I can—because who knows how much I'll appreciate having gotten that rest later."

"Good point." I glanced toward my bedroom. Despite the coffee I'd drunk, my head was getting heavy. It'd been a long day, and I couldn't say I'd been sleeping well in general. "Maybe I'll turn in for the night too."

It might have only been because of Morgan's comment, but the small space of my room did feel eerily lonely once I was inside it. I curled up under the covers, wishing I knew for sure I'd get a future where I could snuggle in bed with all four of my lovers around me, no more worries about the fate of our entire society hanging over us.

* * *

A squeal that carried through my bedroom door yanked me out of sleep. I sat up, blinking blearily in the morning light that crept past my curtain, my pulse racing faster. Was something wrong? Had—

"It really worked!" a breathless voice said, and I realized the squeal must have been in excitement rather than distress. My heart kept thumping, but in a more upbeat rhythm now. I kicked off the sheets, pulled on my bathrobe over my nightgown, and headed out.

Victory, Cressida, Morgan, and a couple of Morgan's friends were all huddled together around a laptop set on the dining table. Seeing the two haughty fearmancer girls in such close proximity to a group of Naries threw me for such a loop that it took me a moment to remember why I'd come out in the first place.

Morgan glanced up at me and beamed as I hurried over to see what they were looking at. "Those jerks must be running scared now," she said.

"What's going on?" I asked.

Victory was smiling too. "The Nary newscasts are reporting that some of the recent turmoil may have been caused by terrorists, and they're showing photos of the fearmancers who went out there, asking if anyone has information on their activities."

"All the government law enforcement agencies have got to be on their case after this," one of the other Naries said. "They're going to have a lot more trouble using their voodoo on anyone."

My spirits lifted. It wasn't a total triumph, but it was a huge step in the right direction. Now we'd just have to wait and see how the barons responded. At some point, surely, no matter what my mother and Baron Nightwood felt they owed their supporters, they'd have to realize it was too much trouble to—

A shrill tone pierced the building's walls and rang into my ears, seemingly from all around us. I clutched the edge of the kitchen island with a wince. The others looked around, the Naries' expressions bewildered while a shadow crossed Victory's and Cressida's faces.

"What the heck is that?" Morgan asked.

A lump had filled my throat. I willed it down, pushing myself straighter, even though my stomach stayed clenched tight.

"That's the alarm built into the school's wards," I said. "Someone's trying to break through them."

Apparently we were getting the barons' response right now.

CHAPTER TWENTY

Rory

Victory, Cressida, and I left the Naries behind with hasty words of reassurance I didn't totally believe. We were met by a bunch of other fearmancer students as we burst out into the hall. Even the mages who hadn't heard Ms. Grimsworth's explanation about the warning alert could tell the sound signaled something important —and bad.

I realized halfway down the stairs that I was still only wearing my nightgown, bathrobe, and slippers, but I couldn't imagine going back for proper clothes. I wasn't going to let my outfit be the deciding factor in whether Blood U stood firm or fell.

As we passed the fourth floor landing, Declan rushed out in a similar state of disarray among more classmates, a wool coat pulled hastily over plaid pajamas. His normally neat hair stuck out in irregular tufts, but his hazel eyes shone sharply alert. How much sleep had *he* gotten after he and Brandon had finally finished all their computer trickery?

"Have you heard anything about what's happening out there?" I asked as we fell into step together.

He shook his head. "The alert woke me up. But it doesn't take much to guess who'd be attacking us. No one except our fellow fearmancers even know where the university is." His lips twitched into a tense smile. "Looks like yesterday's stunt caught their attention, if not entirely in the way I'd like."

He wouldn't have seen the news yet. "The Naries are already reporting on the supposed terrorist activity," I said. "It's got to have thrown a wrench in the barons' plans."

A wry voice carried from behind us. "And now they're trying to throw a whole lot more than a wrench at us."

Jude had managed to pull on slacks and a sweater, probably because, knowing him, if he'd come running straight out of bed, he'd have been in nothing but boxers, if that much. His hair was equally rumpled, a pink indent from a crease in his pillowcase crossing his cheek like a scar. The image jolted me back to weeks ago when we'd found him crumpled near death in the west field.

"I'm coming," he added in a taut voice, maybe catching the shift in my expression. "I can do *something*, even if it's just hurling insults to conjure a little emotional distress. I'm not going to be remotely safe if this invasion succeeds."

I couldn't argue with that—and it wasn't as if I had time to anyway. We spilled out into the first floor hallway beside the library, with Maggie, Malcolm, Connar, and Holden catching up with us there. Outside on the green, a couple of our remaining professors stood on the grass with Ms. Grimsworth and a few of our blacksuits. Junior students poured out of Killbrook Hall beyond them. Malcolm made a decisive motion, and both his sister and Noah loped over to join our pack of heirs.

At the same time, the staff were gesturing for our attention and one of the blacksuits was hollering instructions. "We need people by the road and beyond the east and west fields. The wards will hold strong once they're tuned properly, but most of the participants in the current offensive have prior permission to cross them. My colleagues are changing that as quickly as they can as our attackers arrive, but we need help pushing them back in the meantime."

One of the other blacksuits pressed her hand to her ear where she must have been wearing a radio for communication. Her jaw tightened.

"The assault is focusing in on the mid-east field. A few of the barons' blacksuits have pressed past the wards!"

Her colleague leapt into action. He jerked his hand toward us. "Scions, take the east field. The rest of you, spread out across campus."

Before he'd even finished speaking, all of us heirs and a handful of our classmates were moving, running across the green toward the field beyond Nightwood Tower. My slippers wobbled on my feet, and I murmured them more tightly into place with a quick spell. Shouts rang out up ahead, although I couldn't make out any of the fighting yet. It'd be deeper within the forest that bordered the campus.

As we reached the trees, a lanky figure sprinted across grass toward us. The new Baron Killbrook must have gotten word of the shift in the assault. Hector waved us onward. "Get in there as quickly as you can. We've got to try to keep them behind the wards."

We dashed into the forest, dodging tree roots and fallen branches. A flash of magical energy split the dim space ahead, followed by a cry of pain. Our side or theirs? I propelled myself faster, my lungs constricting in my chest.

If the barons' people overran the school and took all of the resisters into custody... nothing we'd done so far would really matter, would it? There'd be no one left to oppose them. Even people who'd been on the fence would hesitate after seeing our failure.

We couldn't let that happen.

Hector had veered through the trees to catch up with us. His voice came out forceful despite his ragged breaths. "Our blacksuits are wearing blue cloths like scarves. If you see any without that, do whatever you can to stop them."

I nodded, gathering casting words for shields and propulsion onto my tongue. Connar and Malcolm were already speaking spells with a quiver of magic around us. Jude snatched up a jagged-ended branch and brandished it like a spear, clearly determined to put up as much of a fight as he could if it came to that.

More flashes of blazing energy highlighted a line of figures ahead of us: blacksuits with the splotches of bright blue Baron Killbrook had mentioned, some of the other professors and staff. I caught sight of Professor Viceport's pale bob and Mr. Wakeburn's shaggy hair.

My toe stubbed against a protruding rock I hadn't seen, and I pitched forward. Maggie caught my elbow before I outright fell. She shot me a firm smile. "Let's show them what Bloodstones are really made of."

Yes. As we charged the rest of the way to the front lines, I spotted other people deeper in the forest. Blacksuits in their standard uniforms and other mages the barons must have rallied to this cause barked casting words and flung out spells in an erratic, crackling wave. A bolt of heat sliced through the barrier the guys had conjured and seared across my jaw with a stab of pain.

Around my wince, I snapped out another defensive spell, and then conjured a blast of wind to slam into the oncoming attackers. Several of the blacksuits staggered backward—a few toppled right over. I rushed on until I was just behind our own officers.

They were chanting casting words in rhythmic tones, their hands twitching now and then toward our enemies. Removing the permissions that had allowed those fearmancers to step past the wards before, presumably. But that would only help us if we could push them back behind the wards to begin with. Once they were in, there was nothing to do but fight.

Voices rang out all around me: more shields, more whirlwinds and lurches of the ground to toss the advancing forces farther back. My fellow scions had gathered close around me, most of the guys casting, Jude waving his branch threateningly while hurling his promised insults.

When I glanced back in the midst of my own volley of spells, Maggie was flanking me on one side, Holden just behind me on the other, Noah close to Declan and Agnes hanging slightly back behind Malcolm. Her mouth was pressed flat and her eyes were wide, but she'd taken Jude's lead and grabbed a makeshift spear of her own.

We had other company too. Victory and Cressida had followed us across the east field, along with several other Guard members and classmates. But as I yelled out the words to stir even more magic from behind my sternum, to turn that thrum into a wallop of energy that smashed through a fresh assault of magic and sent the casters reeling backward, the steady sense of our little group of heirs wrapped around me.

It didn't matter that not all of us could cast very much or even at all. It didn't matter that some of us had trained for the barony for years and others had never considered it until months or days ago. We were our families' children, in power if not in goals, and when we put all that power to bear together, the air sang with it.

Why the hell *wouldn't* the pentacle of barons be stronger with every member of age participating rather than squabbling over who got the seat? New problems would come up with that approach, no doubt, but in that moment all I could feel was how right it was for us all to work our magic together. How naturally we wove our spells around each other's, complementing each other's specialties, filling in the weak points.

"There's more!" one of the blacksuits hollered. They threw themselves into their spells to adjust the wards even more urgently. New figures barreled into view, their mouths already moving with castings of their own.

The air shuddered around us. One man, off to the side, whipped a hand through the air to launch a casting so subtle I couldn't see more than a glimmer of its energy —but vicious enough to snap through the barriers in place around us.

He'd aimed it at the bunch of us, but he'd been closest to Jude. The glint scythed through the air, my heart lurched, and without another thought I sprang past Connar to shield the other guy physically as well as with the spell that tumbled from my lips.

The glint shattered against my magic just an inch from my face—sharp enough that a few flecks of its energy scratched across my cheeks. I knocked into Jude, who caught me with his free arm. His gaze caught on my bleeding face, and his eyes narrowed with a glitter of anger.

"I'm okay," I said quickly.

"And so am I," he replied with a pained smile. "Don't put protecting me ahead of everyone else."

I gave his arm a quick squeeze. "I think I can manage both."

After a few more volleys back and forth, the pressure

against us seemed to dwindle. Which didn't mean it was break time. "They're shifting their main force to the south!" one of the blacksuits called out, and the bunch of us raced over to lend our skills near the road to town.

I didn't think we'd taken many of our opponents down. Most of us hadn't been aiming to hurt them anyway, only to force them to back off. Despite the cool air and the forest shadows, sweat was trickling down my neck beneath the collar of my bathrobe, but the oncoming force against us was starting to thin.

The blacksuits' strategy was working. The wards were doing more and more of the work, preventing the invaders from even getting close to us. The protections around the school had held secure against the top joymancers who'd spent decades trying to track down the fearmancer stronghold—they could fend off our own kind too.

At least, until the barons came up with some other strategy to get at us—or forced us to leave the safety of the wards. We could only protect ourselves in here, not out in the rest of the world.

That knowledge dampened any exhilaration I might have felt as the battle wound down. Finally, there was no one left to fling spells at. I let my voice fall silent, my throat stinging from the strain, my jaw still throbbing from that first strike. When I swiped my hand over my forehead, it came away with a thin streak of blood.

My companions looked equally exhausted and relieved. Connar turned and caught me in a squeeze of an embrace. Malcolm set his hand on my shoulder after, as if he felt he needed to make some physical claim as well.

"We're secure for now," one of the blacksuits reported. "Thank you so much for your swift assistance, everyone. We may need to set up more regular patrols than we can manage on our own, but for now, get some rest. Anyone with more serious injuries, report to the infirmary."

We meandered back to the main campus buildings on weary feet. I might be exhausted, but I was also so keyed up from the fighting that it was hard to imagine really resting, let alone getting back to sleep. The blacksuit's comment had been one more reminder that even if we'd defended ourselves once, the war was far from over.

Victory had stuck with us when we'd moved to the south end of campus. She ended up trudging along next to me, a chunk of her auburn hair scorched away over her ear, smudges of dirt dappling her cheeks and hands. After a short stretch of silence, she glanced over at me.

"You're pretty quick in a fight. I'm glad I'm on the same side as you."

I couldn't stop a tired laugh from tumbling out. "I hope that's not the only reason you're on the same side."

She made a face at me. "Of course not. I'm just trying to say—I respect how much you're willing to put yourself out there for the rest of us. Even when it's literally life or death."

She spoke in her usual unflappable tone, but the words held a hint of an apology. It took me a moment to mull over my answer.

"I never had anything against you, you know," I said. "I mean, other than you being a jerk to me. I wasn't out to take your room or undermine your status on campus or anything like that."

"Yeah. I've been figuring that out. I guess a lot of us were stuck seeing everything from one specific point of view, and we overlooked a lot of other things. Like the fact that apparently most of our barons were batshit crazy." She made a spinning gesture with her finger by her ear.

"To be fair, even I only took them for assholes, not outright maniacs, until recently."

"Yeah. Well. Somehow I suspect you caught on faster than I did." Her head dipped as we came into Ashgrave Hall to head back to the dorms. "I never gave you much credit for how hard it must have been to keep standing up to us when you weren't used to the way things worked here. I wanted to see you as weak for being so worried about the Naries and all. But… maybe I was being kind of a coward myself, when things started to get bad, hoping I could live my life the way I always did without getting involved. Expecting other people to pick up the slack so I could stay out of anything tough."

A twinge ran through my chest. I smiled at her, more genuinely than I'd ever thought I'd be able to with the girl who'd once been my nemesis. "You fought just as hard as the rest of us out there right now. I don't think anyone could get away with calling you a coward."

She lifted her chin. "I *am* a Blighthaven. We step up when we're called on."

There was that usual pride. But after the admissions she'd just made, the attitude didn't rankle me.

"I appreciate that," I said. "And if I have my way, there won't be many more calls after this one."

I had no idea how likely I was to make that happen, but the tip of her head and the small smile that crossed her lips made me feel I'd won two battles today rather than just the one.

CHAPTER TWENTY-ONE

Jude

"Mr. Killbrook!"
Professor Viceport's cool voice rang out in the high-ceilinged entrance hall. I stopped on my way to the cafeteria, tensing automatically.

The Physicality professor had never been anything but even-tempered with me, but I'd always spent her classes sharply aware of how much I was faking my supposed third magical strength. Now I not only lacked any magical strengths at all, but she might also have guessed from the family secrets revealed that I'd never had all three to begin with.

I swiveled with an automatic smile. There was no point in drawing attention to my insecurities. Given everything that had gone on today, I doubted she was approaching me to criticize my past classroom performance.

"Professor," I said glibly. "Have I forgotten to turn in some assignment?"

She gave me a sardonic look as if to say she recognized my attempt at humor but wasn't going to reward it. She'd always tolerated my attitude more than encouraged it.

"There's something I wanted to talk to you about," she said. "Unrelated to your schooling—except, I suppose, indirectly. Do you have a few minutes?"

I'd told Mom I'd meet her in the cafeteria to grab dinner, but I'd been restless enough that I'd shown up early. I really didn't have any excuse to decline. And even if I could have made up one, I couldn't help being curious about why Viceport would have approached me of all people for this talk.

"I can find a few," I said. "What's the topic?"

She glanced around, noting the juniors ambling down from their dorms upstairs, and motioned for me to follow her. "Why don't you come to my office?"

Walking down the hall in the staff area reminded me of the last time I'd ventured this way to speak to a professor—when I'd gone to my mentor, Professor Burnbuck, to get contact information for the fearmancers horning in on the film industry. For a little while, I'd had a real plan for what to do with myself when I left this school —something I could accomplish even if I wasn't actually a scion or an especially stellar talent at anything other than illusions.

So much for that. Thank you so much, dear departed 'Dad,' for not just screwing me over from the moment of my conception but all the way into my future too.

The thought sent an unsettling ripple of anger and satisfaction through me. I was glad he was out of the picture, glad I didn't have to worry about any more assassins lurking in the forest, but at the same time his death felt almost too easy. Why should he have gotten off with a short scuffle turned deadly when I'd had to live with the horror of his actions for *years*?

It was done, though. It was all done. I had to focus on what I had and kick the resentment and fractured dreams to the curb.

The staff wing was even quieter than usual now that several of the professors had vacated the building. Our shoes hissed audibly over the carpet. Viceport unlocked and opened a door to a tidy room full of clean-edged furniture that fit her demeanor perfectly. An astringent herbal scent lingered in the air.

She didn't bother with the chair behind the glass-topped desk but rather leaned against the desktop. I considered and decided there was no reason for me not to rest my feet. I flopped into the leather chair opposite and stretched out my legs, waiting for her to get on with things.

"I understand the doctors haven't been able to make much progress in repairing your condition," she said. "And that you've recovered relatively little of your capacity to contain magic."

My hand rose to my chest instinctively. The thin tickle of energy there served mainly as a reminder of how little magic I could hold onto after it passed into me. "That's correct," I said, my voice coming out tighter than I'd have preferred.

"I'm not sure if the doctors were unaware or they simply felt it was too early to mention it, but I thought—presuming you'd like to regain a decent amount of your abilities—you should know that there is an adaptation you could make that I think would help quite a bit."

I perked up inside while keeping my pose languid. "An 'adaptation'?"

"Yes." She went around her desk and opened one of the lower drawers. "A fearmancer losing their ability to hold onto magic is relatively rare, so it's not surprising the doctors might not know of the more external strategies for coping, which don't involve actual healing. But there have been a few cases in the past where healing alone didn't accomplish a great deal. I took the liberty of studying those accounts and fashioned what I think is an appropriate tool. It wasn't so different from conducting pieces I've worked on in the past."

She straightened up with an object in her hand: ivory-pale, egg-shaped, and about the size of her palm. A few ridges and dimples marked the upper half. She'd fixed a silver chain to a notch carved into the stone-like surface. Even if she hadn't said anything, I'd have identified it as a conducting piece of some sort.

My spirits deflated. "I'm not sure a conducting piece will be of use when I can't summon much magic to conduct through it in the first place."

Viceport's lips curved upward. "That's exactly what

this is meant to help you with. As you should know from your studies, many conducting pieces function not just to direct and amplify magic, but also to store it until the function is activated. Imagine you once had a literal container inside you that held magic for your use, which is now broken. This piece will act as a replacement."

I stared at the thing for a long moment. "If I provoke fear in someone, the energy will go in there instead?"

"If you direct it there. And while it's not a perfect substitute and the magic will seep away over time, it'll hold the energy for quite a while, ready for you to draw on."

A flicker of relief shot through me—and faded. Could the answer really be that simple? What, I was going to walk around for the rest of my life with that obvious crutch hanging around my neck, signaling to every mage who saw me that I couldn't handle my own magic? How much better could one conjured chunk of stone make things anyway—enough to offset the embarrassment? I found that hard to believe.

"The transfer will go more smoothly, almost automatically once you get used to the process, if I attune the piece specifically to you," Viceport went on. "The spell will only take a minute or two, and then—"

"No," I said, getting up.

She blinked at me. "Mr. Killbrook—"

"I don't need it. I'm not much of a mage now—that's going to be a fact either way. Better that I get used to it than play around with toys designed to trick me into thinking it's not all that bad."

The professor's mouth twisted. "I don't think that's the most accurate way of looking at the situation. It isn't a trick—it is, as I said, a tool. We all make use of them in various ways. There are brilliant mages who do great work with relatively little power and mages who can gather immense reserves but whose spellwork is nothing but clumsy. How much you can wield has nothing to do with your skill."

"Well, you should know by now that my skills weren't quite on the level the former Baron Killbrook let everyone assume either," I tossed out.

Viceport folded her arms over her chest. "You may not have been the most impressive Physicality technician I've ever encountered, but I've seen your Illusion work too. More importantly, I saw you at the edge of the battle this morning. You can't convince me that you don't *want* to be able to put the skills you do have to use again, in whatever way you can. This is your best opportunity to recover them."

Her insistence only made me bristle. "You don't know me, not really. You don't know what matters to me."

"Perhaps not." She sighed and held out the conducting piece to me by its chain. "Please at least take it. I won't insist on the attuning spell. I made it for you, and it won't be of use to anyone else I'm aware of. Hold on to it, and then you'll have it if you decide to see what it can do for you later on."

I didn't want to give in even that much, but it was clearly the fastest way to get her off my back. "Fine," I said. I took the thing and shoved it into the pocket of my blazer. "I should get going now anyway."

"If you change your mind…" she said, but at least she had the courtesy not to look as if she assumed I would.

When I got to the cafeteria, my mother was already there, just sitting down with her plate. I waved to her in acknowledgment and hurried to get my own meal.

"Sorry," I said when I joined her. "I got sidetracked— one of the professors called me over to talk about something—it didn't end up being important."

"Are you sure?" she asked. "If you've got other business you need to see to, I'll be fine on my own."

Anyone else in the fearmancer world might have said that in a passive-aggressive way, intending it as a dig that I didn't seem devoted enough. But Mom… She didn't have an aggressive bone in her body, passive or otherwise. She looked genuinely pained at the thought that I might be missing out on something to be here with her.

It was those sorts of little things that made it hard for me to stay mad at her now that she wasn't scurrying around after Baron Killbrook trying to make him happy. That was all she'd ever wanted, really—for everyone around her to be happy. And there hadn't been any way she could manage that for both him and me. So she'd chosen the baron over the bastard.

I couldn't imagine what her lot would have been like if she'd run off with me to escape him. It probably hadn't seemed like much of a choice at all. He might have decided to end us both and simply start over with the whole raising a family thing rather than risk her giving away what she knew.

Now that he was gone, she'd come to me, not to the families of pricks who'd curried his favor or his baron colleagues. That was going to have to be enough.

I waved dismissively. "It's all dealt with now anyway. How are you doing?"

"Worried, but all right." She touched her belly. "The baby's moving around a lot these days. Maybe she can pick up on all the tension in the air. Not the most stable events for her to be emerging into."

Comments like that brought up the jab of jealousy that I hadn't completely conquered. There had never been a good time for *me* to "emerge" into the world.

I bit back the rancor and managed a crooked smile. "Who knows? We might have it all fixed up for you before she arrives."

I made another flick of a gesture, this one a touch too jerky. My fingers brushed my fork and sent it skittering off the table. Mom reached out with a hasty word. Her casting caught it in the air before it hit the floor.

A month ago, I could have done that myself. I'd already gotten out of the habit of even trying. The back of my neck heated as I snatched the fork from its magical hold. "Thanks."

Mom gave me a considering look as I busied myself with the stuffed chicken breast the school chefs had provided me with. She wet her lips and then ventured, "Is there nothing else the doctors can do?"

I didn't need to ask what condition she thought they might help with. "No. They said if it's going to improve, at this point it will on its own. And it hasn't, so… This is me now."

Her gaze slid away from me and then back, her eyes going watery. "I didn't—I had no idea he was taking things so far. If I had, I would have said something, to try to stop him, to warn you…"

Maybe she should have been able to guess. She'd known what her husband was like. But she'd pulled the wool over her own eyes for so long, deceiving herself must have become second nature.

"He wanted to kill me," I said, stabbing a piece of chicken. "He didn't get that. So, that's something."

"I just wish… I wish I'd known what else to do. You deserved so much better, Jude."

She'd already apologized for my childhood and for the secrets she'd kept more than once since she'd arrived. Still, something about the words made my throat close up. I forced down the morsel of chicken and considered chucking the rest of my meal in the trash.

Before I could make up my mind, another member of our bizarre family made an approach. The new Baron Killbrook stopped a few feet from us and stood there awkwardly and not at all baron-ly, clutching his plate. When Mom looked at him, he dipped his head.

"I hope you don't mind the intrusion," he said, with more grace than showed in his stance. "I've been meaning to find a chance to talk to you for a while."

I couldn't read the emotions that crossed my mother's face, other than that there were a lot of them. But as always, she was accommodating. "Of course," she said. "Sit down."

He left a careful space between him and her as he took his seat, setting down his plate as if he wasn't sure why he'd gotten it in the first place. He swiveled toward Mom with his head still bowed.

"What happened with Edmund—I'm sorry. It's not how I ever wanted things to end. I stayed out of politics for so long to make sure— But excuses don't justify anything. If there's anything I can do to make your situation easier from here on, please don't hesitate to let me know."

Mom smiled at him, tight but soft around the edges. I could see the forgiveness in it already. Abruptly, I felt like an intruder at the table. She and I had already talked through so much. I wasn't going to force him to have an audience while he made his amends.

I gulped down one last piece of chicken and got up. "Lots to do. I should check in with the scions."

Mom glanced at me with wide eyes, but I gazed back firmly to say she didn't need to worry about me. As she turned back to her brother-in-law, I scraped the rest of my dinner into the trash as I'd imagined doing earlier. Then I stopped, watching them from the edge of my vision, as he spoke more and she nodded, and something like a sense of peace settled over the table I'd left.

My supposed father had been the storm cloud that had

darkened both of their lives—making Hector feel he had to back away from the whole family to prove he wasn't a threat, making my mother desperate to find some way to finally please him. All because he held the goddamn title that made him one of the five most powerful fearmancers around.

I never wanted to end up under someone's thumb like that. No way in hell.

How exactly was I going to make sure that didn't happen when at this point I was relying on Rory and the other scions to protect me? The memory of the battle and my ineffectual part in it made me grimace. I headed out of the cafeteria, but my hand slipped into my pocket to close around the conducting piece.

It couldn't hurt to see exactly what it could do, just once, could it? I should gather all the available information. No doubt that's what Declan would have said.

In the hall, I pulled out the carved stone and slung the chain around my neck. The piece settled against my sternum as if it'd always been meant to rest there. I swallowed thickly and looked around.

A few juniors were meandering toward the cafeteria. Normally I'd have taken a subtle approach to teasing a little fear out of them, but that was beyond me at the moment. Instead, I'd have to bulldoze it.

I strode toward them with my mouth dropping into a scowl. One of them noticed me, and a quiver of nervousness reached me just from that. When I was just a few feet away from them, I snapped out a casting word and slashed my hand through the air as if I meant to sever them in two.

It was a meaningless word, and I didn't have the power to sever much more than a spaghetti noodle anyway. They obviously weren't sure of that, though. A rush of terror hit me from all three as they dashed around me for the shelter of the cafeteria.

Normally, these days, the sensation would have washed through me and right back out again. This time, working on instinct, I caught it with a real casting word that pushed it toward the conducting piece against my chest.

The energy flowed through me and into the piece like water sucked through a straw. I expected to feel nothing afterward, but instead, the impression of power lingered. More distant than if I'd held it inside me, but still there, like a tingling aura with its most condensed point just below my collarbone.

It'd been weeks since I'd felt that much magic within my grasp for more than a second or two. I stood there, soaking it in, torn between a laugh and a sob.

Fucking hell, I'd missed this.

Before I'd even thought about it, my feet were turning me around. I marched through the halls to the staff wing. Even after I recognized where I was going, I didn't stop myself.

Fuck embarrassment. Fuck maintaining some stupid image of imperviousness. Baron Killbrook had spent his whole life trying to convince everyone around him what a hot shot he was, and where had that landed him in the end?

To my relief, Professor Viceport opened her office door shortly after my knock. She nudged her glasses up her nose with a puzzled look. "Mr. Killbrook?"

"I changed my mind," I said. "Let's get this thing tuned up."

CHAPTER TWENTY-TWO

Rory

Jude swiveled on his heel to take in the green, his face lit up despite the cloudy dreariness of the autumn day. The ivory conducting piece that hung from his neck swung lightly with the movement. "Hmm," he said in a playful tone. "Who shall I terrify next?"

Even if I hadn't known he wasn't out to cause anyone that much distress, it would've been hard for me to ask him to back down. I hadn't seen him in spirits this high in ages. I'd almost forgotten how much buoyant energy he could exude when he was in his element.

"How much do you figure that thing can hold?" I asked with a smile.

He rubbed his hands together. "That's what I'm aiming to find out."

Once he'd replenished his store of energy a little, he'd been able to put that magic toward stirring up even more fear for fuel. Considering the tense state we were all in after recent events, he'd been careful not to go overboard with his illusions and steered clear of the Naries, but he'd gotten some yelps out of our fearmancer classmates over the last hour with little pranks here and there. So far he hadn't seemed to top out the piece's capacity.

"You could get Mischief in on the fun," I pointed out. Whenever Jude's ferret familiar startled anyone, that energy would pass on to him.

"Oh, she had a nice little romp last night," Jude said with a wink. "I think she was almost as happy about it as I was."

Thunder rumbled faintly in the distance, but the clouds overhead held onto any rain they meant to spill. Jude spotted a couple of juniors coming out of Killbrook Hall and intoned a word under his breath that made the grass in front of them ripple with the impression of dozens of tiny snakes. From the one girl's squeal and Jude's chuckle, he'd gotten a good rush from that.

He waved the illusion away a moment later and called out, "Sorry! Just testing some things out." The juniors gave him a skeptical look, but then they laughed and continued on along the path.

I shook my head in amusement. "Does it feel very different from the way you'd have drawn on your magic before?"

"It's a little more distant," Jude said. "Like I'm pulling it up from farther away. I can't work the spells quite as fast as I used to. But once I've got the magic, I haven't noticed any change in what I can do with it. As long as I stay topped up, I think I'll be able to pull off just about anything I could have before—I'll just need to make sure I'm refilling the well a lot more regularly than I used to need to. No marathons unless they're fright-fests too."

He didn't look all that bothered by the limitations—unsurprising given how much more limited he'd been before he'd gotten this accommodation.

As he scanned the area for a fresh target, footsteps whispered over the grass behind us. The one dormmate I didn't know all that well who'd stayed on campus instead of taking off with Ms. Grimsworth's announcement—a quiet, sallow girl named Torrin—came over to me with an intense expression.

"Rory?" she said hesitantly, as if she wasn't sure whether she'd offend me by presuming to use my first name.

My instincts immediately went on the alert. "Is something wrong?"

"I'm… not sure." She looked at the grass and then at me again. "I thought I should tell you just in case. Last night, Pauline—you know, who was in our dorm before—she texted me asking about the Nary girl who left. Shelby? The one you hung out with sometimes. Pauline couldn't remember her name."

I frowned. I wasn't completely sure which of our four absent roommates Pauline was, but the girls who'd left hadn't been at all friendly to the Nary students. Three of them had started tormenting Morgan the second she'd moved in. "Did she say why she was asking?"

"She said Baron Bloodstone had been asking about it.

I don't think she realized I'd mention it to you—I didn't tell her I'm still here and not at home."

Why would my *mother* care about a Nary student who hadn't been at the school for weeks now? Uneasiness coiled around my gut. I managed to offer Torrin a smile. "Thank you for telling me. I really appreciate it. If Pauline contacts you again, let me know."

She nodded and scurried back into the building. I guessed she'd been the sort of fly-under-the-radar, not-making-waves type, acting as if she agreed with whoever was nearby, so Pauline had assumed she was an ally. Maybe she hadn't even totally sided with us yet, but at least she'd cared enough to reach out with this information.

I dug my phone out of my purse. Jude watched me, his joy fading. "Do you think Shelby is in trouble?"

He had a personal stake in my friend's well-being too. After one of his more elaborate pranks had accidentally resulted in Shelby breaking her wrist, he'd taken a huge chance to arrange for her to get magical medical treatment so she could return to school.

"Hopefully not. But I can't imagine my mother wanted to know about her so she could send her a gift basket." I worried at my lip with my teeth as I brought up Shelby's number. I'd arranged for her to get the job with the orchestra because I'd thought she'd be safer that way, back when the fearmancer students had first been given the go-ahead to torment the Naries. Now, knowing she was two hours distant and well beyond any protections our wards could offer made my skin itch with nerves.

Shelby picked up after the second ring. "Hey," she

said, sounding a little breathless but not disturbed. "What's up? I don't have much time to talk—we've got an afternoon performance in half an hour."

"I just—" How could I even explain the reason for this call? Her memory had been wiped of anything to do with magic—as far as she knew, Blood U was a perfectly normal if elitist school. Well, maybe it didn't matter if I sounded weird. "I had a bad feeling. It might be nothing. You haven't noticed anything strange today?"

"No, it's been a pretty good day so far, really. Are *you* all right, Rory?"

Her concern for me when she was the one so much more vulnerable brought a lump into my throat. I didn't hear any other sign of distress in her tone. "I'm good, other than a little paranoid, apparently," I said. "I hope your performance goes well! And just... be careful and keep an eye out just in case, okay?"

"I can do that."

Her reassurance barely dulled my apprehension. I shifted on my feet as I tucked my phone away, a helpless sensation prickling over me.

I *wasn't* helpless, though. I had to at least take a look around and make sure she was safe.

"She hasn't seen any reason to be worried yet," I said to Jude. "But she wouldn't know what to look for. I'm going to drive out there and check for any signs of magic use nearby, and then put down some protections around the concert hall and her apartment. I can't just leave her hanging."

I turned to head toward the garage the moment I'd

finished speaking. The sooner I went out there, the sooner I could make sure Shelby really was safe—and stayed that way.

Jude fell into stride beside me. "Should I call the cavalry?"

As much as I'd have liked to tackle this with all of the scions by my side, or even a few of the blacksuits, I couldn't be that selfish. "I think the campus will survive without me here for a few hours, but we don't know when the barons might launch another attack. I can't risk taking people with me, especially when there's a good chance it's nothing."

"You're taking at least one person," he said. "You can forget it if you think you're ditching me."

When I shot him a stern look, he held up his hands. "Hey, I didn't contribute much of anything during the last attack, so it's not like I'd be all that missed. And you shouldn't go out there completely alone. It's probably nothing—great. Doing some detection and warding spells will be a good warm-up for when I really need to put this to use." He tapped his conducting piece.

I couldn't argue with that—and I didn't really want to. "All right," I said, reaching for my keys. "Can you let the other guys know where we're going and that we'll reach out again if we need backup after all?"

Jude tapped away at his phone as we hustled into the garage. I jumped into my Lexus and started the engine the second I'd clicked my seatbelt into place. Jude lowered his phone with a dry chuckle. "They don't sound all that happy about it, but Declan says he understands your reasoning even if he'd rather you had more protection. And he makes a good point—are you sure this isn't some kind of trap to lure you off campus?"

I paused, turning the question over in my mind. "I guess I can't be totally sure, but it doesn't sound as if my mother meant for me to find out that she was poking around. If the point was to draw me out, she'd have made a lot more sure I'd get the message and made the message a lot more threatening. But why don't you start that warming up right away by scanning for magical activity around the road while we're leaving?"

"Aye aye, captain."

He spoke his casting words quietly as I headed toward town. I focused my own attention intently on the forest around us and then the buildings up ahead. No enemies leapt to confront us. We turned onto the main street and then onto the highway without any interference.

"Looks like we're home free," Jude said, but his expression had turned grimmer. The fact that this *wasn't* a trick made it more likely that Shelby really was in danger.

I drove well over the speed limit, faster than I'd ever have dared go when Jude had first been teaching me to drive, with an occasional murmured spell to distract the attention of anyone who might have taken an issue with that minor crime. Jude peered out the window, making cheeky remarks about the drivers we passed and occasionally casting an illusion toward people in their front yards to rebuild his supply of magic.

We'd been on the road about an hour, with still at least thirty minutes left before we'd reach Shelby's new home, when my phone chimed in my purse with an incoming text.

"Can you check that?" I said to Jude.

He fished it out and clicked the screen awake. His face stiffened so abruptly that my pulse stuttered. "What?"

"It's from your mother," he said slowly. "She says… 'When you tie yourself to the weak, you make yourself weak too. Destroy things other people care about, and you'll be paid back in kind.'"

"Shit." Panic flashed through me, sharp and dizzying. That didn't sound like a trick or a warning. It sounded just vague enough that she'd hope it'd unnerve me and then I'd understand later what she'd meant. Because she didn't expect me to have any idea just yet. She wouldn't have wanted to risk me figuring out what she was up to in time to stop it. Whatever she was going to do, it was happening soon.

"Tell the blacksuits on campus that there's likely to be an attack out here any minute now. If they can spare anyone—"

But what were the chances any of them could get here in time? I wasn't sure even we could reach Shelby before my mother rained down the destruction she'd planned.

Jude had already made the call even though he must have realized it was pretty much hopeless too. He relayed what we knew as I pushed the gas pedal even harder. The roar of the engine and the whir of the tires speeding over the asphalt made my heart thump harder.

Please, let us not be too late. Hell, please let me be wrong about this whole thing.

"A few of them are coming out as quickly as they can," Jude said when he'd hung up. He swiped his hand across his mouth, his face gone even paler than usual. "You said Shelby has a performance, didn't you? They wouldn't attack her in front of an entire audience."

"They wouldn't have before now," I said. But after all the stunts the barons had already pulled and how free they wanted to be with their magic, I wasn't willing to count on their caution.

My hands gripped the steering wheel tighter as we passed the city's welcome sign. I forced myself to slow down, not trusting myself to keep up the same pace amid city traffic and pedestrians. As I wove through the streets toward the concert hall, I watched for any hint of disaster.

We were just a few blocks away when a billow of smoke rushed up into the air over the rooftops ahead of us.

My stomach knotted. I shot straight through a red light, ignoring the honks of the cars that had slammed on their brakes. People ran past us in the opposite direction.

The concert hall was on fire. Its roof had already partly collapsed to release that torrent of smoke. Flames flickered in the windows of the lobby where Malcolm and I had met with the director just weeks ago.

I threw the car into park in the first empty spot and threw myself toward the building with Jude at my heels. With a few quick words, I shielded myself from the worst of the heat and smoke—and cast a similar spell back toward him so he wouldn't have to use up his own smaller store of magic just to follow me. We dashed into the burning building.

Only a few bodies lay in the lobby, their heads blasted open or burnt to a crisp by more than just regular flames. Shouts carried from the auditorium beyond. I ran for the inner doors, wincing at the heat that penetrated my bubble of cooled air.

The performance must have recently finished. When I burst past the auditorium doors, the seats were mostly empty, only a few figures scattered among them—slumped and lifeless.

But the orchestra hadn't left when the attack began. Bodies lay strewn across the stage amid their blood-splattered instruments. A few still had life in them, crawling farther back on the stage to seek shelter, and a handful of others were scrambling along the walls, dodging flames as they searched for an escape route.

Four figures in blacksuit uniforms stalked along the aisles. With barked casting words, they smashed the survivors off their feet one by one, leaving more blood and the smell of singed flesh in their wake. My heart wrenched as a man toppled with a crunch of his skull just ten feet away from me.

In the time it took me to catch all that in a glance, the blacksuits jerked toward us. I grasped Jude's arm as we ducked down behind the nearest row of seats. The smoke seeped through my shield and seared my throat.

"There's no way we can put out a fire this big," I said hoarsely.

Jude nodded, his expression queasy. "Did you see Shelby?"

I hadn't spotted her mouse-brown hair among the sprawled bodies, but between the blood and the cinders it was hard to be sure. "We have to try to get anyone we can out of here."

He nodded and then stiffened. "We've got company."

Footsteps were rasping across the singed carpet to our left. We scuttled to the right, swinging around to the far aisle just as another man crumpled with one of the blacksuits' spells.

In just the short time we'd been here, the mages had taken down all of the people attempting to flee on this side of the room. But a few others were crouched low like us beside the rows. I caught sight of Shelby's face behind another girl, and my hopes leapt.

Now we just had to get them out of here.

Jude peeked over the top of the nearest seat and spat out a quick casting word that shoved a blacksuit who'd been closing in on us across the room. I sent a punch of magical force to fling aside another. The flames licked closer, slashing across Jude's shoulder. A pained hiss escaped him, but he motioned for me to move toward the huddled forms ahead. We murmured together, thickening our defenses, although scorching ribbons of heat still managed to dart across my skin.

At a shout from across the room, one of the boxed seating areas overhead cracked. The railing and a significant portion of flooring careened down, ready to crush us.

There wasn't much room left for stealth. I sprang forward, hurling every casting word I could think of to deflect the falling debris from both us and the survivors. Jude's voice rang out too.

Magic tore from my chest, but my effort wasn't quite enough. The chunks of metal and plaster whipped to the side and crashed over the guy at the back of the huddle.

My gut lurched, but I kept barreling forward. I grabbed Shelby by the shoulder and Jude clutched the wrist of the other girl. We tugged them with us back toward the main doors.

Shelby stared at me, but as startled as she must have been by the horror around us and my arrival, she kept her mouth shut. She could obviously realize questions could wait until we got out of here alive.

If we got out of here alive. As we bolted from the last row of seats toward the flame-edged doorway, the blacksuits flung a barrage of spells at us.

The first few cracked through our shields. The last raked across my leg like a dozen white-hot knives. I stumbled and fell to my knees, barely managing to push Shelby on toward the doorway.

Another vicious spell slammed into the chest of the girl Jude had been helping, punching in her ribs with a burst of blood.

Jude reached for me, his hand trembling, casting words sputtering from his lips as quickly as he could speak them. He managed to get another shield up in time to fend off the next assault. I snapped a word to numb my leg enough to dull the agony and staggered with him through the doorway.

Shelby was waiting for us in a small patch of clear floor outside, sweat trickling down her face and firelight wavering over her stiffened form. We swept her up in our escape, half running, half limping toward the outer doors. I forced casting word after casting word from my smoke-stung throat to keep off the worst of the heat and the spells thrown after us.

A fire engine was just wailing into view several blocks down the road when we tumbled out onto the sidewalk. I propelled myself on toward my car, my teeth clenched against the pain breaking through my numbing spell.

Jude got there first. He unlocked the doors with a hasty spell and leapt in to start the engine the same way. As I urged Shelby into the back seat, two of the blacksuits charged out of the burning concert hall. I jerked my hand up with a gasped casting word just in time to smack back the worst of their renewed attack.

The second I dropped into the car, yanking the door shut with me, Jude hit the gas. We roared away from the scene of my mother's crime with the sound of our ragged breaths filling the air—one life saved, so many I could hardly bear to think about it cut down and left behind.

CHAPTER TWENTY-THREE

Rory

Several minutes into the drive, Shelby finally broke out of her shell-shocked state enough to speak. Her voice came out scratchy. "I don't understand—who were those people? Why would they have— What the heck were they even *doing*?"

They'd been acting out my mother's revenge on me—for caring about the Naries more than I was willing to stand beside her, for arguing on their behalf. For a second, my nausea overwhelmed the pain creeping up my leg from my wound.

"They're assholes," Jude said before I had to figure out my answer. "That's all you need to know. Fucking psychotic assholes." A tremor ran through the words despite the acid he put into them.

"They almost—The guy right beside me—" Shelby sucked in a ragged breath. "If you hadn't called me and told me to keep an eye out, I'd probably be dead now. I got a bad feeling as soon as one of them came in. I ran the second they attacked. How did you know?"

"It was a guess," I said. "There were some signs... It's complicated. I'm sorry. I wish I could explain it all properly. They are just assholes, like Jude said, and right now they want to hurt me and everyone who's been associated with me or my friends. When they find out we saved you, they might come after you again. For now, you should come with us back to the university. It'll be safer there."

"It doesn't make any sense," she murmured, rubbing her forehead. "They're all... They're all *dead*." Then she lapsed into a haunted silence.

My chest clenched up at the thought of all the people we hadn't saved. All the people who'd just been collateral damage in my mother's campaign of vengeance. Did she even recognize that she'd torn lives apart, or was it impossible for her to see a Nary's existence as even that valid?

Partway through the drive back, Shelby started to cough. It began as a periodic sputtering and grew into a continuous, raw hacking in between apologies. I didn't want to think about how much smoke she must have inhaled.

As soon as we reached the campus, I helped her out of the car, and all three of us tramped across the grounds to the infirmary. The staff took one look at us with Shelby and exchanged a glance.

"She's already been forced to see more magic than she

should have had to," I said before they could protest about using magical healing on a Nary who was no longer even a student. "It won't help anyone being coy about it now. Do whatever you can to make her better."

"And, ah, the Bloodstone scion here is forgetting to mention that she could use some patching up too," Jude put in.

He looked as if he regretted drawing attention to that fact when a doctor escorted me off to a separate room. Where the spell had raked across my leg, the fabric of my jeans appeared to have melted into my skin in ragged slices from my ankle to halfway up my thigh. The doctor murmured a spell that left my mind floating off onto some distant plane while he worked on my wounds.

When he finished his work, that leg of my jeans was left in tatters, but my actual limb only stung slightly when I stood up. The daze of the anesthetic spell was wearing off.

I emerged into the reception area to find Jude waiting. One of the staff led Shelby out a few moments later.

My friend wasn't coughing anymore, but she had the same spacey look that'd come over her in the car. Scorch mark and flecks of blood dappled her clothes. The sight of her made my throat constrict all over again.

"I've put her under a mild calming spell to help her rest," the woman who'd brought her out murmured to me. "If she seems to need more help coping emotionally once that's worn off, you can encourage her to come back here. We'll do what we can." From the horrified strain in her voice, I suspected Shelby had relayed at least some of what she'd been through.

"Where are we going?" Shelby asked in a distant, wavering voice as we left the Stormhurst Building. I kept a gentle hand on her elbow.

"You can stay in the dorm for now, until we figure everything out," I said, summoning the most soothing tone I had in me. "There are a few unoccupied rooms right now. I'll find you some extra clothes and things."

"My apartment, back in— Do you think those people went there too?" A shudder passed through her.

"We'll check on it as soon as it's safe," I said. The fact that the blacksuits had gone all-out in their destruction of the concert hall suggested they'd known Shelby would be there and had focused their energies there, but I couldn't promise her they hadn't done even worse.

Jude followed us all the way up to the dorm, sticking close by my side. To my relief, the common room was empty. I wasn't sure I was up to trying to explain what had happened to anyone else just yet.

I checked the abandoned rooms and led Shelby into the one that held the fewest remnants of its previous inhabitant. She stood uncertainly by the desk while I made the bed with fresh sheets from my own room.

"Do you want to lie down and get some rest?" I asked. It was late in the afternoon, not quite evening yet let alone night, but she looked like she was barely holding herself up. I didn't know how much of that was the trauma and how much the calming spell.

"Yeah," she said. "Yeah. If I could just lie down for a little bit…"

She sat down on the bed, and her fingers curled around the sheet, clutching it hard.

"If you need anything and you're not sure where I am, you know how to call me," I said. "I'll come right away."

"Right. Thank you." She hesitated and then lay down. As she tucked herself under the covers, I left her to her rest.

Jude was standing in the common room, his stance awkward, his face still more wan than usual. "Do you think she'll be okay?" he asked

A broken laugh sputtered out of me. "She just lost her dream job by having all her colleagues slaughtered and her workplace burned down. I don't know if that's something you get over." The anguish that had formed in the pit of my stomach before swelled to fill my chest. I swallowed hard. "I don't even know what happened to her cello." The loss of that beloved instrument suddenly seemed like the tipping point between tragedy and total catastrophe.

Jude wrapped his arms around me, and I hugged him back, clinging to him tightly. His body trembled against mine. I wasn't sure who needed the support more—him or me.

Voices sounded in the hall outside. I didn't know if they were even heading to this dorm, but I tugged Jude toward my bedroom rather than take the chance of facing a conversation I wasn't ready to have.

As soon as I'd closed the door behind us, the weight of the day's events collapsed over me. I sank onto the edge of the bed, and Jude dropped down beside me. He tucked me into another embrace, his arm around my waist, my head against his shoulder.

Images flashed through my mind: flames, blood, burnt flesh. I winced and buried my face deeper into the crook of his neck.

Jude squeezed me to him and dragged in a ragged breath. "They would have killed you if they'd had a good enough chance. They came too fucking close. I almost lost you."

I tipped my head to look at him. His expression was so utterly distraught that I brought my hand to his cheek, an ache twisting around my heart. "You didn't. I'm okay. *You* helped make sure of that. I don't know if I'd have made it without you."

"I never want it to be that close a call again," he said with a sudden fierceness, and lowered his mouth to mine.

Unlike his voice, his kiss was nothing but tender, his touch teasingly light as he skimmed his fingers down my side. I held on to him, giving myself over to the kindling desire, a temporary reprieve from the terrible memories lurking in my head.

Jude kissed me again and again, each time claiming a little more of me, until the tingling of my lips and the warmth of his body against mine overwhelmed every other sensation. He tugged up my blouse and eased it off me before guiding me back on the bed.

His mouth charted a scorchingly thorough path along my neck, across my shoulders and my collarbone, down to the curve of my breasts. He marked every part of me with the heat of his lips and tongue and the gentle scrape of his teeth, as if confirming to both himself and me that I was still entirely here, that no part of me had been left behind or burned away.

When he slipped off my bra and brought his mouth to the peak of my breast, his fingertips skimming over the other, the rush of pleasure shocked a gasp from my throat. I managed to mumble a quick casting to stop any sounds we made from seeping into the common room. My fingers tangled in his soft hair as he worked me over with exquisite, torturous care.

My body quivered with anticipation as he undid my ruined jeans. He kissed my stomach and the dip at the base of my belly, hooking the waist of the pants and my panties together and drawing them down. Then he was pressing his mouth to my core with a swipe of his tongue that left me moaning.

Bliss sang through me in waves, but he felt too far away now, barely close enough for me to touch. I rocked into the pulse of his mouth for as long as I could stand it, wanting to receive everything he was so intent on giving. When the need to hold him overrode the pleasure, I pulled him back up over me.

Before he'd even captured my mouth again, I was fumbling with the buttons on his shirt. He helped me strip it off and yanked off his pants in turn. A growing urgency gripped me as it appeared to have caught him too.

He lay down next to me, tucking his conducting piece on its chain behind his back, and turned me onto my side to face him. His hand slid from my hip to my sex, testing the slick arousal he'd already inspired. At the flick of his thumb over my clit, I let out a needy growl and hooked my leg over his thigh. He made an equally hungry sound as he positioned me against his cock and slid straight into me.

The position, face to face on equal ground, felt somehow more intimate than any moment we'd shared before. I leaned into him with a moan as he thrust even deeper. One of his hands lingered on my hip to steady our rhythm, while the other stroked over my breasts to provoke even more sparks of pleasure. I ran my fingers down his lean chest and up his back, wanting to offer up just as much bliss in return.

Jude tilted his mouth away from mine for just a moment to murmur a casting word. A quiver of magical energy coursed down my spine and formed a soft but solid pressure at my other opening. I clutched him harder as it eased inside, perfectly smooth and warm, setting off a heady jolt through my nerves.

He'd filled every part of me like a statement of his devotion. With that perfect friction radiating through me from every direction, I couldn't do much more than hold on and rock with him. His cock hit the most sensitive spot inside me, and the force of his magic plunged in and out of me from behind with teasingly blissful friction.

My orgasm raced up on me so swiftly my head jerked back with the force of it, my legs shaking. A cry reverberated up my throat.

"Love you," Jude whispered against my cheek, as if that were a casting too. As if the strength of his affection could shield me even when no other spell would. "Love you, love you, love you."

A second wave of release surged through me, leaving me too breathless to answer right away. Jude groaned as he followed me.

He swayed to a stop, his head still bowed next to mine, his own breath rough. His lips grazed my forehead in one more kiss.

I reached up and tugged his mouth to mine. We kissed long and hard.

"I love you too," I said afterward. "I'm not going anywhere, not if I can help it."

His hand balled against my back. "Neither am I."

I heard the promise in his words, all the more meaningful for the times he had pulled back or struck out on his own, thinking he wasn't worthy of anything else. I snuggled against him to soak up the last bits of joy and comfort before I had to face reality again.

The larger world came calling sooner than expected with the sound of an alert from both our phones. Jude grumbled and shoved himself up to fish his out of his slacks. At the sight of the text, his mouth went crooked with a sheepish sort of annoyance. "Your fellow scions want to know what the hell happened. Maybe we should fill them in before they send an emergency search party."

I wanted to get into that topic in writing even less than I wanted to talk about it. But I definitely owed the other guys some sort of account. I sat up reluctantly and reached for my clothes. "Tell them we're okay and that we'll meet them in the lounge?"

As I lifted my blouse, I realized the smell of smoke had saturated everything I'd been wearing. It was on my skin too; my nose had just adapted to it. I had the urge to run to the showers, but we'd already kept the others waiting long enough. I settled for grabbing a totally clean outfit while Jude typed out our response.

I stopped by the door to Shelby's current bedroom before we left, but I didn't hear any sound that would indicate she hadn't simply fallen asleep. Hopefully the rest would take the edge off her distress, as much as anything could. We headed downstairs.

By the time we reached the lounge, the other three scions had already arrived. Malcolm's expression hardened the second he saw us.

"We should have come with you. You knew something was wrong."

My smile came out pained. "I had no idea it'd be that wrong. It *could* have screwed over everyone on campus if we'd all been gone." I sat down on one of the armchairs. "Anyway, I don't think having more people to help would have made much difference. Most of them were already dead when we reached the concert hall."

I recounted the scene we'd found there with halting resolve. Jude stayed behind me, resting a reassuring hand on my shoulder and interjecting a comment as needed. Before I'd even made it halfway through the telling, Connar had sat down at the edge of the sofa next to me and grasped my hand. Malcolm and Declan hovered over us.

"My mother must have ordered them to do it," I

finished, my voice gone raw in my throat. Guilt swept through me, even heavier than before. "She was so angry the last time we talked... Maybe I shouldn't have tried to push things with her. She never would have gone after any of those people if it hadn't been for me."

"Hey." Connar squeezed my hand, his jaw flexing. "How many times have you told me that I shouldn't blame myself for things my parents did—even things *I* did under their compulsion? This isn't your fault. No one's responsible but her."

"And the fucking blacksuits that followed her orders," Jude muttered.

Malcolm's eyes blazed. "That's it," he said. "That's goddamned *enough*. Fuck proper protocol and respect for the baronies and all the rest. They can't come back from this. Whatever happens, we're taking the pentacle away from them. Both of them, my dad and your mom— they're too far gone. We can't have people who'd pull shit like that calling any of the shots."

I'd never wanted to feel like I was fighting not just to stop my mother's plans but to outright replace her, but I couldn't argue with the vehemence in his voice. If she'd been willing to order the attack I'd seen this afternoon, how could I ever trust her to look out for anyone whose interests didn't perfectly align with her own? Or, forget about *looking out* for them—to not savagely destroy innocent lives in punishment?

Leaving her in power wasn't safe for anyone. Maybe not even herself.

"How do we take it?" I found myself saying.

"We've screwed up their plans. They're going to lose even more supporters. Between us and the other heirs, there's ten of us now to their two. When we get the right moment, we'll march in on them and arrest the both of them for all the laws they've already broken."

"Things have been pretty quiet today so far," Declan said. "And we had a few more families turn up looking to join us—or at least seek refuge." He pulled out his phone. "If the momentum the barons' people were gaining among the Naries keeps dwindling, then in a day or two we could probably—"

His voice fell away, his fingers clenching around the phone. An icy prickling shot through my gut. "What?"

"Apparently we didn't throw as much of a wrench in their plans as we thought." He lifted his gaze, his expression so stricken that anxiety clutched me twice as hard. "The barons must have gotten to the president himself somehow. He's just declared martial law and announced that he's passing all recently proposed policies immediately. We'd better get everyone together to figure out if there's some way we can step in before we're out of time."

CHAPTER TWENTY-FOUR

Rory

By the time everyone willing had gathered in the gymnasium, the situation in the wider world had escalated from critical to fatal. Protests had risen up after the president's announcement. On his orders, military troops had stormed the major cities and started shooting anyone who wouldn't immediately disperse from the rallies. The protests turned into riots, more bodies fell—and all at once, as the last bunch of our allies hurried in, a series of startled noises filled the room where people had been following the news.

"The broadcast just cut out," Declan said, knitting his brow. He tapped at his phone's screen, and his expression turned even more serious. "It looks like the whole website is down."

Malcolm frowned. "The one I was following is too. What the hell?"

"Holy shit." Noah looked up from where he'd been sitting cross-legged on the floor, a laptop balanced on his legs. "I hopped over to social media. People who worked for the major news organizations are reporting that soldiers marched in and ordered them to shut down operations."

"That's ridiculous," I said. It was hard to wrap my head around the fact that anything this extreme could really be happening. It felt like a movie. "They have to know that just shutting down some official channels isn't going to stop people from hearing what's happening. There's no way to control the entire internet."

"They don't want to control the entire internet," Declan said grimly. "The barons don't *really* want the president to take over."

Jude let out a hollow chuckle. "Of course not. What do you figure the plan is? Make the current leadership look so horrible that everyone will cheer when a bunch of fearmancers step in?"

"That would be perfect, wouldn't it?" Connar said quietly. "Set up a horrible situation so they can swoop in and 'rescue' the Naries from it."

Hector Killbrook, who'd been silent in thought as he followed our discussion and others around the room, nodded at that. "This has got to be the crux of their plan. They don't have the power to stage a forced takeover against the entire government. But if the majority of people would welcome someone coming in and cutting down a tyrant, they might have a chance."

I wasn't sure it'd be all that easy even in the current

scenario, but that didn't help the Naries being mowed down by the figures who were supposed to protect them while we stood here talking about it. "It wasn't enough—sending our own people out there to counteract the barons' influence, arranging the terrorist alerts."

"They must have pulled out all the stops to speed things along this quickly," Maggie said. "Barons Nightwood and Bloodstone might have gone out to Washington themselves to set this in motion."

Both my mother and Malcolm's father did specialize in Persuasion. How many politicians and soldiers had they already managed to infect with their scheme?

I hugged myself, rubbing my arms. We'd gathered all our supporters together, but I had no idea what to tell them now. The barons had managed to stay a step ahead of us from the beginning. What did any of our plans matter if we'd never get the chance to see them through?

I couldn't let that hopelessness overwhelm me, though. The Naries deserved better than that. I turned to Hector. "I think everyone's here."

As the only semi-official baron in our midst, it made the most sense to let him lead the discussion. Many of our classmates would have responded to us as scions, but the older fearmancers would respect his authority more than ours. He nodded and leapt onto the raised platform at our end of the room.

"I can't believe Dad would go this far," Agnes said to Malcolm with a shiver. "It's like he's gone crazy."

Malcolm grimaced. "He's either desperate or deranged or maybe some of both. Once they'd committed to a certain point, there was no going back. Either they make this work, or they're done for—with everyone, even the assholes who liked the plan."

If they'd just backed down sooner. If they'd just *listened*… But I couldn't do any more to make that happen now than I'd been able to back when simply talking it out was still on the table.

"All right," the new Baron Killbrook said, raising his voice so it carried over the conversations around the room. "We've got a hell of a mess on our hands now. The most obvious way to put an end to this situation is to remove Barons Nightwood and Bloodstone from their positions and end their authority over the other mages they've employed in their machinations. Has anyone had contact with the families who've been standing with them to get a sense of how many will still defend them? I don't want to send us into a battle we can't win."

It really was coming down to that, wasn't it? Figure out where the barons were, leave the safety of the wards, and do whatever we could to remove them from power. We'd hoped to do that only temporarily the last time we'd confronted them, and they'd sent us fleeing. Did we have enough people on our side now—and had they lost enough—that we stood a chance?

Several of our allies spoke up, but only with vague observations. "There were quite a few unsettled murmurs going around before we left," said a man from one of the handful of families that had joined us today. "Most people weren't brave enough to share their doubts with the barons, though."

"We managed to convince the blacksuits to arrest Ambrosia Ashgrave," someone else pointed out. "Can't we turn them against the other barons?"

A defected blacksuit at the edge of the crowd shook her head. "The acting Baron Ashgrave made a clearly unprovoked attack on a minor and in a setting where she lacked any significant defenders—and even to arrange that arrest, we had to choose who we reached out to carefully. They're holding her in a separate facility away from the blacksuit headquarters, because they know some of their colleagues would let the barons overturn the charges and free her."

"The barons can't constantly have an army around them," said a guy from the Guard. "Is there a way we can find out when they'll be traveling and, I don't know, ambush them somehow?"

"That could be a viable strategy—if we can get that information quickly enough to act on it," Hector said.

A few more ideas volleyed back and forth, but nothing that sounded concrete enough to settle my nerves. I shifted my weight on my feet. "What if we could draw the barons *to* someplace ourselves?" I said, only loud enough for the cluster of heirs around me to hear. "Like, I don't know, if I put myself out somewhere as kind of bait—my mother would come, at least."

"Your mother and half an armada," Jude said. "Do you really think she'd take the chance of coming unprepared after everything that's already happened?"

"No, I guess not." I just wanted to *do* something that didn't depend on watching the barons' next moves.

"Maybe if we distracted a bunch of the blacksuits who are with them, got them to charge off someplace else to split up their powerbase... But I'm not sure how exactly we'd do that."

"They're going to be pretty skeptical of anything we put out there," Malcolm said.

"Well, let's think on it." As their children, we'd seen more of the barons than anyone else had. There must be something we could use.

The meeting wound down with agreements of various people to ferret out what information they could from friends and colleagues on the other side of the wards. As we left the gym, people drifted apart into their separate clusters. Noah and Agnes headed back toward the junior dorms, Noah in emphatic conversation with a few of his classmates. I meandered toward the green with Jude and the other scions, not feeling ready to turn in for the night yet.

The clouds still hung thick overhead, blotting out any moonlight and stars that might have brightened the evening. The only illumination came from the lights mounted on the campus buildings. Adding to the ominous vibe, a raven soared past us with a flap of its expansive black wings.

"How long do you think the barons will let the Nary situation fall apart before they announce themselves?" I asked.

Declan cocked his head as he considered. "They'll want to make sure the Naries are completely unsettled and desperate for a solution—but I'm not sure how long they can keep directing a catastrophe on this scale. I think we're looking at a matter of days, and few of them."

"Which doesn't give us a whole lot of time," Jude said with a kick at the grass. "Is there anything else that computer hacker of ours could contribute, do you figure?"

I frowned. "If branding the barons' most important allies as terrorists didn't work... I don't think the barons would have their travel plans or anything like that on a server he could get into."

We fell into silent contemplation as we strolled on. After a minute, Connar raised his head. "What about—"

At the same moment, a dark shape swooped into view. Declan stiffened. "Stop that bird!" he said with a jerk of his hand toward it, immediately tossing out a casting word of his own.

His spell either missed or bounced off some defense on the animal, but the one Connar flung at it stopped the creature in mid-flight. With another string of syllables, he brought it down to our level, its body still paralyzed.

It was the raven I'd noticed earlier. Only there was more to it than I'd realized then. A thin black harness was fitted around its chest—and at the center of that harness was a dark gray object I immediately recognized as a conducting piece.

Declan swore and spun around to scan the area the bird had been flying back from. Malcolm murmured a couple of words over the bird.

"The piece is empty, but there's magic in the bird," the Nightwood scion reported. "It's someone's familiar."

"And it carried some kind of spell right into the

middle of campus, we have to assume." Declan continued his survey, but I couldn't make out any sign of a hostile spell affecting anything in the area.

"Maybe it was just spying on us for now?" I suggested without much hope.

"We should report it to the blacksuits. They might have a technique for determining whose familiar it is or even what magic the conducting piece last contained. At the very least, they'll want to be on high alert for similar intrusions."

Declan scooped the raven under his arm and started off toward the staff quarters. He pulled out his phone with his free hand. By the time we'd reached the building, a few of our blacksuits were already emerging from the building.

Declan handed the bird over to them. One of them inspected it with a few spells while another turned to us. "What exactly did you see it do?"

"We were coming up from the Stormhurst Building," I said. "It couldn't have been more than ten minutes ago it flew by us heading west. None of us noticed the conducting piece then. Just a minute ago it flew back to the east. Other than that, I'm not sure where it went."

"Me neither," Malcolm said grimly. "It could have gone anywhere while it was on campus. We don't even know if it kept heading east."

"It's definitely a familiar," said the man examining the bird. "If we had access to our database—"

A shout rang out from farther off by the western forest, followed by a shriek. All of us jerked around toward the noise.

Without any spoken decision, we took off to find out what had happened. The blacksuits barked orders into their radios. A few of the staff and some of the junior students spilled out of the building as we passed the farthest entrance, drawn by the commotion like we'd been.

As we raced across the field, a girl stumbled out of the forest, clutching her arm. "They're *taking* them," she babbled. "All of them."

Declan caught her by the shoulder. His voice came out in its most soothingly even tone. "Who's taking them? Just tell us what happened."

"One of my friends started walking off toward the forest." The girl gulped back a sob. "She wouldn't answer me when I asked what she was doing. I followed her—a bunch of other people were all going out there too. They went so far, I started to get nervous. I grabbed her arm and tried to make her come back, but she pushed me back with a spell that really hurt. And then I saw—there were other people in the forest, waiting for them—I think they must have been on the other side of the wards."

The second she got to that part, most of us listening started running again, on into the woods. I gasped out a few words to conjure a ball of light to help us find our way through the thicker darkness between the trees. The only sound was our rasping breaths and twigs crackling underfoot.

"Take it slow," one of the blacksuits said. "We have to take stock before we engage."

She'd only just finished speaking when my light caught on a few figures marching along some fifty feet ahead of us. One of them had a familiar fall of blond hair. Beside me, Malcolm swore.

"Agnes!" he yelled, sprinting faster despite the blacksuit's caution.

She was too far away. I pushed myself harder too, but in the space of a few stuttered beats of my pulse, she stepped into a shroud of shadows so thick they completely swallowed her up.

One of our classmates who'd run this way called out someone else's name and leapt ahead of us. He barged between the trees—and was yanked away into the same curtain of shadow.

It must have been magically conjured, I realized. Here and there, I spotted vague figures moving behind it.

They must have set it up along the boundary of the wards. A woman who'd gotten a head start on us dashed toward it too, reaching for a boy who was just stepping into the haze. In an instant, they both lurched forward into its grip.

"Stop!" one of the blacksuits shouted. For a second, I thought he was yelling at the mages beyond the shadows. Then he thrust out his arm, and a rush of wind knocked all of us on his side backward. I fell on my ass, the breath jolting out of my lungs.

Malcolm grunted as he tripped over a tree root but managed to right himself. Before he could fling himself after Agnes again, more of our blacksuits rushed in to form a line between us at the wards' boundary.

"We can't win like this," said the man who'd warned us

before. "They'll just snatch us away one by one the second we cross the wards."

"My *sister* is over there," Malcolm snapped. He moved to push past the blacksuits, and three of them spoke at once, casting a wall that halted him in his tracks.

"We pull back," the man said firmly. "We pull back and decide how to handle this. It isn't going to help anyone if they draw you in too, and if we attack them without a clear view of them, we're just as likely to hurt the people you want to save. They *want* us to rush in. Don't you think that's why they're doing this?"

Connar touched his friend's arm. "Don't play into your dad's hands, Mal. He's not going to hurt Agnes. He needs her."

Malcolm exhaled raggedly, his hands clenching at his sides. I ached to reach for him, but I wasn't sure he'd accept that kind of comfort right now.

"Fine," he said. "But we are going to fucking fight." He hurled his voice toward the unnatural shadows. "You'd better believe I'm going to crush every one of you bastards."

CHAPTER TWENTY-FIVE

Connar

It took an hour, pulling everyone on campus together in the huge foyer of Killbrook Hall, to fully count our losses. Our enemies had used what I had to admit was a smart tactic. It looked like they'd sent the raven familiar to target the junior dorm area with a contained persuasion spell that had activated in the students' presence. The younger mages wouldn't have been as practiced at keeping up their mental shields, making them more vulnerable.

Along with Malcolm's sister, six other juniors were missing, plus a few seniors and two parents who'd either been in the vicinity and unprepared or who'd chased after the younger students like Malcolm almost had. There hadn't been a huge number of staff and students left at Blood U after we'd lost over a dozen allies in our last confrontation with the barons and said a temporary good-bye to those who'd left for the capital and elsewhere to try to interfere with their plans. Tonight, our enemies had taken nearly a quarter of those who'd remained, not counting the Nary students.

Which didn't make anyone all that optimistic about our chances of getting the victims of this assault back.

"We can't let the assholes get away with this," Malcolm was saying, his normally cool voice gone hot with anger, though no less commanding than usual. "Who knows what the hell they're going to do to those kids?"

"There's a significant chance that's exactly the move they want us to make," Jude's uncle said. The new Baron Killbrook frowned as his gaze traveled over the assembly. "They want us to charge after them carelessly like some already did so they can pick us off easily, and then there'll be no one left to oppose them."

"So we don't do it 'carelessly,' then. But we don't stand around waiting to check on their next moves either. What's next could be even worse."

"We still have the same problems we did before," Jude pointed out. "Except now we've got even less manpower on our side, *and* we know they'll be expecting some kind of counterattack."

Holden had been watching the turmoil play out with a thoughtful expression. Now he said, in the warm, mostly steady voice I was still getting used to, "We can start with what we know and work from there. Do we have some idea where the barons are, or where they'll have had the people they captured taken?"

Hearing those reasonable questions sent an uncomfortable prickling through my chest despite myself.

The more time I spent around my brother, the harder it was to picture me standing at the table of the pentacle next to him, no matter what Rory and the guys said. He saw the big picture. He approached it with care but determination. And here I was, a million times more familiar with the school and the people here than he was, with nothing I could think of to say.

"If they're hoping that we'll come after them, they won't have gone too far," Rory said. "We could find out, couldn't we?" She looked to a cluster of blacksuits standing nearby. "When you were searching for my mother before, you used me to help because my family connection made it easier to identify her—and that was across the country. It shouldn't be difficult to figure out where she is now or where Malcolm's father or sister are when they're at least in the same state as us."

A couple of the blacksuits nodded. "We could determine where they are within a fairly small range. That would certainly be a starting point for making any plans."

"Good. Let's get on with it." Malcolm made an authoritative gesture, but I knew him well enough to see how much his sister's disappearance was eating at him. He was the one who'd brought her here, thinking she'd be safer—of course he felt responsible. If the barons had ripped Holden away from the school for whatever malicious purposes, I'd have been wracked with guilt too.

"Now?" the one blacksuit asked.

"We might as well get that confirmed," Rory said, taking Malcolm's arm. "We could use one of the staff offices so you can work the spells without distraction." She glanced at the rest of us. "No matter where they are, we'll have to take some of the same things into consideration. Keep hashing it out while we figure out this part."

"Can we use our familiars in any way?" Noah asked as the Bloodstone and Nightwood scions walked off with a few blacksuits. "Turn their own tactics around on them?"

"If they've used a tactic, they'll be prepared to guard against it," Declan said. "We need to come up with an approach that neither the barons nor the blacksuits will have considered."

"What if we go straight into a full-out offensive?" I said. "Before, we've always taken the time to try to talk things out, which gave them time to, I don't know, size us up."

Baron Killbrook rubbed his jaw. "I definitely think we should plan on bringing all the power we can to bear from the start. The question is how to use that power most effectively—effectively enough to overwhelm their own."

"We do still have quite a few people here." Holden motioned to the crowd of mages in the foyer around us. "Some of them are professors who are experts at their subjects, and of course the scions. What special talents do we have among them that we could use?"

Jude clapped me on the arm. "Connar's got his excellent Physicality skills. We've got Professor Viceport on our side for that area too. And between almost-Baron Ashgrave here and Rory, we've got Insight well covered."

"You can't downplay your Illusion skills," I said.

He shrugged, without the wince I might have expected if I'd made that comment a few days ago. His hand came up to touch the conducting piece Professor Viceport had given him. "I'll do what I can, but I don't think we should make any plans that revolve around me. I still can't count on sustaining any spell for longer periods."

"Persuasion is where we're weakest," Declan said. "As strong as Malcolm is, he can't face off against two barons who specialized in it—and both of our Persuasion professors left to join the barons too. Not that we'd necessarily have wanted to use that as a major combat tactic, but we'll need to be on guard against them using it on us while we're launching our efforts."

Jude tapped his finger against his lips. "Rory did have a good suggestion about breaking apart our enemies' attention. Divide and conquer and all that. There've got to be some other strong Illusion mages here—Professor Burnbuck would know who's the best. If we could conjure the impression of a whole additional army coming from a different direction…"

"Illusion is my strength just as it was your fa— Edmund's," Hector said. "But the barons will know that. If we show up in much greater numbers than they'd expect, the first thing they'll do is test for illusions."

Jude let out a huff. "Too fucking clever for their own good—or ours, anyway." He aimed a crooked grin at me. "It's too bad you can't conjure a whole actual army to do our bidding. A squadron of golems or the like?"

I could maybe have constructed three or four humanoid figures and kept enough control over their movements for them to join a physical attack, but that was hardly a balance-tipping force. "It's not really physical might we need anyway," I pointed out. "It'll just take one spell to blast a conjuring like that apart if we're trying to maintain a bunch of them at once."

Some of our other allies drew closer to join the conversation, and I let myself drift back a couple steps. If they came up with an idea that would require a large Physicality effort to make it work, they'd let me know. Declan had a good sense of what was possible or not in pretty much every realm.

My gaze drifted across the room and caught on a bunch of pale faces in a huddled group that had just slipped into the room. Some of the Naries had stopped bothering to wear their scholarship pins regularly, but it was easy to tell from their demeanor that these weren't fellow mages. I spotted Rory's dormmate Morgan and her friend Brandon who'd helped us out the other night among them.

Seeing them stirred something in my mind—the first glimmer of an idea that had hit me as we'd been crossing the grounds this evening. I went over to see what they'd come for and whether being around them might shake more inspiration loose.

A couple of the Naries recoiled a bit at the sight of me, but I guessed that wasn't surprising given what they'd endured at the hands of many of my classmates recently. I was used to my presence unnerving even fellow fearmancers. I kept my stance as relaxed as I could manage and pushed my mouth into a mild smile. "Hey. Is everything all right?"

Brandon stepped forward, apparently the most

confident of the bunch after spending as much time as he had working with us directly. "We were just wondering what's going on. The news has been crazy—what we can get of it now. You're obviously making plans." His gaze slid past me to take in the rest of the room.

"We're going to be making a move against the barons —hopefully very soon," I said. "We just want to be sure it's one that'll work. As far as I know, there isn't any major threat to the campus itself right now." Although the Naries were the most vulnerable of anyone here, I didn't think the barons were likely to bother hassling them because of that exact same weakness. "If you see anything unusual—more unusual than things have been the last few weeks—let one of us know right away, though."

He nodded. "If there's anything *we* can do to pitch in, we're happy to step up."

He made the offer with such confidence that I had to admire him. Here he was, a guy without magic surrounded by mages, witnessing the breakdown of his society because of some of those mages and unable to stop it even with his non-supernatural talents, and he still said those words as if he didn't doubt for a second that he could contribute something.

Why wouldn't he want to? It was his people even more than it was ours out there, hearing their leaders making horrific announcements, watching the violence as those who protested were mowed down...

A memory of one of those videos flickered through my head: the rattle of gunfire, the sparking of a fallen electrical wire. My breath caught in my throat.

"There might be something, actually," I said. "If we wanted to buy or make things you can't buy in a regular store… you'd have some idea how to look up where and how to do that?"

Brandon's eyes glinted with curiosity. "If anyone's ever done it before, there's probably a record of it on the internet somewhere. And if it's on the internet, I can find it."

I hustled back to the main knot of discussion. Declan was saying something about negotiation tactics, with Holden nodding along. The word made my entire body balk.

Barons Nightwood and Bloodstone and those who stood with them had lost any right to negotiation. They deserved to *fall*.

"I know how we can turn the tables on the barons," I said the second there was a brief pause in the talk. "And it's a strategy no one there will be prepared for."

Several pairs of startled eyes shifted to me. The weight of those gazes made my chest tighten, but I barreled on to answer the question in them.

"We used Nary strategies before, hacking into their law enforcement and putting up those profiles. That was the first effort we made that really slowed the barons down, even if it was only temporary. So, we want to distract the blacksuits and the others who'll be fighting for them, and not in a way they'll immediately detect or diffuse magically? Let's blow some things up the old-fashioned way."

Declan stared at me. Jude blinked and then started to

laugh, but it didn't sound derisive, maybe even a little impressed. The blacksuits who'd joined our group frowned, though.

"We aren't going to run at them with literal guns blazing," one of them said tartly. "Once they catch on, they can use their magic to turn weapons on us just as easily."

Holden was watching me, waiting to see how *I'd* respond. Trusting that I'd have a good answer. I drew myself to my full height, bringing all the authority this body afforded me to bear.

Maybe I wasn't an idea guy a lot of the time, but sometimes I saw things other people didn't. And I knew with a certainty that ran down to my gut that I'd hit on the key this time.

"We won't bring guns," I said. "We'll bring one-time explosives and other devices like that—enough to make them *think* there's a huge magical attack happening from various directions. We force them to scatter to deal with that, and then we march in and do things *our* old-fashioned way."

A small but pleased smile split Declan's serious expression. "You know, I think that could be just what we need."

Baron Killbrook looked around at the group. One of the blacksuits started to protest again, and he raised his hand. "We don't have a lot of options," he said. "In fact, until a moment ago, it wasn't clear we had *any* viable options at all. Let's at least determine how this approach would play out before we debate its merits."

He tipped his head to me as if to say, *You have the floor*. A mix of anxiety and pride rushed through me. I was really leading our people too. In that moment, it didn't feel so ridiculous to take on that role after all.

But if I was wrong, then I'd have screwed us out of our last chance to preserve our society and the Naries' the way they were meant to be.

CHAPTER TWENTY-SIX

Rory

W hen we were just five minutes from our expected destination, the blacksuit who was sitting next to me in the van cast his locating spell for the last time. It didn't seem likely that my mother or her colleagues had moved in the past half an hour, but considering the explosive entrance we intended to make, I wasn't going to argue against being one hundred percent sure.

His magic rippled through me with much less force than the spells Lillian and her crew had used to find my mother in joymancer custody. This time we were only reaching across a few miles rather than thousands. And he was reaching out through me tentatively, not wanting my mother to sense the brush of magic as it identified her.

I caught a whiff of her presence, a celebratory energy shot through with undercurrents of frenetic hostility, and then the blacksuit was easing back.

"Still on the Nightwood property," he said. "I'm sure they're in the main building now."

In the seats ahead of us, the blacksuit who'd been performing a similar spell on Malcolm nodded. "I agree. And the younger Nightwood heir isn't right with her father but nearby."

"We'll have to be careful with how we blow things up," Malcolm muttered, but his eyes gleamed in the darkness with an eager if cool light. He was looking forward to this plan, to seeing how much we could throw off the barons and their supporters.

In a way, it was perfectly fitting that we'd be using tools created by the people they felt so superior to in order to bring about their defeat.

As soon as we'd determined that the barons were at Nightwood manor, Ms. Grimsworth had pulled out a blueprint from the library archives for us to analyze. It didn't include any of the magical enhancements or wards the Nightwoods would have laid down over the years, and the structure itself might be somewhat outdated because of renovations, but Malcolm had been able to contribute plenty of additional information. We'd plotted out every step of this plan in detail.

It was nearly midnight now. We couldn't have gathered the supplies we needed in any nonmagical way at this short notice. But Brandon had helped us find instructions for the creation of the sorts of rockets and other explosives we wanted to use, and Connar, Professor Viceport, and a few of the blacksuits who specialized in Physicality had gotten to work conjuring our arsenal to those specifications.

I just hoped that arsenal was enough to give us the edge we needed. We were going all-in tonight, and if the barons got the upper hand… I didn't want to think about what would happen to us and our allies.

As anticipated, the driver pulled the van off into a secluded forest lane before we came into sight of the mansion. A couple of the other vehicles with us parked nearby. Several blacksuits hopped out into the night and gathered at the start of the lane, canvas bags that held most of our new equipment slung over their shoulders.

"Are you all ready?" Hector Killbrook asked, his expression tight. Even when he'd agreed to support us in our initial campaign against the barons, I didn't think he'd imagined he'd end up leading a charge into actual battle. He hadn't wanted this any more than we had—but he was stepping up, and that was what mattered.

The blacksuits all nodded, faces taut with nervous anticipation. The unofficial baron gave them a thin smile. "Launch all the devices as soon as you get in place. We don't want to give their security people any chance to catch on and interfere."

The bunch of them set off with spells cast under their breaths. Before my eyes, they wavered and faded into the shadowy landscape around us.

Malcolm, Hector, and I left two of the vans behind and climbed into the one closest to the road. The driver cruised a little further until we reached a small hill that hid us from view of the driveway just beyond it. The vehicles carrying the rest of our force were already parked on both shoulders, waiting for the signal to race in.

As soon as the explosions started, we'd gun the engines and tear right through the gate onto the main Nightwood property. The rest—well, it was difficult to predict how the barons and their companions would react. All that mattered was making sure that if they left the property, it was in cuffs.

Or in coffins.

I swallowed hard, not letting myself dwell on that thought. After the way they'd slaughtered the joymancers and Shelby's colleagues, I couldn't summon much in the way of guilt about turning that violence back on these people to stop them from doing even worse. I still didn't enjoy the idea.

The barons had pushed us to this point, I reminded myself. My mother had forced the situation. If we didn't put all the power we had into stopping them now that we'd seen just how far they'd go, we'd have as much blood on our hands as they did.

Malcolm sat tensed next to me, his gaze trained on the windshield, even though he couldn't see the house where he'd spent most of his childhood yet. Even this road must have been so familiar. I was going up against a woman I'd only known as my mother for a month. He was facing off with the parents who'd raised him. I couldn't imagine what he was feeling right now.

"I'll kill him," he said in a quiet, strained voice, without looking at me. "If it's him or us, which it basically already is—I will."

I couldn't tell whether he was looking for agreement or an argument. Before I could offer anything at all, a cracking sound split the air. Orange light blazed against the darkness up ahead—a flare of it here, another over there. My pulse hiccupped as the driver hurtled us forward.

The mages in the cars in front of us had been prepared to batter our way onto the property. Our van roared down the driveway in the midst of our allies, and those at the lead would have been launching the spells they'd prepared. With a screech and a clatter, the gate burst right off its hinges. We raced past the wall.

Flames surged amid the trees on either side of the expansive house. The multi-car garage had collapsed in on itself; glass and other debris lay strewn across the crumpled roofs of the vehicles that'd been parked outside. More fire licked up one side of the house itself where the windows had shattered and the stones were cracked and blackened.

Enemy blacksuits streamed from the front doors to run across the property in every direction. Our allies knocked several of them to the ground and pinned them there with a few quick castings allowed by surprise.

We all leapt out of our vehicles. At the same time, more people careened out of the house under the glow of the entry light, most of them looking a little dazed. Baron Nightwood's guests wore the same sorts of finery as I'd seen when Baron Stormhurst had hosted a gala weeks ago. A couple still clutched champagne glasses as if those would shield them.

This hadn't been a strategy meeting. The barons had

been *celebrating* with their allies, toasting to their victory that was destroying the Naries' society more with every passing hour.

Anger flashed through me, as hot as the wafts of heat and smoke carrying on the breeze. I tossed out one spell and then another—the ones the blacksuits had coached us on—to lock this woman's legs and topple that man to the ground.

Several of the mages hurled spells back at us with much less restraint. Cressida cried out as a bolt of energy drew a gash across her cheek. A punch of energy sent Declan staggering back into the hood of a van with a pained grunt.

A few of our blacksuits charged into the house to look for the prisoners. I couldn't tell for sure if they made it very far. A few seconds later, the remaining barons strode out with more of their supporters. My mother's hair whipped in the wind, and magic shimmered around her body. In that first instant, she looked as if *she* were on fire.

A roar broke through the chaos. A huge scaled shape rose up over the battle with flaps of its massive wings. Connar had shifted into his dragon form. He plowed through the mass of fearmancers in their fancy clothes, sending them toppling. Even the barons stepped back.

The sight distracted me enough that I wasn't quite prepared for the next spell that hissed my way. Someone yanked me to the side while they snapped out a casting word. The attack crackled away with a stinging spray of sparks. Maggie let go of me with a quick squeeze of my arm.

I didn't have time to say so much as a thank you. The mages who'd managed to avoid Connar's sweep were throwing more hostile magic at us, fast and furious. The flames around the fringes of the property were dying down. The blacksuits who'd run off to investigate the explosions emerged from the woods to join the fighting. Even with the people we'd managed to paralyze or been forced to deal fatal wounds to, there were more of our enemies still fighting than there were of us.

Jude let out a battle cry and flung a couple of our smaller conjured devices across the courtyard. They blasted through the asphalt and toppled several more of our enemies. Connar's dragon lunged down at the crowd again, slamming through those still standing. A clear space opened up between us and the barons poised on the house's front steps.

Both of the barons were shouting casting words of their own. Baron Nightwood's face had turned blotchy with anger. His lips curled with what looked like a snarl as he flung his next spell, one that slashed through the shields we kept bolstering and flayed open the chests of two juniors just a few feet from where Malcolm stood, by one of the other cars now.

The Nightwood scion's arm jerked up, but the rest of his stance stiffened with momentary hesitation. He'd defied his father and told him off to his face, but he hadn't outright attacked him before. And he'd been so horrified by the thought of following in his parents' footsteps, of somehow becoming as vicious as they were.

I barely thought, only acted on instinct. A casting

word that had become familiar slipped from my mouth. I focused on Malcolm with the curl of my fingers toward my palm and propelled that sensation with my magic to his free hand. Not teasing or challenging the way we used to play this game—just extending a simple gesture of my support and love.

Malcolm's head twitched, but he was too wary of the enemies ahead to risk looking back at me. His fingers curled too, and an answering sensation brushed across my hand, as if he'd squeezed it back.

He stepped toward his father, and a couple of the blacksuits who'd rushed into the house emerged behind the barons, several of the mages who'd been stolen from campus among them.

Agnes was hurrying in front. Her gaze locked on Malcolm. I couldn't tell if something passed between them or if it was only *her* instincts guiding her, but her jaw set and she lunged forward to shove Baron Nightwood with all the strength she had in her.

The baron stumbled down the steps and barely caught his balance when he fell to one knee. Before he could push himself upright again, Malcolm heaved his raised hand forward with a casting word that sizzled with its emphasis.

The spell rammed straight into the baron's chest, so hard his whole body lurched backward with the spasm of an electric shock. His eyes rolled up. He sagged on the ground, his head smacking the asphalt. He didn't move again, only sprawled there limp and lifeless.

A shriek that barely sounded human broke from my mother's lips. She marched down the steps, her tongue flying with spell after spell. One cracked open the head of a guy from the Scions' Guard. Another ripped through one of Connar's dragon wings all the way to where the thin flesh met his body. He crashed to the ground amid the cars.

"Mom!" I yelled before I even knew I was going to speak. My legs were moving of their own accord. I thrust myself to the front of our group, with my hands lifted in a pleading gesture, as if any entreaty would be enough to stop her.

She did stop for a second, at least. Her gaze found mine, burning with intensity, but she paused.

"Please," I shouted over the barrage of noise around us. "Let this be over. You can't keep going like this."

But she could. I saw the moment full resolve hardened her features. It set off an answering resolve in me.

This was who she was—possibly made worse by her awful treatment by the joymancers, but still her. I wasn't enough to change that. All I could do was be who *I* was and not let her change me.

Even if I'd wanted to try to beat her to the punch, there wasn't time to spit out a casting word before she'd already barked hers. From the whine of the energy as it seared toward me, it would have smashed straight through any shield I conjured. But I wasn't conjuring a shield.

"Mirror, rebound, back," I said as quickly as I could, the casting words tumbling out with all the power I had in me. A wallop of magic wrenched from my chest and flung itself to meet the spell.

It caught that blaze of magic, stretched with it, and

whipped it back toward my mother with the same force she'd put into it.

Baron Bloodstone only had time to part her lips before her own spell crashed into her. Her ribs cracked, and her head snapped back with a crunching of her spine. Her body shot backward against the steps. She hit the stones with an even sharper smack of broken flesh and bone. Every limb slumped at an unnatural angle.

My stomach lurched with a rush of nausea, both for her and because that was what she'd meant to do to me. A tremor rippled through me. I took a step forward, not out of any hope—or fear—that her broken body might still contain life, but out of a bone-deep impulse to see, to bear witness and not look away.

She was who she was, and I was who I was, but she'd still been my mother. There'd been something human and caring in her, even if it hadn't been powerful enough to offset the rest.

That momentary urge was almost my undoing. One of the blacksuits who'd been on the barons' side charged at me with a hiss of rage and the flash of some magical weapon in her hands. My arm jerked up to shield me, and my casting word tripped over the heirloom ring on my right ring finger.

The razor arc of magic slashed across her face, cutting across her lips and, from the sound she made, right into her tongue. She flinched, clapping her hand over the wound—and then our blacksuits were on her, yanking her away from me.

I touched the ring as I braced myself for another attack. A weird melancholy sensation rose up over me.

My mother had tried to kill me, and then she'd saved me, whether she would have meant to now or not.

Malcolm caught my shoulder. When I turned to face him, Declan joined us too, rubbing his back. I grasped the Nightwood scion's hand for real the way I had with my magic minutes ago, and he tugged me closer with a ragged exhalation that said he'd found the battle just as wrenching as I had.

Holden had bent over Connar where the Stormhurst scion had shifted back into human form, his chest bleeding from a shallow gash his brother and Professor Viceport were working to seal. His eyes were alert enough to reassure me that the wound wasn't life-threatening. Jude was standing a little unevenly a short distance from us, another small explosive in his hand, but rather than throwing it, he was watching his uncle.

The fighting had fallen off as the barons' allies had registered the deaths of their leaders. The remaining blacksuits and other mages wavered on their feet, watching us with uneasy expressions but much less conviction than before. Hector Killbrook strode into the space between our opposing groups and let his voice ring out.

"The pentacle is fallen. It is up to us to rebuild it and everything they fractured during the last part of their reign. Anyone who backs down from the fight and shows their willingness to work with us instead of against us will face no sanctions. Let's not tear apart our community any further. We have quite the mess to clean up as it is."

I waited, braced. Our attackers who'd stayed in an aggressive stance slowly lowered their hands, their stances slumping. A few drifted closer to the barons' bodies as if needing total confirmation, but their faces showed only hopelessness. They had nothing, really, left to fight for.

"It's over," Jude said, coming up behind us, his voice thick.

It was. That fact sank in slowly as the mages who'd been fighting us a few minutes ago came up to Baron Killbrook on their own or in small groups and made their gestures of acceptance.

We'd ended the assault on the Naries—or at least, we would fully once we sent for the fearmancers who'd gone out to spread the chaos. Things were going to be unsettled for a while, but not like they had been the last several weeks. Not like they had been for me since the moment I'd arrived here.

My greatest enemies, the three barons who'd done everything they could to undermine me and control me as soon as I stepped on campus, were all as gone as they could be.

My shoulders sagged with the wave of relief. Malcolm's grasp and Declan's, reaching for my arm, held me steady. But I didn't need reassurance. From beneath the anguish and the grief for what I hadn't been able to save, a much more joyful emotion was bubbling up through my chest.

I was free.

CHAPTER TWENTY-SEVEN

Rory

Six months later

The sculpture was more figurative than a literal representation: a waist-high piece of marble shaped into two vaguely human figures in an embrace, with a small mousy form at their feet. I'd been afraid I couldn't capture my joymancer parents' faces accurately with all the time that had passed since their deaths, and the symbol mattered more than a perfectly detailed portrayal. It formed the focal point of the sort-of shrine I'd created here just beside the main Bloodstone home.

A week ago, as soon as the spring weather had turned warm enough to ward off any frost, I'd planted flowers around the base of the statue and the wooden arbor that arched over it. Now, I sent a tendril of magic to urge the roses around the arbor to cling more tightly to its slats. With a little supernatural encouragement, I hoped they'd cover the entire structure by summer.

Those blossoms hadn't opened yet, but the violets in front of the statue gave off a tangy scent. I bent to encourage them to shift a little to the sides of the words carved into the marble base: *In loving memory of Lisa and Rafael Franco and Deborah Isaacs.*

I didn't know what future Bloodstones would make of this display, but I intended to keep the story of their sacrifices alive as long as *I* was alive to tell it.

I brushed my fingers over the mouse figure with a bittersweet twinge, but I didn't think my late familiar and friend would have resented my plans for today. No, Deborah probably would have said something in her brisk voice like, *It's about time you moved on with this, Lorelei.*

As I straightened up, my gaze fell on the other, smaller memorial I'd set up beside this one. The glossy stone held my birth mother's name, the dates that had marked the start and end of her life, and the only other two words I could bear to add: *Remember family.* I meant to remember *her*, even if many of those memories were uncomfortable. And I hoped all future Bloodstones would listen to each other instead of letting ideas of power and glory color over everything else.

I'd come from two places—fearmancer and joymancer, with love given and secrets kept on both sides—and it felt only right to honor both.

Footsteps whispered across the grass. Maggie came up

beside me, a leather portfolio case tucked under her arm. As the current acting Baron Bloodstone, my cousin had come along on the trip out here to check for some records among my mother's old things. I'd offered her a place on the property if she'd wanted to live here, since it was plenty big enough for both of us even once our families grew, but she'd opted to keep the apartment she'd been living in while she'd still been presenting herself as a Duskland.

"I found what I needed," she said. "Ready to get going?"

"Yeah. I think I'm good." I let out a slow breath through the easing jumble of grief and nostalgia inside me and followed her back to the car.

"Have you got everything set with the blacksuits when it comes to security arrangements for tomorrow?" I asked as she put the car into gear.

Maggie nodded. "We'll be well-covered if the joymancers try anything sketchy." She glanced over at me. "You've interacted with their people a lot more than I have. Did they give you any bad vibes when we talked with them before?"

Over the last few months, our coalition of barons and heirs had tentatively but steadily patched together a peace agreement with the joymancers' Conclave. Tomorrow the two groups were meant to meet up to finally bind ourselves to the conditions we'd agreed upon.

"I don't think they trust us completely," I said. "Maybe they never will. But I've gotten the sense that the leadership is at least a little impressed that we were willing to stand up to the old barons as adamantly as we did. They've lost people in this conflict just like we have. They must see that it helps them as much as it helps us. And it's not as if we haven't made plenty of concessions."

The agreement mainly amounted to staying out of each other's way, which was perfectly fine with me. After the way the joymancers had treated my mother—and me —I wasn't sure I'd ever completely trust them either.

"It'll be nice not to have to worry about them breathing down our necks and assuming we're up to no good," Maggie said. "*I'm* impressed that you got them to listen."

I shot her a quick smile. "We all worked together on that one. Seeing how well we're cooperating, within our own families and with them, has to have reassured them."

After the final battle at the Nightwood residence, Maggie had revealed her true heritage, and she and Hector Killbrook had gone through the ceremony to confirm their places in the pentacle. We'd adapted the barony ceremony to confer a similar authority to each of us heirs not yet old enough to take our full place at the table yet. Other than Jude's little sister, who had been born happy and healthy but obviously wasn't making any decisions as a newborn, and Hector's young daughter, all blood members of the barony families had participated in the meetings of the pentacle and gotten a say in the decisions made so far.

Cleaning up the chaos the previous barons had left behind had been our first and most intensive task. When their allies moving through the Naries' political circles heard about the barons' deaths, they'd returned quickly enough, but Nary society had been in a lot of turmoil even after the persuasive spells had worn off and the politicians affected had retracted their statements and orders.

We'd sent blacksuits out to all the major urban centers to help settle the lingering hostile feelings, and arranged donations to the families who'd lost loved ones during the violence in anonymous reparation. The president had ended up stepping down all the same, and his former vice president was now in charge, which appeared to have worked out all right. Life seemed to have reverted back to normal from what I'd gathered when I checked the news, other than moments of confusion when the Naries reflected back on that brief period of horrible unrest.

As if triggered by my thoughts, my phone rang. At the sight of the name on the screen, I smiled and answered the call.

"Hey, Shelby!" I said. "How did the symphony go?"

"It was *amazing*," my friend said, breathless with awe. "I can't believe—having that many people listening to *me* —well, I mean, it wasn't just me, but you know." She paused, and her voice faltered. "I still feel a little selfish enjoying this after what happened to get me here."

As with all the Naries who'd been on campus after our battle with the barons, we'd made the decision to wipe any memory of magic they'd seen from their minds. It was either that or ask them to keep a secret that would weigh on them far more than was fair. The infirmary staff were monitoring the students closely with regular check-ups to address any lingering trauma, but Shelby's story had been all over the news. Even as a non-paranormal incident, a group of attackers slaughtering an entire orchestra was shocking enough to draw a lot of attention.

Being the only survivor of the attack, even if her memories of it were a bit muddled by our intervention, Shelby had been asked to speak on talk shows and give magazine interviews. With the therapist Blood U had paid for her to work with, it'd taken her months to shake off the worst of her distress, but she'd benefitted from the spotlight too. Last month, the Boston Symphony Orchestra, which was apparently one of the best in the country, had unexpectedly required a new celloist, and they'd invited Shelby to audition. She'd just completed her first large-scale performance with them last night.

"They wouldn't have hired you if they didn't think you were incredibly talented," I said. "And it's not as if you came away from the tragedy without any scars. What happened to the others wasn't your fault." I still had to remind myself it was my mother's, not mine.

"I know." Shelby sucked in a breath. "The counselor I'm seeing here has been really good, so I'm not dwelling on the past *too* much. But anyway. I wanted to see if you can come and visit sometime. My apartment isn't the biggest ever, but the pull-out couch is pretty comfortable."

I smiled. "Definitely. I've got to hear you play with your new colleagues. Let me check my schedule for the next few weeks, and I'll get back to you about when I can fit that in."

When we reached the university, Maggie parked in front of Killbrook Hall, right around the spot where I'd first stepped out onto campus when I'd barely known who or what I was. "Good luck," she said, flashing me a grin, and went into the building for a meeting she'd arranged with Ms. Grimsworth.

I set off across the grounds to the Stormhurst Building, my heart beating a little faster already.

There wasn't anything to be nervous about. This was a totally standard spell, and I was sure of my choice. It just felt more momentous than it might have otherwise with everything that had come before—with the fact that I *could* make a choice now.

Professor Viceport was waiting for me in the gymnasium where we'd decided to perform the casting, and so were my four lovers. I raised my eyebrows at them as I came in. "I didn't think this was a big enough deal to warrant an audience, especially one that includes two barons."

Declan, who'd taken the Ashgrave barony after he'd graduated back in January, let out a laugh. "We thought you might want to celebrate afterward. Easier if we're already here."

"I'm looking to be reassured that you picked a good one," Malcolm said with a teasing note in his smooth voice. He'd graduated to take the Nightwood barony only a few weeks ago, but the air of authority already fit him just as well as I'd expected it would. "Then I can explain to Shadow why he's not getting a hunting companion."

My gaze slid to the carry case by Viceport's feet. Malcolm had amicably pushed for me to follow his example and take a wolf as my new familiar, but I'd wanted an animal I could keep with me in my dorm and anywhere I traveled. I hadn't settled on exactly which one until I'd been talking with a fearmancer woman who bred cats as a hobby. She'd bemoaned how she hadn't been able to find a home for one of the kittens from her most recent litter, which by now was pretty much grown, because he didn't have the hunting instinct that most fearmancers wanted in their familiars and pets.

I swear he's made friends with the rabbits in the gardens instead of terrorizing them, she'd said, and my mind had tripped back to my early lessons with my first mentor. To help me come to terms with the need to strike fear to power my magic, Professor Banefield had tried having me protect a rabbit from a stalking cat. The idea of taking in a feline that chummed up to bunnies instead had struck a chord deep inside me. I'd gone to see the cat the next day, and within ten minutes he'd been purring on my lap, both of us committed.

Viceport had held onto him for a couple of days to prepare him for the magical bond. The moment she opened the case, he bounded over to me, his black fur gleaming under the harsh lights. *A proper witch's cat*, she'd said with a hint of humor when I'd first brought him to her. I scooped him up, and he snuggled into my arms as if he was made to fit in exactly that spot.

"Looks like we've got some competition, guys," Jude said, shaking his head with amusement.

Connar made a humming sound. "I think Rory's proven she's got more than enough affection to go around."

Viceport looked as if she'd restrained an eye roll, but

the corners of her lips curled upward as she stepped closer to me. "The main spell should only take a matter of minutes. Close your eyes so you can tune out everything else, and focus on the connection you want to form with this animal. Have you chosen his name?"

I followed her instructions, stroking my hand over the cat's soft fur. "Archie," I said. Banefield's first name had been Archer. It seemed a fitting tribute.

The professor started to pace in a circle around me, intoning casting words in a rhythm that shivered over my skin and into my chest. Archie's back twitched, but he nestled against my shoulder with a hitch of a purr.

A faint sense of the cat's impressions drifted into me as my consciousness must have been seeping into his head as well. I caught contentment and curiosity and a whiff that might have been relief. Maybe he hadn't been any happier stuck with the breeder who obviously disapproved of his habits than she'd enjoyed his company.

Slowly, with a finality that brought a lump to my throat, a hum of magic filled the empty space inside me that had ached so badly in the early weeks after Deborah's death. I had my familiar, and he had me. Even if we couldn't engage in actual conversations like the ones I'd shared with Deborah, I could already feel how right he was for my life—and hopefully me for his.

The energy washing over me rose and then ebbed, until my sense of the familiar connection was only a faint tickle I wouldn't have noticed without reaching for it. When Viceport stepped back, I opened my eyes.

"The bond is complete," she said. "It may take a little

getting used to, especially for him. I recommend giving a new familiar as much space as they want to take in the first few days while they adjust."

"Of course," I said.

The guys headed out with me. Archie stayed tucked in my arms until we came out into the warm spring air. Then he squirmed from my grasp, and I let him leap onto the ground. He sniffled the air, took a glance back at me as if to check whether I was going to protest, and trotted off to explore with his slim tail held high.

"Look at that independent spirit," Jude said, elbowing me lightly. "Definitely a good match."

I laughed and glanced at Malcolm. "Maybe he can go hunting with Shadow after all. They can work out some joint strategies."

"Sure, if your familiar ever wants to hunt rather than cuddling up to every other animal in the world," Malcolm muttered, but his tone was good-natured. He motioned me toward the western woods. "Come with us? We made a few plans for this afternoon."

"Without telling me?" I said, but I went along, my curiosity piqued. We didn't get together just the five of us as often as I'd been used to now that Declan and Malcolm were finished with university. They generally tried to make the most of what moments we did get to share, and in ways I quite enjoyed.

"You've seemed pretty fond of surprises in the past," Jude said with a grin.

As we ambled between the trees, I settled into step

beside him. "How did your meeting with the studio go? Do you think they're on board?"

Jude's grin grew. "Hell, yeah. It basically means lots more funding for them, so they're hardly going to argue with that. They'll just add a new production or two every year with that money to cater to our intentions."

He'd been taking part in the meetings of the pentacle even though he couldn't be officially initiated, since he did have plenty of experience to lend to the discussions regardless, but he didn't expect to keep up with that forever. When he graduated, he was still hoping to find work with one of the few fearmancer film studios, conjuring special effects with his illusionary magic.

His affiliation with that industry had sparked an idea as our new pentacle had been brainstorming ways for us to help our people stoke their powers without causing the Naries any further harm. My memory of the way I'd drawn fear from my Nary roommate while she'd been reading the scary novel I'd bought for her had stuck with me, and I'd realized that effect could help us on a much larger scale.

We'd tried it out in a very small way a couple months ago, having several fearmancers including myself and Jude fund a short horror film that then showed at a local festival. The rush of emotion from the audience had been intense, even spread out between the bunch of us. Now we were in the process of arranging feature length horror productions that dozens or even hundreds of fearmancers could get in on at a time. Whenever anyone watched those movies, enjoying the scares they brought, our magic would be fueled at the same time. Win-win for both sides.

"What's next after movies?" Connar asked. "Do you think we should try Noah's amusement park idea?"

"He's pretty set on giving it a shot," Declan said with a chuckle. "I told him we'd work on that if he can find a place to build it and figure out how to deal with the red tape."

Malcolm rubbed his hands together in anticipation. "I wonder what roller coaster terror will taste like." He'd been on board with the innovative approach as soon as Jude and I had suggested it to the rest of the pentacle.

I'd seen wobbles in his confidence after the final battle with our parents as he'd grappled with the choice he'd made, but with every decision he was able to make out from under his father's shadow, every step he'd taken toward making the Nightwood name stand for integrity rather than tyranny, those lingering worries had fallen away. It was as if he'd recovered a piece of himself that'd been stolen away and now was whole in a way he'd never quite been before.

Glancing around, I realized the path we'd taken led toward the Casting Grounds. Declan paused to activate the wards that would prevent any other students or teachers from coming this way while they were being put to private use. Even more intrigued about this "surprise" than before, I searched his expression and the others' for some clue, but they were keeping very good poker faces. Only Jude's hint of a smirk suggested how much he was looking forward to it.

We stepped out into the large clearing used for practicing particularly expansive spells. My gaze shot straight to the shape marked in the grass—a pentacle, maybe ten feet in diameter, each point perfectly equal. It was a slightly larger version of the symbol that marked the pentacle table that belonged to the barons.

Connar took my hand and led me to one of the points. "It'll be more than a year before we've all graduated and can make official commitments," he said. "And maybe it'll take longer than that to find a way of presenting this kind of marriage so that it won't cause any political or other sorts of problems. But in the meantime... we thought it was time we made our own kind of commitment."

"I designed the ceremony," Declan said quietly. "It takes elements from the traditional fearmancer marriages and from the baron consolidation ritual, which seemed appropriate given the circumstances."

"All that library time does come in handy every now and then," Malcolm said with a playful glance at his fellow baron.

"This is all assuming you *want* even an informal commitment to us," Jude put in, an eager gleam in his eyes despite the caution in his stance. "You're totally welcome to tell us all to take a hike."

Emotion swelled in my chest, so fast and giddy it overwhelmed my voice for a moment. I hadn't known I could love these guys more than I already did, but in that moment my heart panged in the best possible way, as if it were so full it was about to crack open. "Yes. Of course I want to. I wasn't expecting—none of *you* should feel like you have to."

None of them had shown any signs of concern before, but since we'd stopped any attempts to hide how close our relationship had become, we'd certainly gotten some odd looks and the occasional skeptical comment from those bold enough to challenge a scion's judgment. Even once we figured out a way to adapt the rules, it was going to take a while before everyone accepted what we had.

Malcolm scoffed and stepped close to brush a kiss to my temple. "It's a fucking honor, not an obligation."

"None of us has the slightest doubt, Rory," Connar said. "The hard part is going to be waiting for the full ceremony."

"All right then." I dragged in a breath, unable to hold back a grin that stretched across my face. "What's the ceremony? How does this work?"

Declan motioned to the pentacle. "We each stand on our own point and focus our magic around the key elements of commitment: dedication, loyalty, cooperation, and love." A soft smile touched his lips as his bright gaze held mine. "We'll all send out that energy to you, and you'll send your own back to us. As we maintain that exchange, we'll each speak, making a personal statement of how we mean to uphold those elements. We've already prepared ours. If you need a little time to consider what you'd like to say…"

I shook my head. So many words were already clamoring at the back of my mouth to come out. "I already know."

"And then we end with a binding spell to enforce our commitment. I think we can use the standard marriage wording: 'I swear to stand with you while you stand with me, in faith and love.'"

The promise sent a tingle of rightness through me. "Yes," I said. "That's perfect."

Jude clapped his hands. "What are we waiting for, then? Let's get hitched." He winked at me before he moved to one of the points on the pentacle.

The other guys spread out around the symbol. I trained my awareness on the thrum of magic behind my collarbone, remembering the principles Declan had mentioned and coloring the energy inside with those emotions.

I'd already dedicated myself to being there for these guys in every way I could. I would have defended them loyally to the bitter end. I wanted every move we made to be born of cooperation and unity. And love? It radiated through me without my even summoning it. I adored them each so much in their commonalities and their differences.

"Let's begin," Declan said.

I didn't want to take the chance of skewing the spell by using my own made-up casting words when I still wasn't completely solid on using those. This was too important. I murmured the words to propel four streams of magic from me to my lovers. "Dedication. Loyalty. Cooperation. Love."

Their lips moved with their own casting words, ones of their own creation, but I heard the emotion in them all the same. And then I felt that emotion, tingling through me as their magic coursed from them into me.

I looked at the guys in turn, willing the magic I was sending them to flow with even more strength. How could even this act completely capture all the love I felt for them? Connar with his balance of ferocity and gentleness, each quality coming out when called for. Declan with the unshakeable devotion and studious curiosity he offered all of us. Malcolm with his kingly power and the generosity that hid beneath it. Jude with his playful tongue and the depth of emotion I'd discovered in him.

Without any signal between them, they launched into their statements in turn, their magic coursing steadily on.

"I want to share every part of my life, for the rest of my life, with you," Connar said, his gaze intent on me. "You saw parts of me that no one else did and helped me believe in them."

Declan inclined his head with his eyes still trained on me. "You bring light and hope into my world that I hadn't realized was possible. If I have my way, I'll never stop bringing the same to yours."

Malcolm's mouth curved with a softer version of his usual cocky grin—the version he saved just for me. "You're everything I could possibly have wanted, more than I knew *was* possible before I met you. If I can spend every day admiring the strength and the compassion you wield so well, it'll be time well-spent."

Jude's voice came out slightly hoarse with feeling. "Even when I thought I was nothing, you showed me I could be so much more. I don't know that I believe in better halves—what you do is bring out the best I have in me."

My throat had tightened with each expression of love. It took a moment before I could work my own out onto my tongue.

"Before I came here and found out who I was, I'd never been in love with anyone, let alone four people at once," I said, shifting my attention around the circle to encompass all of them. "You made me realize how much I was capable of. You trusted me when I struck out on my own path. You let yourself consider things from my point of view, even when you'd been so sure of your own. You grew with me in understanding as you helped me understand my own people and powers so much more. Even though we went through a lot of pain along the way, there isn't a single moment with any of you I'd wish away. I may be a fearmancer, but more than any amount of fear, it's the love that's bloomed between us that raises me up."

My four lovers beamed back at me. With their magic rippling into me, a lightness came over my body as if I might float right off the ground.

"The next words we each speak, we are bound by," Declan said with the pulse of a spell in his voice.

"The next words we speak, we are bound by," we all repeated, adding our energy to the casting.

"I swear to stand with you while you stand with me, in faith and love," Connar said, and then Declan, and Malcolm, and Jude, the words ringing out the same and yet shaped by their individual tones.

"I swear to stand with you while you stand with me, in

faith and love," I said back, again and again, until I'd given my word to all of them. The certainty of the moment snapped tight around me, but not in a constricting way. More like a comforting blanket wrapped close around me.

The magic fell away as we released it. My mouth curved into a smile so wide my cheeks ached with it. I stepped into the center of the pentacle, and the guys all moved to meet me at the same time. They encircled me, their hands slipping over my body, their heads bowing close to mine. Right then, it was hard to tell which reverberated through me stronger: affection or desire.

"You know," Malcolm said in a low voice, "we may not be able to christen the actual pentacle for a while, but I think this one right here would make a pretty good substitute."

I grasped his shirt as my other hand slid up Declan's chest. My head tipped to the side for Jude to kiss my neck, and my body swayed into Connar's caress across my belly. "I'm in total agreement," I said, and anything I might have added was lost to the press of Malcolm's mouth against mine. I gave myself over to the moment, soaking in and offering back every bit of pleasure I could to each of them.

How many odds had we beaten to end up in this place together, with so much devotion and passion between us? More than I suspected I could count. But here we were, and here I knew we'd stay, standing together for both the people we were meant to lead and for each other, with all of our hearts.

ABOUT THE AUTHOR

Eva Chase lives in Canada with her family. She loves stories both swoony and supernatural, and strong women and the men who appreciate them. Along with the Royals of Villain Academy series, she is the author of the Moriarty's Men series, the Looking-Glass Curse trilogy, the Their Dark Valkyrie series, the Witch's Consorts series, the Dragon Shifter's Mates series, the Demons of Fame Romance series, the Legends Reborn trilogy, and the Alpha Project Psychic Romance series.

Connect with Eva online:
www.evachase.com
eva@evachase.com